OF MAIDENS & SWORDS

MELISSA MARR

Signed Copies:

To order signed copies of my books (with free ebook included in some cases), go to MelissaMarrBooks.com

Adult Thriller

Pretty Broken Things (2020; psychological thriller)

Adult Fantasy

Graveminder (HarperCollins, 2011)

The Arrivals (HarperCollins, 2012)

Cold Iron Heart (2020; *Wicked Lovely* adult)

The Wicked & The Dead (2020; Urban Fantasy)

The Kiss & The Killer (2021; Urban Fantasy)

Young Adult

Wicked Lovely series (HarperCollins, 2007-2012)

Made For You (HarperCollins,, 2013)

Seven Black Diamonds (HarperCollins, 2015)

One Blood Ruby (HarperCollins, 2016)

Middle Grade

The Hidden Knife (Penguin, 2021)

Loki's Wolves (with Kelley Armstrong, 2012)

Odin's Ravens (with Kelley Armstrong 2013)

Thor's Serpents (with Kelley Armstrong, 2014)

Collections:

Tales of Folk & Fey (2019)

Dark Court Faery Tales (2019)

This Fond Madness (2017)

Co-Edited with Kelley Armstrong (with HarperTeen)

Enthralled

Shards & Ashes

Co-Edited with Tim Pratt (with Little, Brown)

Rags & Bones

CONTENTS

INTRODUCTION

Sometimes the short form is the right one--to extend a world, to clear my mind between novels, to explore an idea. In January 2019, I started to sort through some ideas about violence, about the perils of life as a woman, about folklore, and about the dangers of love, life, and politics.

"Of Roses and Kings" springs out of my love of *Alice in Wonderland.* I still have my childhood copy, pages falling out, inscribed to me with the date of the gift (1977). I was five, and yes, I could and did read it at that age. Repeatedly. *Alice* was formative. This Alice-inspired story is about falling into that mad, mad world and how sometimes we fill the role we are assigned the best we can. I wrote it as a gift for my partner, whom I met via swordfighting, but then sent it to an editor (who bought it for Tor.com). It might be a love story—or madness.

"The Nameless," likewise, came from reading. This time, both Red Riding Hood and *Herland* (a 1915 feminist novel) played out in the story. What if there were people in a village whose role was defending the community from the wolves? It's a bit dark, but for the first time since selling my very first novel, I sent a story to *The Magazine of Fantasy & Science Fiction*. They published it (January 2020), and thereby fulfilled a career goal of mine. It's a story of sisterhood and survival.

The influence for "Knee Deep in the Sea" is a different animal. Not fairy tale. Not literary. It's rooted in Orkney, on beaches I've walked and pubs I've visited. It may be the tale of a woman sick of "mansplaining," or it could be a murderess of mythic origins. It might *also* be a love story—or madness.

My dark streak continued in "The Devil's Due" wherein a young woman must cope with a nagging ghost, missing sisters, and a vicious man—a Bluebeard figure. There is love, family, and survival. Again, there is sisterhood.

And at the very last minute, I included a story that exists nowhere else. "Not Unlike a Child" is a bit of darkness rooted in the mountains where I was raised. I don't often look long at the Appalachian roots that created me, but this is about that place, magic that may or may not be, and the lengths one goes to for motherhood. Like "Knee Deep in the Sea," it's offering a read that is either about magical paths or sheer madness. Or both.

To round everything out, I added a prequel *Graveminder* story because some maidens carry pearl-handled pistols in the land of the dead.

But not everything is dark or fairy tale!

I've included three "love stories" from my Wicked Lovely world. "Love Hurts" is a sequel, telling of Irial, Leslie, and Niall—who coexist together at the end of my series. Theirs was never a triangle about "choosing one." It's a story about three people who find love together. This story takes place after the original series, and it includes wrestling with a world-shifting secret. That secret sets up *Cold Iron Heart*

(NOTE: That's why this short is thus included in the back of that novel).

"Love Hurts" was followed by a sequel story, "Summer Bound," that was also set after the series. The Summer Queen meets a long lost relative, an advisor to the court finds love, and pieces are in places for a series sequel novel.

This collection also includes the prequel story, "Winter Dreams." That just released in ebook in December, but as I was inundated by requests for a print version, I made that available in this collection, too. "Winter Dreams" is set in the 1990s, when a young Moira Foy met faery kings—and Donia still had hope for Keenan's love.

These three Wicked Lovely stories are all stand-alone pieces, but they—as with the other WL stories in years past—add to and expand the series world.

In all this collection offers some maidens, swords, madness, love, and the occasional murder ahead...

Melissa

2020

"OF ROSES AND KINGS"

"To the dungeon." Those were the last words she said to me, and the reasons for them should be what I ponder. Instead all I can think about is the way her mouth curved, the tip of her tongue between her parted lips as she spoke.

The Red Queen controls everything. Such is the power of money, of influence, of her lovely, lying lips.

"It's not my fault," I protest, even as I step outside the palace into the dusk.

My escort, one lone guard, glances at me curiously.

"It's not my fault," I repeat.

He shoves me, hand between my shoulder blades. "Keep moving."

"I'm not guilty."

He doesn't answer. I could kill him if I had a mind to, but I don't. He's just doing his job. It's not personal. I'm accused of . . . well, honestly, I don't know the list of charges this time. All I know is that I was in the Red Queen's chambers, and now I'm in custody.

"I'm not *innocent*, but neither am I guilty," I explain, more to myself than him.

He's no one. His opinion means less than nothing.

He keeps silent as I follow him through the garden. My shoes are gone, and the road we follow is anything but soft. Knowing her, I wouldn't be shocked if she had extra rocks or shards of glass carted in to cover the path. She's always quick to remind me she's in charge.

I lift my gaze from the path at a soft chuff of laughter to my left. The guard doesn't notice the sound, but he's not paid enough to notice. Or maybe he's simply one of the rare Wonderland-born people. They never find the oddities worth noting, not the way those of us who came from the Original World do.

I stare into the wild foliage. There, nestled among rose blossoms as big as a child's head, is Tom. With his dark skin, the garden, and the flowers, all I see is his eerily wide smile. No one else has such a grin, though, so there's no mistaking him.

"Who goes there?" he calls out, official-like, as if he has the authority to question my transportation. Perhaps he might. Politics are a peculiar thing in any world, including this one.

The guard halts and peers into the greenery. "Guard 39, sir."

Tom steps out with a bit of a pounce. He always gives the impression of something feral, grinning as he does, popping out of unexpected shadows more often than not.

If I were to like a man, I suspect it would be him.

"Ahhh, you have Rose." Tom looks me up and down.

"Beatrice," the guard corrects.

"But a rose by any other name is . . . If you are not a rose, what *does* that make you?"

The guard scrunches up his face in a most unflattering way. "This is *Beatrice*, the Red Queen's maid."

"Today." Tom's grin vanishes. "There are tomorrows and yesterdays, though. Are any of us both who were *then* and *now*?"

The guard nods as if this makes sense. I suppose, in a manner of speaking, it does. Once, a very long while ago, my name was not Beatrice. Before that, in the Original World, it was something else entirely.

Tom sidles up next to the guard and takes the keys from where they hang at the guard's hip. The guard watches him, as do I. Who can resist such a being? Tom moves the way the loveliest music comes into being, as if it's suddenly woven from nothing into something remarkable. Tom is like that— except he knows things in a way that makes me suspect he's sometimes here when he's not.

"I shall take Rose," he pronounces.

Guard 39 looks perplexed at this. "Did the queen change the orders?"

Tom's wide grin flashes back into being, and we all three undoubtedly know that whatever comes next is not the whole truth.

"Ah, does she ever *not* change them?" Tom asks.

The guard hands me over with no more than a cursory glance at the castle. Tom, for all his deceits, is trusted as few beings ever are in Wonderland. He is not in her employ, but he is not her enemy. Truthfully, I think he's as much in charge as she is.

As the guard leaves, I feel Tom beside me, nearly vibrating with the difficulty of stillness. We stand there, watching Guard 39 return along the path we've traveled. I'm not sure if he's going to the castle to ask for clarity or simply resuming whatever task he should've been attending if not for my sudden arrest.

Once the guard turns a bend in the garden path, Tom extends an elbow to me. "Come, my dear Rose. We shall walk a while."

He doesn't unshackle me, so linking my arm with his is not possible. I rattle my restraints slightly in answer.

"I see."

Instead of removing the manacles, he twines his arm around mine, and we perambulate through the jungle-like growth. Tendrils seemingly reach out, snagging my hair and skirt. There's a wildness here that suits me.

After several quiet moments, I tell him, "I never lied to her. I need you to believe me. I need *someone* to trust me."

Tom's toothy grin flashes in the dark. "Shall I admit I don't care, dear Rose?"

"Why did you stop him from taking me to the dungeon, then?"

"That, my dear one, is a fine question." He pats my arm as if I have earned a point in a game I didn't realize we'd begun. Unlike me, unlike Alice, Tom is a native of this peculiar world. In the best of moods, he seems to consider if you're worth toying with for a while or if you're beneath his notice. Neither seems particularly pleasant.

"Do you believe me?" I ask.

He laughs, mouth stretching wider than human mouths ought to stretch.

"Alice would not like it if I believed you," he says, bluntly getting to the lone truth of things. "Of course, she would not like it if I doubted you either."

"I serve her best interests," I tell him. "Whatever name you call me, or she calls me, I serve Alice."

This is the truth that has left me here, chained in the garden, plucked from her room. It is also, apparently, the answer Tom sought. He peers at me, and then he reaches out. I don't flinch—although any man reaching toward me is cause for discomfort. The side of his hand grazes my face as he plucks a dripping rose from a wild tangle of vines and thorns. A good third of the petals rain over me as he frees the blossom and weaves it into my hair.

"I serve Wonderland, Rose. Not this Red Queen. Not the last. Not the one before her . . . or the one who will follow Alice some day."

"She *trusts* you." It's all I can say as we follow the sinuous path toward the dungeon—where, apparently, I am still going.

"More's the pity," he says.

We drift to silence then, broken only when he opens my cell door. The clank of it seems welcoming. Tom's company has become oppressive.

I pull it closed. The keys clatter as he locks the cell and then reaches in to unshackle my wrists and attach the manacle to my ankle.

"Never unchain a killer unless you must," he says cheerily.

"I serve the queen," I repeat.

"No one with a bit of sense doubts *that*. They might not admit they realize it, and you will likely still lose your pretty head, Rose, but those of us who pay attention have always known where your loyalty belongs." He pats my cheek and grins as he backs away, white teeth gleaming out of the shadows.

And then he's gone.

THE FIRST TIME I stood before the queen, I knew she was why I'd fallen into Wonderland. She is my reason. I was meant for her.

I'd been here for four months, not entirely sure where *here* was or if being here was to last forever. Nothing made sense some days, but I'd been keeping my head down and had taken a position as a maid. It wasn't much, but it kept me in tea and jam.

The day that changed my life was a Wednesday. Admittedly, most days here are Wednesday, but still, I noted it. Details matter when the queen is rumored to be a litigious sort.

"You, there." A guard stood over me, close enough that I briefly considered mopping his shiny black boots. "Stand up."

That part was easy enough—welcome, even. Being on my knees wasn't a natural position, especially not before a man. Don't mistake me: I'm not a misandrist. I dislike most people, men and women both. I maybe just dislike men a touch more.

"The queen needs you to clean the throne room," he ordered.

"Now?"

He stared at me as if I were daft. "Of course, now. Everything she orders is *now*."

Months later, I'd understand, but I hadn't yet learned that the Red Queen had made it a *habit* to lack patience. It was part of the illusion she crafted. No one thought her capable of the ruses she set into motion because her carefully constructed persona was that of an impatient, slightly mad, entirely indulgent woman.

But I digress.

The Red Queen had summoned me, and so I went to the throne room. It was a marvel of black and white tile, an elaborate game board where pawns maneuvered for power. She sat like a goddess on high, watching the courtiers seeking her attention and pointedly refusing them. The king, for all that he existed, was a shell of a man. He nodded and spoke as if she crafted lines for him at night and glancing at her with such hunger and fear that I pitied him almost as much as I envied him.

(I know now that *this* was the moment of my demise. She knew somehow, before I realized it, before I could hide. She knew I was hers to use and discard.)

When she turned to look at me, my fate was sealed. Golden ringlets framed a face that sculptors have carved and painters have captured. Her lips tilted into the smile that Helen once used to launch a war. I knew then that Lucifer fell for the same reason Adam did—because *she* willed it.

So, when she crooked her finger, I did what any sane woman would do: I turned and walked out of the room.

That was the first time she had me tossed in the dungeon. I wonder if today will be the last.

IT's midnight when she visits me. I know she's here before the guard slips out of the small side door into a courtyard. Like I said, everyone knows she's deadly, but no one else is mad enough to cross her.

It's an honor I don't have to share.

"Hello, Ally," I murmur as she approaches out of the shadows. She's an angel deigning to walk into the muck, illuminated by the candle she holds just so. It casts light onto her perfect face and bare throat.

"You never learn."

I shrug. She's not wrong. I'm not any more likely to change than she is. I was what I am when I arrived in Wonderland, formed into the raw stuff that landed me here in her domain. No one knows exactly why some people fall into this fantastic world, but we all know there are only two ways to get here—be born to it or fall into it. Those born here cannot leave. The rest of us must constantly worry that we'll break the wrong rule and wake up in the Original World.

"Treason," my queen adds, "is a very serious crime."

"I wondered what the charge was this time," I admit. "One never knows with you."

She presses her lips together, and I see that they're glossy with fresh lip-stain. I'm fool enough to be glad she still finds me worthy of painting those dangerous lips. The words that slide through them can condemn me to death; in fact, I suspect they have already done so if I'm charged with treason. I'd still sell a small country or two to have the Red Queen's lips touch mine again.

"I must protect the crown," she says, as if I don't understand.

"He was a blight, Ally. Killing him was a gift."

She tilts her head, looking at me curiously, and very softly says, "Well, of course, it was. You know that, and I know that."

The Red Queen lifts a hand, summoning the constantly accessible ladies-in-waiting. Then she glances at the ground behind her. A chair—ivory with beautiful carved legs—materializes out of the shadows. Hands are all I see. The light of the queen's candle doesn't extend to the servants. Another woman reaches out of the shadows and places a matching footstool in front of the chair. Hands settle her skirts.

Alice sits without looking.

The chair, the stool, the dress, it will all be consigned to the fire by morning. The proof that she was here in the filth will be burned up like so many other things. My beloved is clever and cautious, despite what the people think.

I glance at Alice's shoes. When she became queen, Alice

adopted a madness that seems to be bound to her role in this world, as if being queen meant some level of madness was inevitable. She *is* her office in ways, but in the heart of the madness, Alice still exists. The *last* Red Queen had no such shoes, but Alice wears strange, lovely ones that defy logic. Today's have a cut-out heel featuring teeth.

"Tell me."

"Why?"

"*Tell* me," she repeats.

I sigh. I want to resist her, but I can't. Maybe in the Original World, maybe if we were both back there, I could resist her charm. Here? Everything in me wants to resist, but I still give in.

"I love you," I begin.

"And?"

"There is nothing I would deny you, Alice. Nothing." I settle into the hard bunk of my dungeon cell. Briefly, I attempt to cross my legs, but am stopped by the clank of shackles. I stare at her through the bars and profess, "You are my world."

"*And?*" Her voice is different now. Softer. Hopeful.

"So, I killed him. For you, Ally. I murdered him because you wanted him to die."

The Red Queen smiles at me in a way that makes me forget the filthy cell where I live now. I know then that I'd do it all again—and so much more—for the joy in her expression. She knows it, too. I suspect she knew before I did. She picked me. She groomed me to be the red hands of the queen.

"I never wanted the king to die, Beatrice," she lies. "He was my husband, ordained so by Wonderland."

And in her lie is the crux of the problem. The truth is that Alice wanted the crown. She won it from the last Red Queen, and so she became heir. She was the new queen, taking the throne, the power, the crown jewels—and the king. It was one almost perfect package.

The king, unfortunately, adored the Red Queen. Not Alice. Not the last queen. Not the one before her. He adored the *queen*—whichever one she was.

My TIME at the Red Castle was illuminating in ways I couldn't explain. I went from nameless maid, ordered about by every guard and courtier in the palace, to *her* maid. She chose me.

That was the result of my first foray into the dungeon: She released me, renamed me, and I was New. I was hired as the Queen's Personal Maid as if I were new to the castle. The head of the maids gave me a tour—including the very same rooms I'd cleaned the past four months.

My new name was Beatrice. I cannot recall the old name. It no longer matters.

As Beatrice I would wear a dress befitting the Queen's Personal Maid. I hate dresses, but the pay was great. I signed my new name on the form presented to me, and so it was to be.

On my second day as Beatrice I arrived to work, and I prepared to clean her royal chambers. I assumed that would require tidying her sitting room, possibly waiting to fetch her tea or her beloved tiny cakes. The queen, for all of her airs and etiquette, was fond of the hallucinogenic bakery—so much so that she'd burned it down and offered the bakers positions in the palace as Royal Bakers.

I was wrong, of course. I arrived to find my employer naked and pacing. The room itself would take half a day to clean. Dresses, stockings, and jewelry were strewn everywhere as if she had thrown them in frustration.

"How am I to dress without my maid?" She stomped her foot, frowned at it as if it ought to make a noise even though she wore no shoe and stood on thick carpet. She picked up a book and tossed it at the wall as she stomped again. When the book made an apparently satisfying noise, she smiled at her foot.

My mouth gaped open in confusion.

"We're all a little mad here, Beatrice," she explained conspiratorially.

I nodded. What else was I to do?

"I need cleaning and dressing." Alice gestured with her left hand.

Women appeared from behind curtains. They all stared at her feet as they glided forward. Each woman was laden down with some sort of bathing supply: buckets, sponges, soaps, and towels. Several slid a large tub toward the windows. None spoke.

They left after depositing the mound of supplies alongside the tub. Once they'd gone, the queen stared at me expectantly. She looked at the tub. She looked back at me. Surely, she didn't require aid to climb into a tub.

"Your Highness?"

The Red Queen looked at me, as if my speaking was a shock.

"Shall I come back or clean now?" I gestured around the room. The clothing and jewelry that were everywhere—except in the path the tub had traveled—should have been my task as a maid.

"Beatrice, truly?" She laughed as if I were ludicrous. "I need cleaning and dressing. Are you or are you not my maid?"

Even then, I was not so unaware of her reputation. The queen's madness was legendary. Her temper, however, was more so. I wasn't about to risk my life if I misunderstood the way she was watching me.

"Will I be sent back to the dungeon for touching you?" I asked.

"Not today."

"For not touching you?"

"No." She offered me a rare, almost honest moment. "I would like you to please me, Beatrice. I selected you to do so, but there are plenty willing to look after my needs if you're not so inclined."

She glanced toward the curtains behind which her ladies-in-waiting stood or sat expectantly. "I have people who exist to take care of everything I seek. All volunteers. I don't see the point in bedding the unwilling."

I didn't ask questions. Not about them. Not about the king. Not about anything. I simply set about doing as the queen desired. I bathed her, and I dried her. I knelt in awe as she stretched out before me on the floor. There—amidst satins and silks, diamonds and rubies, dresses and crowns—the Red Queen asked, "Love me?"

And so, I did.

Afterward, she asked, "Would you do anything I wanted?"

"No," I lied.

She smiled, and I felt my soul shudder in fear.

"That will change," she warned me.

I said nothing.

"You may never leave me, Beatrice." The Red Queen gripped my hands in hers. "Even when I tell you to go, you must not leave me."

And then she sent me to wait with the other ladies-in-waiting and summoned the king.

. . .

"I didn't hate him," the Red Queen says.

I'm not sure if she's lying. I suspect this is one of the strange, precious moments of honesty that can too often be overlooked in the maze of lies and madness that make up my beloved Alice.

It doesn't matter, though.

"Will I be finishing my days in your dungeon or meeting the executioner?" I ask.

"Must you be difficult, Beatrice?"

I smile. She only wants me *because* I am difficult. The hardest task in my life is finding ways to be so. If I am complacent, if she knows I'd sell my soul at her whim, she'd be bored. Alice never meant to be a queen. She chose it over expulsion from Wonderland. In essence, she chose madness over death.

The power, on the other hand, she enjoys far too much to surrender.

"Were you after my crown?" She touches her head. Today's crown is blood ruby and onyx. Like the rest of her crowns, it's a small circlet, so simple it could be mistaken for a headband.

No mere citizen of Wonderland may wear a crown. A "crown" is any metal or jeweled ornament that rests atop one's head. It's one of the gentlest rules enacted by Her Mad Majesty.

"I do not want your crown, Alice." I keep my voice soft as we talk. The darkness makes it hard to be loud. "Nor the weight of it."

"I see."

"If I wanted your crown, I'd have killed *you*, not the king," I point out.

"True," she muses. "But a queen must have a king. That is a rule."

To this, I have no answer. Wonderland is still a mystery to

me. We strangers arrive here with no clue as to what it means, why us, why any of it.

"If I break the rules, I have to go back," Alice whispers. "I can't go back, Beatrice. I can't. I remember enough to know that I would rather die here than return to the Original World."

I want to hold her. When Alice is like this, lost and more frightened than mad, I want to be the knight who rescues her, the person who saves her. I killed the king. I'd do far worse for love of her.

"I HATE HIM," the queen told me as we were having the required afternoon tea. "I eat the little cakes and smoke the flowers to bear it."

I brushed her hair as she spoke. It was an excuse, not the task of a maid. No one really could overrule her, though— except him. I often thought she hated him simply for that.

"He smells." She paused and folded her hands. "He goes off to do who knows what, and I am in charge. I make all the choices. I rule. He . . . I'm not sure what a Red King does, but it certainly isn't helpful."

"Do you need help?"

I watched in the looking glass as the queen pouted. Her reflection did so sooner than the queen herself, who was sitting between my legs on the floor in a very un-royal way. Even now, however, I knew there was a level of dishonesty in her. My beloved Alice was rarely truthful unless we were both naked. Without her royal clothes, without the Red Queen's crown, she was nearly sane. She was even honest in the way of regular folks sometimes.

"I don't need help with anything," Alice lied. "I can do it all myself."

We were interrupted by the arrival of Lord Hare, which was what the pale, red-eyed man called himself these days. One of the myriad guards that roamed the Red Castle stood beyond the curtains and announced, loudly, that Lord Hare had arrived.

Alice stood and shoved her feet into today's absurd red shoes. Through some magic or machination, this pair had long-lashed eyes that stared and fluttered as if someone were trapped within the shoes. Maybe they were.

"I *hate* him," Alice muttered.

I didn't ask which him. She was the Red Queen, and back in her royal garb, her answers were as likely to be true as to be utter gibberish. The magic of the place changed reality. It changed her. If I pondered the matter, I knew I'd realize it had changed me—but why would I dwell on it? I chose Wonderland, and my choice had led me to her. The rest was immaterial.

I would never leave her.

"My dress," she prompted me, dropping her robe to the floor. Her voice was imperious, and the gesture matched. Her eyes, however, told me otherwise. My poor, delicate Alice. She was trapped in ways I could only try to fathom.

I picked up the dress for the day. Pale blue. White sprigs. It reminded her subjects that she was once just a girl, facing an irrational queen. No matter that she'd become just as mad. No matter that she was as likely to behead a teapot as her once-trusted allies.

I buttoned it up the back, fingertips lingering long enough to remind her that I was here, that I was hers, but not so long that she'd need to reprimand me. I straightened her full, heavy skirt by reaching under it with the excuse of a twisted fold of cloth.

Alice stood mute as my hands touched her softly.

"That won't do," she grumbled. "I have meetings. Lord Hare waits."

As I made to remove my hand, she added, "Beatrice, really? Dispense with the posture of gentility."

"Of course, my queen."

Alice wasn't born and bred to be a queen. She was once an impulsive girl who ignored the rules. Such traits make for a temperamental queen—and exactly the sort of lover I cherished.

I dispensed with everything gentle until the mad queen was calm again.

When the Red Queen descended to attend her courtiers and disloyal subjects, I followed with the flock of ladies-in-waiting. I was never quite sure what they did now that she claimed that I was the only woman in her bed, but I wasn't about to ask. My queen would lie, and I would accept it.

"Alice, my dear!" Lord Hare greeted her far too familiarly, and then he turned away from the Red King—who was in attendance suddenly, too—with a meek, "Sire."

The Red King had no concerns, no worry over Lord Hare's manner. The king was too interested in the latest rifle he was being presented. If not hunting, the man was off racing. If not racing, he was with his own ladies-in-waiting. The Red King served no purpose. He existed to create the next heir, to procreate. I had no idea if he'd ever achieved such a thing with the other Red Queens.

All I knew for sure was that when Alice was fertile, the Red King felt pulled by a mighty urge to rut with her. My queen initially had endured it. Over time, however, the king's drink was spiked so he could not inconvenience her.

Briefly, the king smiled in her direction, but his hands were on the hunting rifle.

Lord Hare, however, reached for the queen as if to hug her.

"Bunny," Alice murmured in seemingly fond greeting, but I knew it was a rebuke for greeting her by name instead of her title.

The pale man flushed red and bowed deeply. "Your Highness. I meant no offense. None."

He had concerns that he needed to discuss, and to be honest, I had no interest in hearing them. I watched instead as the king waved off drink after drink. I knew there was trouble ahead. I wasn't sure what was coming, but life in Wonderland taught me to listen to my paranoia and star charts the way I had once watched the news.

My queen was oblivious to the threat, and I was left with a choice.

"Take this to His Highness," I told a passing maid. I pulled a vial of sleeping medicine from my pocket. I didn't use it myself, but I had brought over from the Original World a bit of this and that. Admittedly, a few times I had stirred it into Alice's tea when I had things to do, but I had to protect her—even from herself.

Anyone would've done the same in my place.

"Do you remember before?" the queen asks me suddenly. Her voice and the candle are the only lights in the dungeon.

"Before?"

"Before *here*, Beatrice." Her voice is urgent now, and I want to fix it. Fix all of it. Anything. Nothing. Whatever will make her happy. "Do you remember before Wonderland?"

I shrug. I suspect I could recall it if I wanted to try. There was a life there, a place I'd existed. People. Pain. Pills. There were things in my mind best left ignored, though, and I was certain that this was one of them.

"Who were you?"

"No one," I lie.

We both know I'm lying, though. I'm not good at it here. Before Wonderland I was an excellent liar. My entire world was balanced on the edge of lies, and I felt the end closing in. That's why I took the chance, why I came here.

"You are the only person I send to the dungeon repeatedly," Alice confesses. "I have to, you know. It's a rule. I must send you. I must punish you."

"A rule?"

"Who *were* you, Beatrice?" she asks again.

Images clamber to be given voice. A man dead at my feet. A man bleeding. A man with a knife blade in his belly.

"My hand held the knife," I say quietly.

The Red Queen lacks context, does not see the men—for there are many, not one—whose faces I see. She hears enough, though, to nod.

"Deserving?" she asks.

Alice is, after all, a woman who has shrieked to have the heads of her enemies severed for offenses various and sundry. Spilling blood does not bother her.

I close my eyes and let the stories flow into my mind. Once I was not Beatrice, once I was not in Wonderland—I was a volunteer. Shelters. Hotlines. Hospitals. I watched for men who were not stopped by the law, and I stopped them. No guardian angel. I did it because I wanted to kill, and I had too much religion to kill without cause. Still a murderer. Still a serial killer, if I were to use the words of the Original World.

Without opening my eyes, I nod and declare, "The dead deserved to die."

Another face looms in my memories, one I shove back. I

still hear my father's voice, telling me how and where to press the tip of the knife while my mother prays on her knees next to the man sprawled out in the leaves. I open my eyes to erase that particular memory. His death is one of the reasons I must be sent to dungeons now.

"All deserving," I say in a drier voice.

The ones in my childhood don't count. They never counted because if I hadn't done it, they'd still have died. They could not count, and so I choose to forget them.

The Red Queen stands and steps closer to the bars of my cell. She reaches out and places both hands on the metal cage. So quietly that no one else—even the ladies-in-waiting—would hear, she tells me, "The Red King deserved it, too."

"Beatrice!"

"Beatrice!"

"Beatrice, Beatrice, Beatrice!"

I wake to the strange in-tandem voices that seem to be caught in a call-and-response loop. While it *is* my name they call, they are not currently interested in my reply. I'm not sure what to do. I could interrupt, but it's dreadfully dull in the dungeon. The only other alternative is to wait until they notice that I am awake. I sit in my cell and watch.

"We'll miss teatime," Mark Hare says as he stares into his teacup.

"Hush, dear. It's always a grand time to have tea!" His companion, oddly, is a stranger to me—or at least I think he is. A ridiculous hat, oversized and garish, perches on his head and obscures his face. In the dim light of the dungeon, I would venture to say that the hat is puce, but I suppose it might be eggplant. I'm certain it's *not* brown. Nothing quite so ordinary as brown will do for any of the natives of Wonderland.

Mark, whom I only know because he is a lesser cousin of Lord Hare and has been lingering around the palace far too often, leans on the wall beside my cell and tosses his teacup over his shoulder. "Clean cup, if you please."

From the shadows a pale, shaking hand reaches out with a cup of tea in a saucer. Tea sloshes over the sides of the cup.

"Without any biscuits?" his hatted companion asks in a tone that can only be called scandalized. "You barbarian! You . . . you . . . *animal*."

Mark flashes teeth in the sort of smile that is more feral than not and says, "Hop, hop."

The hatted man *tsks* at him—and then at me. "Eavesdropping. Quite the worst sort of behavior, you know."

"Worse than lacking biscuits?" I ask.

The men both hum and mutter, lost easily in a curious sort of riddling that the Wonderlandians are prone to. Mark taps a finger on the teacup, sloshing the liquid over the edges in a rhythmic way. The hatted man paces and has a little chat with himself. Suddenly, as if responding to signal that I missed, they both say in unison, "Quite so!"

I nod. Really, what else could I do? For all the ways that being here changes a woman, at the heart of it all, I am still me. I see no need to engage more nonsense or nuisance than necessary. Mark and the hatted man are not rational; few of the inhabitants of this place are. In truth, I rather *like* it. A bit of madness makes the things that one must do seem sane sometimes.

At least that's my theory.

Mark watches me as he holds out a hand and demands, "Biscuit!"

The same pale, quivering hand as before extends. This time it holds a biscuit. A key-shaped biscuit is placed gently onto his open palm.

Mark extends the key-biscuit to me almost the moment it touches his palm. "Will you have tea with us, Beatrice?"

"Indeed," I murmur with as much enthusiasm as I can.

He hands me the key-biscuit and . . . waits. No instructions. No anything.

"What do I do with a biscuit?"

"Marvelous riddle!" the hatted man exclaims with a clap. He claps several more times, muttering a series of queries that my question has sparked as he begins to pace. "A biscuit . . . What does a biscuit do? What *is* a biscuit?"

"Does it signify?" Mark asks.

"A biscuit?"

"A biscuit," Mark confirms with a nod.

As they pace and ponder, I decide that there are—as happens regularly in this weird world—only a few choices. One, I eat the biscuit. Two, I see if the biscuit is a key. Three, I do nothing. I'm not great at nothing, and I have been starving since I was left to rot in Alice's dungeon. On the other hand, if it failed as a key, I could eat the rest.

"Key it is."

I reach between the bars of my cell with the biscuit key, shove it in the lock as carefully as one can with a biscuit, and try to turn it. Baked brown pastry flakes to the ground. Inside the key-biscuit is an *actual* key, solid, metal, and effectively granting my freedom. The lock turns.

"She said you'd know!" the hatted man exclaims. "She said it true."

Mark looks at me, shrugs, and smiles.

I shove the door open with a squeak and screech—not the door's sounds, mind you. Mark Hare and his awkward hat-wearing companion provide sound effects as the door opens.

The dilemma, unfortunately, is what to do next. Leaving the cell or-- No, there is no dilemma. I love Alice, cherish her in a way that a fish loves water or an oyster hides a pearl or any number of explanations. The point is that she is both essential and my treasure.

But I do not want to die. I've held on to my head despite everything. This time, perhaps, I will not evade the executioner unless I leave. Then I might *literally* evade him. It is my best hope.

THE KING IS A PIG. Some days I thought he might become so in form. He is a bore, a vulgar, rutting thing, voracious in appetite. In so many ways, the Red King is porcine. Yet Alice titters and laughs when he makes crude jokes. She pats his cheeks. She ruffles his hair.

I hate him.

"I don't want a brat," Alice exclaims as I rub oil into her skin. "If he continues as he does, I'll be fat and mad."

"Plenty of women—"

"What if I get sent back?" Alice asks softly. She is prone under me, belly down on her bed, naked but for another pair of absurd shoes and a jagged crown crookedly affixed atop her head. "What if I have a child, a native of this place, and I get sent home?"

I cannot tell her she won't. None of us who've fallen into this world know when our time will suddenly end. In full truth, I wonder sometimes if we are all in a shared coma, or if we are dead, or highly medicated. There have been times in my life when injury, death, and medication were all likely.

"I don't want him to touch me," Alice admits. "Even if I wanted a squalling infant, I wouldn't want him to touch me."

"He's the king. Shouldn't you . . . want him, or whatever?" I'm not completely clear on how the Wonderland things work, but if he wants the queen—every queen regardless of the woman under the crown—shouldn't she want him, too?

"I've tried," Alice says, almost calmly.

Then, she screams. Once. Twice. Several more times. She's still on her stomach, naked under me.

Guards come. A knight, tall and polished and far more dignified than most of the people here, enters the room.

"Are you in danger, m'lady?"

"Every day," Alice says. "Bring me something to please me. Plan a ball. Find me a new dress. Burn it all down."

"Your Majesty?" the knight asks.

The Red Queen stands, spilling me to the floor in her fit of temper. Two ladies-in-waiting begin to dress her. No one is surprised by her fits or moods. She stares at them all, gaze fixated on the knight.

"You. Come at midnight."

He says nothing, simply bows and leaves.

I wonder at the plan she has in mind, but Alice answers me before I ask: "Perhaps if I watch him rut with you—"

"No."

"I cannot stand the king's touch," she says. "If I am aroused—"

"No, Ally."

"What am I to do?" She looks lost, the confused girl who sometimes peers out of the mad queen's eyes stares at me.

"I'll fix it." I know before the next heartbeat that my plan is deadly, that there are no answers here that will not result in disaster. However, for my queen, there are no lines I cannot step beyond. She is my life.

I have killed for far less rational reasons.

"Tonight?" Alice looks as if she's holding her breath.

I nod and think of my options. I have a king to kill, and there are no guns in Wonderland. It's messier without the slick, simple finality of a bullet. Simple maids have no need of sharp knives or swords, but there was a knight here moments ago.

"At midnight, you will seduce him," I order my queen.

"The knight?"

"It's treason to touch the queen," Alice reminds me. "My maid might do so, but a knight . . ."

"I did not say to fuck him." I shake my head. She's not so daft as this. "Seduce him and have him sent to your lovely dungeon. I will collect the weapons he leaves behind."

"To keep me safe," she adds.

We do not discuss what we both know I'll do once I have his weapon. That is too direct. That is, in its truest terms, treason.

When I leave the cell and the dungeon, both Mark and the hatted man take off. Whatever plot they agreed to did not include staying in the company of the woman who murdered the king.

"Regicide makes a girl a bit of an outcast," I announce, knowing Tom's there. I'm sure of it before his teeth appear in the dark. Tom, for all that he claims not to be the puppet master of this world, is nearby.

In the Original World, in the Crescent City that was my last home, I would have thought that Tom was a tour guide dressed up as Baron Samedi. If ever there was sexier man, I'm not sure where or when he was. Tom, unfortunately, is also the single most terrifying man in the whole of Wonderland. Like the finest bluesman in all of New Orleans or the pirate at the helm of a cutthroat crew, Tom is a force unto himself.

"The queen must have a king," he announces. "There is a necessary order."

"And? Will I be calling you the Red King soon?"

Tom laughs, and I am reminded of my father when he was luring victims to his traps. He was the spider, entrapping fly after ladybug after lesser spider. They all died because he willed it so. Those who lived, who avoided his lair, did so at his whim. Tom is more like that man who raised me than anyone I've ever met.

"I am not interested in surrendering my power, Rose." He extends his arm, and we begin to walk.

A woman is dragged toward the dungeon as we continue down the flower-lined path. "My name is *not Beatrice!*"

"Shame about the queen's maid." Tom glances at her. "Treason is such an ugly thing."

I miss a step. My feet tangle. "What?"

"She'll be beheaded at dawn." He shrugs. "We must protect the throne, Rose."

"She'll die?" I glance in her direction. "That woman will *die?*"

"Indeed." Tom gestures for me to go ahead of him. "Someone must."

And I know that this is one of those moments, a test of my character. Do I let another woman die so that I might live? I can't say that I want to die. I can't even say that I haven't taken lives. None of them were truly innocent, though. No one is innocent.

"Would it help if you knew she wasn't, either?" He smiles, seeming genuine for a change, even trustworthy. "Innocent, I mean."

I stare. "How did you know I . . ."

"You are as readable as a book in a language I almost know, Rose." Tom's voice is light. "You ought to be grateful I'm not scandalized by your salacious thoughts in my direction." He leans in, kisses the tip of my nose, and adds, "And that I don't tell Alice."

"I love her," I say. "You wouldn't be the first man I was willing to kill to make her smile."

And there, in the dark garden, Tom laughs. "You'll make a fabulous consort."

"A what?"

"A king, dear Rose. The role is unfilled, and the queen is useless since she has lost you." Tom shook his head. "We have options. You could become queen, but then I'd still need a king to fill the vacancy you created. I could let Alice descend in madness and bring in a new queen to oust her, as Alice herself did with the last regent. Or . . ."

He looks down at me, and I realize I've slid to the ground.

"*You* become the king. Adore Alice and keep her in check, or if you prefer, I could make you a knight. Move a knight into the king's position."

There are words. Millions of words I know. Most of them aren't available in this instant.

"I'd kill him," I whisper.

"Kill the knight, too?" Tom sounds aghast. He puts his hand to his chest in faux shock. "You truly are bloodthirsty enough to be queen, Rose. That was my plan, you know. Alice seemed so promising, but she became mad. They all do—such is the nature of queens."

"And Wonderland," I add with more bite than I ought.

He laughs again. "I simply want a world as beautiful as can be, and it gets so dreadfully boring if it's only Wonderlandians here."

Suddenly, I realize with strange certainty that this world is *his*. We are all Tom's puppets. Me, Alice, Lord Hare, Mark, the nameless knight, all of us. Maybe it should bother me, but we are puppets with lives and opinions.

"If Alice is to be queen, she needs a king," Tom says.

"Yes." My answer is neither enough nor too much. It is all that is left to say when the question is Alice. I will serve her. Not Tom. Not his world. I exist for Alice.

THE CORONATION IS A LAVISH AFFAIR. In true Wonderland fashion, there are as many impossibilities as can be. The band plays late into the night, and Lord Hare decides to replace the water for the teapots with white liquor. Tall, leggy women in pink dresses walk with the exaggerated elegance of drunken flamingoes, and an assortment of men who look like bloated, sullen toads sit at most every table.

"They wish they were you," Tom whispers as he escorts me to the rose-covered archway where the king's crown rests on a pink velvet cushion.

"I'd kill them," I whisper back. I glance to my side and clarify: "Each and every one until there were no men left to bother her."

Tom gives me another toothy smile.

At the front of the crowded gathering, we stop. Beside Alice is the knight who was almost chosen to be king. He gazes at Alice in awe, and she smiles briefly in his direction.

I kneel before her and make a mental note to kill the knight after all.

She extends her left hand and takes his sword.

When my beloved lifts the blade into the air, I see blood-lust in her eyes. My Alice is mad. She debates my death. It is neither the first nor the last time.

Then, steadily, she lowers the blade and pronounces, "I knight thee, Lord Rose. Stand and be recognized."

I stand, face the assembled crowd of both Wonderlandians and imports from the Original World. None of them matter. They are background at my union with the perfect woman.

I take Alice's hand. "My love. My queen. There is nothing I won't do for you. No life I won't end. No obstacle I won't conquer."

"Such is the nature of the Red King," Alice murmurs.

She's not wrong.

"I'll be better, though," I swear. I stare into her perfect face. "For you, my love. I'll be better."

Tom steps up to my other side.

"Bow and be named," he says.

I can't look away from Alice, but I bow my head as directed. The crown feels heavy, a part of me now as if silver thorns are slipping from the beautiful circlet and driving into my skull.

"I present to you Lord Rose, Red King of Wonderland," Tom pronounces.

As our subjects cheer, I lead Alice to the dance floor and take my bride, my queen, into my arms.

"No children," I swear to her. "No ignoring you for this or that lord or hobby."

Alice looks at me in hope.

"And if Lord Hare or any of the rest offend you, my beloved, I shall serve you their heads on jeweled platters."

The Red Queen laughs gleefully, and behind us, under the rose-bedecked arbor, I see Tom tip his head to me.

Ours is a mad, mad world, and I am grateful to serve my queen.

Our village is nestled on a ledge. Our houses are fashioned of the wood that the land provides. Our byways are woven of root and vine, strung from soil to canopy. We *should* be safe, but still they come, a never-ceasing barrage. The constant anxiety, the threat of wolves always pacing near: it's not how things should be. I am as sure of this as I am that the moon will be dark tomorrow. I cannot tell you how I know, only that I do. Some truths live in the meat and marrow of our bodies, passed from mother to daughter, carried forward in our breath and blood.

And so I hunt. This is what I was raised to do.

I scan the undergrowth, watching for the enemies that scale the cliffs to reach us. No matter how many we stop, how many arrows are loosed, the wolves still come. They came before my aunt Mila held the sword in her hand, before I drew breath, and they will still come when our bodies are rotting in the earth.

"Hello," my aunt Mila says from somewhere behind me.

Whatever route of vine and branch she traveled brought

her touchably close to where I stand. No one but Mila would be able to get this close without my notice.

"Wolves?"

"None so far," she answers. "The archers think they've stopped all of them."

I snort. "They always think that."

They aren't always wrong. Sometimes, the archers are thorough enough to leave no enemies to fight. Other nights, though, Mila and I bloody our weapons as we stand at the edge of the woods. The wolves are a relentless tide.

"Glenda was taken this morning," Mila says.

"At the river? There were archers and--"

"No. Gathering roots." My aunt's hand is resting idly on her sword hilt. Her fingers curl around it as if she's about to draw the blade. "Her daughter was in the birthing hut. The medic's roots weren't easing her pains."

"Some births are hard," I point out.

Despite best intentions, it's a difficult subject for me. Choosing to birth the young is risky. Not everyone survives. My womb-mother didn't. The elders try to choose the fittest of us for the task, preferring those who are built for a full womb. Sometimes, we must risk to bring forth our daughters.

The birth lines are carefully minded. As with any crop we grow, there are those who track the origins to be sure there are healthy yields. What we cannot control is gender. We have only daughters. Once, I suspect our ancestors made a choice to make this so. We are a village of women, and we bear no sons.

When we select womb-mothers, we work to be sure there are no traits we value that are lost in the breeding. It's harder when we must rely on the few men who stay in our breeding huts, but keeping too many men in the village leads to problems. We breed with the ones we capture, set them free, and then wait until another invader has the traits we need. Capture. Keep. Repeat. It is how things have always been.

They seem happy, as if the constant stream of women seeking a filled womb is a gift. Rutting is what they seek of us anyhow. We explain our terms; they agree or we send them back to the ground where they can rejoin their own tribe. There is never force. We don't believe in mating by force.

If they didn't keep trying to invade our village, we'd need to figure out another way to handle breeding. For now, though, we kill easily ten times as many as we capture. Unlike them, we never go out raiding to fill our breeding huts. They come and steal my sisters to birth their young. We simply defend our village--keeping some, killing most.

That is my function. Not breeding. Not teaching. Not preparing meals. Aunt Mila and I were chosen to hold the swords. We keep the wolves from the village. We will die in the service of our sister-mothers-aunt-daughters some day. Each and every woman in our village has a role, and in exchange for fulfilling ours, Mila and I are fed and loved. We are valued.

And we will value our sister-mothers-aunt -daughters until our bodies have no blood or breath remaining.

A rustling in the brush to our side has both of us sliding steel from sheath. Our swords are often nourished with the blood of our enemies. We are not hesitant to draw or to make use of our blades.

Above us are archers. They can kill at a distance, but the canopy is so thick that anyone who reaches the edge of the village is ours to handle. Once the wolves scale the mountain, fighting up close is often the only recourse.

More noise comes from the dense cover.

Something is in there. The foliage is so thick that the best we can do is watch and wait. The forest is not willing to be restrained. We would not ask it to do so either. We coexist with the earth, not at odds with it.

A shrill cry from the growth--and we relax. A peccary's coarsely furred flank is visible. Fortunately, the feral pigs are no threat to us. If the animal charges, we'll cut it down and deliver the meat to the village. If it ignores us, we'll ignore it.

Mila and I aren't hunters of animals. Only men. Only wolves.

By morning's light Glenda hasn't been found, and no wolves have scaled the mountain-side, so we descend to the river far below and patrol there. Typically, we only go this far if our sister-mothers-aunt-daughters are going to collect water. The archers are on alert, but Mila and I descend with them so as to protect them.

One of our own was taken, though. This, too, we must address.

Swords drawn and ready, Mila and I explore as far as the paths into the forest have been carved. No one truly expects us to find Glenda. If the wolves take you, there is no reason to hope.

Only one of ours has survived, has returned, and she has become a lesson we will not soon forget. There was a girl, back when I was no more than a child with a dagger to train with instead of a proper sword. I was only seven then.

Her name . . . we don't speak it.

When we found her, her lips were bleeding. Her body was covered in scratches, bruises, bites . . . and I wished her an easy death. A part of me--one I was ashamed of afterwards--thought that I would choose death over survival.

But the body heals. Bruises fade. Bones knit.

We thought the Nameless had healed. Voiceless but alive, she survived--and in her womb, she carried her child to the safety of our village. The wolves had stopped tormenting her when they realized their cruelty had put a child in her womb. They let her rest, but they had already severed her tongue. They took her words just as they'd impeded her freedom and invaded her body.

So she escaped. The Nameless returned to where our archers could see her, and my sister-family killed the wolves. We brought her home.

Her eyes were different, though. After her return, the Nameless looked into every shadow as if the wolves might hide there. She was a hunted thing. We brought water to her. We fed her. We clothed and healed her body. The village elders did not ask her to work, to speak, to care for herself. She was safe within our village, protected from everything but her memories. No one could slay those.

But her feet did not need to touch the forest floor.

Not long after her return, the Nameless birthed a child. When the child was born, she named the girl Victorie. The elders feared that the babe would be a boy, that they'd need to decide if it was going to be allowed to survive, but fortunately, Victorie came. The Nameless gave birth to a daughter.

The Nameless nursed Victorie until she was sure the child would thrive. One day, when the girl was weaned, the Nameless handed the babe to one of the aunts, walked to the edge of our village, and stepped into nothingness.

Only then did her feet again touch the soil.

"Victorie!" Mila's rasp of a voice carries across the ropes as clearly as if I were already in the sword hut with her. Aunt

Mila is rarely loud, but Victorie tries the resolve of even the most patient of women.

The girl has just turned ten. At her age, I had already moved from dagger to sword. Victorie still has not been taught much beyond defense. It is not my place to argue, but when I can, I do. The girl is meant to fight. It is in the marrow of the bones that were made in blood and violence. I see it. We all do.

Only Mila and I are not frightened by it.

Silently, I step into the hut where I have spent so many of my hours and days. In some ways, the reed covered floor is more comforting than the small hut I share with Mila. This is the one space where all I am asked to do is to create the violence that is my nature, too.

"Auntie," Victorie says in greeting.

She takes a fighter's stance. Her form isn't bad.

"Victorie." I have no words that are permitted. The elders had decided that the girl would not be raised in the care of Mila. Instead, Victorie was passed from mother-hut to mother-hut, her presence a treasure beloved of every mother.

All but us.

And yet, she was meant to be ours. The motherless daughters are given to the blade, raised to protect our village. This has always been so--until Victorie.

Victorie's feet are steady, and her crouch is deep. The bladeless hilt she holds is gripped correctly, too. "I want to fight. I *need* to."

As she has so many times, Mila starts, "You are to be practicing letters, basic defense, and—"

"Why do you all act like I am a child?" Victorie doesn't swing the hilt, nor does she stomp her foot. "I am meant for this."

Mila's gaze meets mine over Victorie's head. The

unspoken question: do we go over the elders' heads? This is not a choice Mila can make alone. I will bear the weight of the elders' reaction, too. The daughter of the Nameless is sheltered. Victorie is our prize, the treasure we stole from the wolves. The elders want her to be kept safe, and those who defend our village from wolves are not safe.

I nod. The choice to train her in the weapon was always inevitable: Victorie will be taught the sword, or she will injure herself trying. We will hide her lessons as best we can, as long as we can.

She should have been ours anyhow. The girl is motherless. I had been a motherless child. Mila had too. Sure, the village is still one family, and sure, we are all raised as family. "No girl has a true mother," so say the elders, but there is a bond between womb-mother and child that still exists. A girl who grows inside the flesh of another feels a tie to her, and so, too, do the womb-mothers. Those without womb-mothers bond together. Victorie is not mine or Mila's the way a womb-daughter belongs to her mother, but she is ours in the way of sisters, of motherless daughters, of those who survived.

"There are reasons, good reasons, no one wants harm to come to you, Victorie," Mila says.

"You all pretend that I don't know, but I do." Victorie lifts her chin.

There is a fighter's spirit in the girl. It was born there when her womb-mother crawled through dirt and over rock to return to the village. It was born there when three-year-old Victorie saw that no other child had fire-tinted hair and blacked the eyes of several children for calling her "wolf girl."

We may be a family, but we are not one without squabbles.

"Form matters, Victorie," Mila begins.

I take up the two-handed sword that is my own, the sword

I have named and bloodied, and I begin to move slowly through the positions. Neither of us tell Victorie to follow my moves. I may execute each guard and cut slower than usual, and Mila may silently correct Victorie's form, but no one says that we are teaching her.

No one says she is the newest of our sword-sisters.

#

OVER THE NEXT THREE YEARS, Victorie makes progress faster than either of us could hope. Mila and I hide it. We lie for her. Something about the child makes us want to protect her above ourselves. If I ever were chosen to be a womb-mother, I expect that it would feel like this. This feral girl makes me want to slaughter every wolf, even as I see their presence in her. She has a ferocity that is unlike the daughters of the village. No other had been born in violence, and her womb-mother's rage seems to be a part of the very bones of Victorie.

The elders pretend not to see that trait flourish. They do not remark that she clings to us like a welcome shadow. Maybe they explain it as motherless ones finding each other. Maybe they choose to ignore it because they, too, see that it was inevitable. Either way, we are not stopped from training her in stealth. It is not endorsed, but we are not told to stop.

And Victorie takes to the sword the way I had hoped to when I was a girl. I don't recall a time when there wasn't a blade within my reach, but I was never the natural fighter that she is. Weapons seem to be an extension of her body. I have begun to fear her sometimes when she fights, but even at her most frightening, Victorie will pause and smile at us. We are not in danger. The village is safer with such a fighter preparing to join us at the edge of the forest.

But that is not what she does.

Her plans are larger.

"Have you thought about going on the offensive?" Victorie asks one evening as we break bread.

"We strike the moment they enter our village," Mila says.

"Take the fight to them. If we trained some of the others, we c--"

"No," I say. "We protect them. We do not ask them to risk their safety."

"They'll keep coming." Victorie paces away from us. Back to us, she adds, "The only way they'll stop is if they are no more. Send a spy. Send me. I look like them. I can get information and--"

"No." Mila follows and tries to touch the girl's arm. "We defend. We do not attack."

Our Victorie is of the wolves as well as of our village, so we ought not be surprised that a year later, the girl slips away to seek the wolves. We ought not think it strange that she has the drive to slaughter those who cost her a womb-mother. We ought not be surprised that she wants to protect us: Victorie is a weapon in a way that no one expected.

#

WHEN WE REALIZE that Victorie has gone, Mila and I gather our weapons and descend. We leave our village in silence; perhaps it is in guilt. The child, young woman now, has done what we've dreamed of. At only fourteen years, she's gone to attack the wolves. She did not tell us before she left. She did not ask to have our swords at her side. In some way, we have failed her. We have lost Victorie because we were not willing to change.

"The elders--"

"Will not need to know," Mila insists. "We find her. We bring her home."

It does not occur to either of us that Victorie cannot be found. It does not seem possible that she will be kept by the wolves. She is ours, and we will bring her home.

At the base of the mountain, we look at the river where we get our water. If there were a way to draw it up to the canopy where we live, we would not need to descend at all. This is our weakness. We can collect that which falls from the sky in basins and barrels. It is not enough. The earth provides, but not always in the ways that we would like.

I did not hesitate when we descended to the river's edge, or when we crossed beyond the paths, but as we reach the edge of the forest and step into a vast open space, I grow anxious. The land where the wolves live is different than our dense forest. The difference, the sheer openness, fills me with fear.

Still we go, knowing that they will see us. In such space, there is no cover. If they had archers, we'd be bleeding by now. However, it is not our death they have ever sought. What they want is not a thing my mind understands. Our wombs. Our flesh. Our obeisance. I am unsure.

But I feel exposed as we cross.

When we see their village, my fear flashes into terror. There are more wolves than I knew could exist. They watch us. Mouths slit open like mad animals whose tongues loll out. They step forward. Weapons not in hand ,as if we are no threat. Perhaps against such numbers we are not.

There are women, too. In the wolves' village, I see girls and women. No crones are in sight, but there are a lot of women here--enough to bear their young. They look away, and they turn their backs to our approach.

The horror slowly washes through me like venom sliding

into my veins, making its way to my heart. The wolves had no need of our wombs. The wolves could stay here and never seek out my village. My sister-mothers-aunt- daughters were never essential to the wolves, not for creation of life. We had thought they had no women of their own. We had thought they were like us, a village of one kind. Seeing their village sends the venom from vein to heart.

They chose to come for us. They chose to bring their violence to my people. I understand rage in a new way. My sword lifts in tandem with Mila's.

And they begin to raise weapons and surge toward us.

Mila and I train daily. We have killed many wolves. The sheer number of them now makes it unlikely that we can survive.

"Do you see her?" she asks.

I'm looking, scanning the village, seeking the girl. "No."

"Victorie!" Mila yells.

No one answers. She is not to be seen. If she is here, I'm not sure where she hides.

"If she comes, get her out of here." Mila does not add that we will not both survive. In truth none of the three of us may return to our home. I think briefly of the village, of no one with knowledge of swords or fight, of only manuals as a teacher.

"Go back," I urge. "I'll look for her--"

"There! She's over there."

Mila and I are back-to-back now, and I see a glimpse of a girl I think is Victorie. She blends into the group of children in a way she never has in our village. Our daughter-by-choice is alive.

A wolf comes. He is unarmed. Foolish, arrogant wolves. We end him, and several more, before we see wolves with staffs. They've taken young saplings and turned them into weapons. Rather than allow the trees to grow, they destroyed them.

"Safe?" Mila's voice is taut with worry, but I hear her blade making contact with our enemies all the same.

And then Victorie sees us. Her feet are like a dance across the earth, and she comes. A staff from a fallen wolf is in her hand before she is fully at our side.

"Aunties," Mila says as she joins us.

"We must go. Victorie, you--" A cry of pain from Mila interrupts my words.

Mila orders me, "Go. Take V--"

But Victorie is a child of our village as much as she is a wolf-born girl. She has an arm around a wolf, a dagger from Mila's side at his throat before more words can flow.

"Back up."

This one wolf matters to these monsters. He speaks, "Obey her!"

Mila and I stand at Victorie's sides. She orders their retreat, and we do likewise. With a wolf as our captive, we three retreat to the forest, to the river, to the base of our mountain.

Women descend. They do not question. They simply treat Mila.

Victorie stands guard, watching the wolf depart. Her arms fold as if she, too, must hold her pieces together. No one needs to say a word to know that Mila isn't going to survive. The aunts fuss, cleaning wounds, wiping blood, gathering sutures. It won't work. Mila knows it. I do too.

She holds out a hand for me. "Come."

I obey. The aunts are all my family. That's how we are. One family. The village is all one family.

But Mila is mine. I've slept on her floor, and I've shared my meals with her for my life. I was raised as if I was her own child. My duty, my role in our village, was to become Mila so that when today came, the village would be safe.

"Victorie," Mila says.

"No," the girl says.

"Victorie," Mila repeats, but she is looking at me as she adds, "Take her home and train her."

Several of the aunties gasp.

They collect their essentials, and steadily they ascend. Mila goes home with effort. The last one on the ground with me is Victorie, and despite how often I've done this very thing with Mila, this time it goes awry. Perhaps the archers are busy with Mila. Perhaps they did not watch as carefully as they ought. Either way, no arrows come when the wolf grabs me.

Mila is far above me, ascending the mountain when she sees. She begins to descend.

"No!" I yell, not at the wolf but at her. "Protect our home. Train another."

I am not sure if it's my scream or hers as she watches me lose my sword to the wolves that leap from the undergrowth, as I am stolen, as my sister- -mothers-aunt-daughters are help-less to save me.

And I am in the grip of wolves.

TIME PASSES, and my ability to fight is limited by the lack of food, the lack of rest, the wearing down of hope. After the first passing of the moon, time begins to slip and blur. I do not think of how long it has been--until I feel the tenderness in my breasts and my blood does not flow.

I think of the Nameless, of my long ago wish that she would find an easy death, and I understand how wrong that was. I do wish for death, easy or otherwise. Not for me. Not for the seed of a child that I carry in the cradle of my hips. If I die, I die, but I will not choose it. I do not seek it.

I do not wish my death. The wolf who trapped me, who has told me that he fathered my sister-daughter Victorie, who has foist his body onto mine. . . his death I wish.

I am in a tent of sorts. The prison where I am kept. The ground is hard, and the packed earth has left many bruises on my skin when I have been forced onto that unyielding earth. The wolf stands over me, smiling, with a slash of white in a worn and wrinkled face.

"What sharp teeth you have," I say.

He snarls at me, as if I will be frightened. We are so far beyond the time when I might cringe. I look down briefly, though, hiding my hatred.

"What bright eyes you have," I add once I've tucked my vitriol in the corner of my mind.

He smiles. Perhaps he thinks my words a compliment. They're not. I see the madness in his eyes. I've seen it in the many wolves I've cut down when they came into our forest. He is simply another wolf. Worse than some, perhaps, but at the end of it, he'll close those monstrous eyes just as they did.

I've no other choice. That truth has settled in my womb alongside my growing child. I was not meant for breeding, but my daughter will not be a motherless child. Not because I am any stronger than Victorie's womb-mother, but because Victorie and the child I carry will need to be taught the lessons Mila once taught me. My family needs women with reddened swords; my aunties, sisters, mothers, daughters need those of us who are willing to slay the wolves.

And I am willing.

His hand strokes my face, my breasts, my thighs. I do not move. I do not speak. Not this time.

"That's better. I like to look at you, girl." He looks down at my already rounding belly. I am too thin now for my growing child not to be obvious. He puts his other hand on my curve. On me. On the flesh that shelters my child. It is the closest he will ever come to touching my daughter.

"I could eat you up," he says. "You'd like that, wouldn't you? That's what you girls do up there, isn't it?"

"It is," I say quietly.

He stops, surprised that I spoke. I often ignore his taunts. I've never spoken as carefully, as gently as I do this day.

"And, yes, I like it," I add softly.

The dagger he's left by the tent flap is still too far too reach. I know it's there. I know it's out of reach. There is nothing I wouldn't do to reach it. Nothing.

He smiles, teeth again bared in an expression I know is to mean that he's happy. I need that, his happiness. I need him to believe I am but a harmless girl.

"I could do it better," he boasts.

I smile but lower my eyes. Modesty. Meekness. Fear. That's what his kind wants. It is not what my people teach, but I've watched it in the women in this village. They expect to be hit. They expect to bleed.

"Probably," I lie.

He laughs and hauls me to my feet. "Rutting would lose the babe, but this . . ."

"It's safe," I agree. Rutting is, too, but the only mercy a woman finds in the wolves' den is this: they think that mating must end during these months. I will not tell him this is untrue.

"You'll do it, too. For me." He says it like it's an order, but it's not a thing he can order, not unless he knocks out all my teeth. A wolf foolish enough to place his weapon in reach of my teeth would be made harmless. My teeth may not be as sharp as his, but they'd do the job. No other women would be forced under him.

For a moment, I consider it. I let the thought of the barbarism of it roll through my mind. I can't. Not because I am too kind, not because I am above revenge, but because he'd scream. That would bring the others. They would never let me survive if I unmanned one of them.

I lift the edge of the blood-stained dress they've forced me to wear. "Do you want to?"

He laughs, and I think it's the happiest I've heard him sound.

I am on my back again. I've been on my back so often these last four-month cycles. I squirm and praise him, lying to him about how wonderful he is, and as I do I ease ever closer to the dagger. My fingertips brush it finally.

I let out a fake noise of pleasure to cover any sounds as I pull the blade to me, secreting it under my shoulder. The sharp edge against my upper spine brings me far more pleasure than the man rooting under my skirt ever will. I roll my hips in the lie he is seeking, pretending joy.

When he's done, satisfied with his work, he sits back on his haunches and looks at me. His hand covers the bump on my belly again. Then he stands and gestures to his trousers. "Well?"

Slowly, I start to come to my knees, but I continue to my feet instead. The blade I've stolen slides across his throat. The only sound he makes is a gargling noise, which I cover with another loud exclamation of pleasure. This one, however, is genuine.

He tumbles to the ground, bleeding. My clothes are bloodied, and my blade is too. It is not a sword, but edges still cut. Blood still flows. I am whole again with a hilt in my hand.

"Now your eyes look like most every other wolf I've met."

Once I'm sure he's dead, I slice a hole in the tent and slip into the darkness. I follow the sounds of the water until I reach the river at the base of the cliffs.

I know the archers watch. I signal to them even as I don't see them, and I wait. I wash away the blood that coats my body, the saliva on my thighs, and then I discard the dress I've been forced to wear. I would rather be naked than in clothes chosen by wolves.

I save one strip of the dress to tie the dagger to my leg. Spoils of war. It will belong to my daughter one day.

When the long twist of vines falls down, I begin to climb, back to my home, back to my sisters. I am not broken. I am not defeated. I am Nameless, but I am Mother. I am Protector. I will keep my voice and my child.

I'll raise her to be strong, to fight the wolves, to protect our village. She will not be motherless, neither will Victorie. I am without the name I carried before now, but I am a Mother now. My daughters will fight, as I did, but not because they are motherless. So, too, will my sister-aunt-mothers.

It is not enough to have two women stand against the tide of wolves. We must all lift our swords, not only to protect those who wander from paths or linger where wolves prowl. I will be called Protector, Mother, and Teacher, all names I choose.

Until every piece of earth is safe, until all the soil is as a safe path, we must stand with swords raised.

"KNEE DEEP IN THE SEA"

I woke early--or perhaps didn't sleep. My body is still adjusting to the time zone hop from Southern California to the islands north of the Scottish mainland. Orkney. A series of islands, many of them uninhabited, in the cold North Atlantic Sea. To the east is Norway. To the West are Iceland and Greenland. In other words it's chilly even in the summer when there is endless light.

It's stunning, aside from the dead guy currently at my feet.

Still, it's just one dead guy. If no one was going to be judgmental, I'd admit that my favorite sort of man is a dead one.

This one is sprawled on the rocky beach as if he's been rejected by the sea, tossed back like rubbish that the tide returned to its origin. He's not dressed for swimming, and a clear set of fingerprints bruises his throat. I don't think they're mine. They could be, but I don't think I killed him. *Jason*. I'm sure he had a surname, but I didn't catch it. I'm fairly sure he was alive when I last saw him. We argued at a nearby pub. I may have kicked him. He may have called me a few ugly words.

Honestly, it doesn't matter if I did it. If I get arrested,

they'll have my fingerprints, and even if they *don't* match the ones on his throat, it'll be trouble. All it would take is one quick fingerprint match and everything I've built would be gone.

I'm not good at jail. I never have been—and if I'm ending up there it will be for a good reason. Not this.

JASON WAS NOBODY, a stranger I crossed after a few too many drinks. I'm not going to end up in jail for his death.

You need to do whatever it takes to make it in this world. Mama explained that fact of life right regularly, often before the lesson that *Men think with their willies, so smile pretty and lead with your bosom.*

I check his pockets, retrieve his wallet and mobile phone. I pull out the SIM card, toss it into the water, and then toss the phone, too. I empty the wallet. Far too many credit cards, a few membership cards, and some receipts. They scatter like bits of sea grass tossed into the waves. I hope I'm not damning some poor sea creature to death by adding Jason's trash to the sea, but the sea should erase his identity soon enough, and I'd rather not leave identifying evidence with the body. Without it, the police are left with fingerprint and dental records if he washes ashore or gets caught in a fisherman's net.

Dental records *can* be great to proof identity, but there's no database.

Still, it's better to be safe. I search for a heavy rock. A few moment later, Jason has fewer teeth, a fractured jaw, and a higher chance of being nothing more than an Unknown Male Victim if he returns to shore.

That leaves fingerprints.

I pull out my Leatherman and slice off most of the skin and meat at his fingertips. It's easier than the last time I did this. I rinse my hands, toss the teeth and bits of skin into the sea, and continue with my task.

Jason was obviously successful to some degree. I found plenty of money in his wallet--$112 in U.S. money, plus another £800 and €200. It's damp, but usable. I fold and shove it all into my pocket. There's no sense throwing cash into the sea. I don't take his watch or ring. Those are traceable and likely filled with DNA.

After another few moments of handling details, I roll him out into the icy Atlantic, wading far enough that I'm soaked to my hips and shivering. The sea, thankfully, is churning today, and in a few moments, the body is gone. A few credit cards blink like misplaced tropical fish before they're carried away.

The only witness to my actions is a seal. There is always a seal watching. I meet her gaze, seeking censure and finding none. Wild things are practical in ways that humans fail.

"I'm sorry about the credit cards," I say, not that she'll understand or hear me. The wind from over the sea seems to whisk the words away, leaving my lips cold. I hope she forgives me.

Unlike my silent watcher, I am not made for the cold wind or waves. She's why I'm here at this early hour, standing with my rain boots in the edge of the surf, watching the sun rise up over the cold waters. For a flicker of a moment I wish I could join her, dive into the surf and swim out to the deep waters where she is so at home. It's a foolish impulse, likely caused by too much whisky and not enough sleep. I'm shivering already from only a few moments in the icy water.

My entire body is off. Still. I can't seem to find my rhythm in this strange climate. The light lasts for most of the day this time of year, offering around five hours of darkness daily. It's completely destroyed my internal clock after not even a week.

The weather here tilts toward windy and wet, and the whole series of islands has only twenty thousand people.

It's not a place I'd have thought to visit on my own, but now that I'm here, I want to stay forever. I feel a calm I'd not realized I wanted. The sea is everywhere. Archaeological ruins seem to crowd the islands, and aside from the tourists pouring out of their busses to see some of the bigger sites, I have found myself alone for hours in wide stretches of stunning land. I don't recall the last time I'd been so far from crowds. Finding that solace was one of the reasons I applied for this job. Life in SoCal is just a bit too crowded for me sometimes. Orkney is an incredible escape.

Being here means that for the first time I love my new job. Most days, I question my sanity. Personal Assistant to a man whose upcoming documentary is called *Pinniped!* Most people call them seals, not pinnipeds, but my boss is pretentious. Given half a chance, he devolves into lecture on how people reduce both seals and sea lions to the singular term of "seal."

When I'm alone on the beach, the seals swim near enough to entice me into the water, and more than once I've found myself knee deep in the cold sea. I want to go with them, touch them, be in the water. What began as an extra for my job has become a strange love affair with the chilly waters and the creatures that watch me from the waves. I am . . . happy.

Aside from the dead guy.

Working in L.A. is far from glamorous. In the land of film, personal assistant to a documentary filmmaker is even less glamorous. Grants fund his work, so job security is nonexistent. Although, admittedly, this isn't forever: What I really want to do is write. Go ahead. Laugh. Every third person in LA wants to be a writer, thinks they're a writer, or is pitching something soon. The rest are actors or wannabe directors. I'm aware that I'm a stereotype, but I'm not the first small town girl who succeeded at her dreams. The difference between me and them is that I'm clever, and there is zero limit to what I'm willing to do to achieve my dreams. *Zero.* Possibly less than zero.

I remind myself of that as my boss saunters my way.

"I thought I'd find you here," he pronounces.

I glance at Jack, grateful that he wasn't here at sunrise. I'd rather not share the seals--or explain the body I rolled into the sea.

Jack Abrams is, in the way of successful men, falsely convinced that he's attractive. Forty-five years old, wrinkles already reaching out from his eyes and lining his forehead, average height, average face, Jack is nothing special. The best I can say is that he's more fit than most filmmakers, but in the looks department, he's average. In L.A. though, if you collect enough awards, grants, and prestige, looks are relative. When Jack looks in the mirror, he mistakenly sees one of the finer Hemsworth men.

"Isabel?"

I realize I haven't answered and try to sound calm as I say, "You missed the seals. I came early to watch them."

He looks at me in the same way I've seen him look at a meal as he decides if he ought to accept it or send it back to the kitchen. "Fascinating, aren't they?"

We stand in comfortable silence for several moments, both staring out to sea. I presume Jack is seeking seals, and I am quietly praying that he doesn't see the dead man or his credit cards bob to the surface.

"I need a local. Find one."

I glance at him. "A local to . . . ?"

"Give me the insider view."

"On *seals?*" I stare at him, not quite sure what he's going for here. It's likely to be some sort of gesture of authenticity. He does that, finds a way to add a touch of humanism to his stories. As much as I think he's an ass, I like that wherever he films he tries to show the locals as appealing. It balances the occasional big budget project he takes on to "fund his art."

If you read "ego" where he says "art," the interview clips are true.

Still, his success fuels my future career, so I nod and listen.

"I need someone with a thick accent."

He looks me up and down again. He hasn't invited me to his bed--yet--but he will. Jack Abrams has a reputation for trading favors for fucks. He's not coercive. I won't get fired for saying no, but I won't get ahead as fast. Truthfully, I just haven't decided if I'm going to say yes when he gets around to offering. I could use a few favors, and I'm not above fucking for them.

For now, I step a little closer and shiver. "Orkney is colder than I thought it would be."

"The old guys at the pub say it's because the Vikings cut down all the trees." Jack's gaze scans the water, again seeking the sometimes illusive creatures we're here to film.

"So, would one of them--"

"A woman, Isabel. Better for optics." He affects a terrible accent and adds, "Why watch old men if there's a pretty Scottish lass to stare at?"

I nod.

"She needs to be camera-ready or close enough to have that 'raw beauty,' like you have when you put effort into it." He smiles as he says this, as if it's a compliment.

I smile back, looking genuine because I've practiced that lie my whole life. "You're always so sweet, Jack."

He continues looking out to sea.

The only way I could sleep with him is if I have a few drinks first--and it's been a good day of filming. The high of a good creative day can make even Mitchell, the key researcher for this project, a *bit* more attractive.

Jack leaves, and I am left alone in the windy weather. For all of my complaints, he's a genuinely talented man, and when he's contemplating the project, not much else matters to him. That's what I want: a story that makes my eyes slip to that far-away place where nothing else matters. I want to be consumed. Instead, I've spent the last two years in pointless jobs just to pay the rent.

———

THREE DAYS PASS in which I realize that no one has mentioned the missing man. He died. Now he's a meal for the many creatures of the sea that feed on the dead meat they find. Likely he ate enough seafood that there's a fairness in his body nourishing them now. Really, if you think about it, by moving his corpse those few feet I gave the sea an offering.

I protected myself.

It's not like I killed him. *Probably.* I'm fairly sure I would have proof if I did. Murder is like that: It leaves a mark on you.

Since I seem to be avoiding jail, I need to focus on the project. I haven't found a single person willing to be inter-viewed--other than the old men who seem eager to tell tales and drink. We put out feelers, and I hung fliers around Kirk-wall, the main city in Orkney. No bites.

Maybe we just need some good public relations.

So, I'm at the pub again. A different one. Tonight is a "peatfire tales" event where locals tell folklore to tourists who sip one free glass of single malt while enjoying the unique scent of burning peat. I came here searching the local or locals who could go on record for the project--or at least some people who might talk to me so I can find some possibilities for Jack.

I started the night determined not to be charmed by either the folklore or the fire, but when I realized that there weren't any "pretty Scottish lasses" to lure into a video spot, I give in and order myself a quality glass of whisky. I am, after all, a writer. Unpublished perhaps, but I am still a writer. More importantly, I'm an excellent liar. That's the trick to success in life: the ability to lie, to con, to manipulate. Well, that and a wee bit of ruthlessness. My mama taught me that part.

Tonight, the only ones here are tourists with family or friends. The only single person here, other than me, is a pretty young woman standing at the back of the room. She's as far from the fire as anyone can be without leaving the room, so she's draped in shadows. She has long brown hair, falling to her low back. Her body is neither slight nor heavy, and her height is average. She wears jeans. a plain cotton top, and a long cardigan. Nothing about her appearance is atypical, except a small smile that says she knows secrets or perhaps is holding back laughter. She holds her body like an athlete, and when she moves to the side to let a server pass by, I can't help thinking that she moves as gracefully as the sea. I wonder briefly if she is a dancer or runner. Either way, I cannot pull my gaze away.

When she smiles, I swear I can feel my body tilt toward her the way the sea follows the moon. Before I mean to do so, I'm across the room, beside her, too near her. She is not the first woman I've flirted with at anonymous bars. She likely won't be the last. She is, for reasons I don't ponder too closely, the first person who has ever been irresistible to me.

"Hello, Isabel," she says with a strange lilt to her voice.

I swear I can hear waves. I glance at the storyteller with her musicians, wondering how they created that sound with no electronics. I look to the window, into the darkness where the sea waits.

"Would you like a drink?" The woman extends a full glass to me. "Or have you had too much already?"

I realize that she has two drinks. She was expecting me. I don't know how--or how she knows my name.

When I try to ask, she touches a finger to her lips and says, "The storyteller is still speaking. Be polite."

Mutely my gaze follows her hand as she points toward the woman at the fireside. The woman at the fire might be speaking Gaelic or gibberish for all I know. Her voice lifts and falls, drifting to a whisper and erupting in a roar. There's music in her words. Scotland seems like a land where music is the pulse that underlies the whole of the landscape. It reminds me of home. Not California, but my real home in the South. The music is different, but in both places, it rises up from the land. Here, the sea's waves move in the people, and the language rolls. The syllables are merely waves that found their way through human lips. It's different than the bayou, where thick air feels like it makes our words and our motions slower. The bayou makes the mundane turn mystical.

And a few moments or hours later, when the woman at my side meets my gaze and simply walks away, I'm fairly certain that she's wrought of music and sea. I could swear I hear it, feel it, moonlight over waves, waves crashing over my head. It's all fine, though, as long as she's there. It's inexplicable. My glass of whisky is full yet again, so I could be drunk. Either way, I follow her, follow the music that slips from her skin, the waves that roll in the sway of her hips, the steady beat of her footfall. As she glances back at me, I want to tell her that I'd follow her anywhere.

I try to say just that.

I turn and leave the few lights of the tiny town behind.

She's there, just ahead of me. She glows like she's swallowed the moon, and I am nothing but water that must follow her pull.

I'm knee deep in the sea when I realize she's gone. She slips away in the darkness, and I am left without her light. I back away until I'm standing at the edge of the sea, cold and alone and still far too drunk.

I sleep or perhaps pass out. When I wake, I see a lump in the dark beside me. It's not as warm as me, but it's not so cold that I mistake it for a rock. *Seal.* I feel like I've been offered a rare gift when I snuggle closer for warmth and it doesn't move away. I'm grateful for the body heat as the liquor continues to hit me. Night is only a few hours in Orkney, so my whisky-soaked mind sees no issue with waiting--especially now that I have the seal to snuggle.

"Thank you," I whisper, carefully patting the slick skin of its back.

When the sun breaks over the sky, I see that I am not, in fact, cuddling the chilly body of a pinniped. I can only surmise that I was drunker than I thought because there next to me is another dead man. This time it's Mitchell, the camera-man, clad in a puffy coat that I had mistaken for seal's skin. He's on his side, and his massive girth makes him seem vaguely seal-shaped in this position.

He's been stabbed. Blood has pooled around the edges of his body, collected in the crevices where the sea has steadily carved its mark. I check myself, seeking clarity. Am I a killer? Well, yes, of course I am *a* killer. I've been a killer for years, but am I responsible for *this* body?

I have no recollection of buying the knife that's caked with sand and crusted blood.

The tide is coming in, and soon the dry spot where I've been cuddled up to a dead man will be in the waves.

"Did I kill you?" I ask, the words no more than wasted air in the sea breeze. "I should remember if I did."

I didn't like him. Our last conversation was ugly. He called me a "glorified prostitute" and said that my only qualifications for the job are that I'm "fuckable and desperate." He wasn't wrong, but I still tried to slap him. He stopped me, shoved me at the wall, and ground his hips against me. His last words to me were "So high and mighty, aren't you? If I offered you enough money, you'd change your tune."

I'm careful not to push him over as I move away. Mitchell is a large man, and he'd be impossible to roll without help. I unzip his jacket, pull out his passport and bills. He has more cash than I would expect. I pocket it, toss the rest, and continue to try to depersonalize his body in case it's found. After enough practice, the process is easy.

Mitchell is the fifth dead man I've frisked.

I worry, briefly, about his disappearance. Muggings happen in Scotland, but Orkney has the lowest crime rate in the nation. Briefly, I hope that means they also don't have any sort of police force able to investigate disappearances. There are so many islands, so many cliffs, that a search seems improbable. And, more importantly, the landscape seems to invite dreamers who just want to get lost. Since I've arrived, I've been battling the urge to wander and maybe find whatever I've lost inside me.

I pat Mitchell again. "I hope this isn't what I lost, Mitch. The urge to kill."

I rip his shirt so I have a way to hold the knife, and then I use the blunt end to knock out his teeth. It's easier than it ought to be. I turn it around, slice off the flesh of his fingertips. Routine. Simple. It's not perfect, but the sea should help hide what the blade doesn't.

Afterward I wipe the knife and handle clean and hurl the knife as far as I can.

I'm not a killer; I'm simply practical.

Once, when I was a kid, I'd killed a man. Okay, admittedly, I killed *three* of them over a couple months, but it wasn't like I did it for pleasure. As far as I know, I haven't done it since. I'm not certain about Jason or Mitchell, but I don't go seeking men to kill. I'm not a sociopath. I killed a few men early in life, but I was just a girl with plans. I was acquitted when no bodies were found. The charges went away, and I changed my name. Met a guy. Daniel. Paid for papers. Then I had a clean slate, a new life.

I did *not* kill Daniel, although he did turn up dead a year later. Part of me didn't so much mind because he knew the old me and new me. I suspect I might've killed him if I'd been thinking clearly, but I wasn't. Fate handled it.

I think.

Is the "real me" what I've found here? Did I kill two more men and forget? Had I killed Daniel after I got my papers from him?

I remember killing the ones whose lives I ended when I was nineteen. I remember the sounds of the bayou when I slipped my tiny boat with dead cargo into the water and went in search of the pigs. They eat more than the gators, despite what television shows say. Eaten by gators is just sexier or something. The pigs are practical, though.

Here on Orkney, I have no pigs. The sea, however, is willing to help.

The tide is coming in, and soon the dry spot where I've been cuddled up to a dead man will be in the waves.

The tidewater starts puddling around my feet, covering Mitchell inch by inch.

In the surf, I see a seal. They seem to be everywhere here.

It's easy to understand why Jack chose this series of islands. The seals bask on rocks that jut out of the water or amidst the rocks on some of the coastal stretches. They haul out on land, but never quite let us approach.

I should've known that it wasn't a seal offering me warmth in the early hours. Maybe they'll offer *him* some warmth as his body finds its final home in the cold waters of the North Atlantic.

SEVERAL HOURS later I'm at a table in the Lynnfield Hotel dining room where Jack has stationed us today. It's mid-morning, past the breakfast crowd and not yet time for lunch, so we are alone in the room. Like many of the restaurants I've visited on the islands, there is a strange out-of-time feeling to the room. The mix of antiques and no-longer-modern but not-yet-antique touches doesn't clash, but there is a strange sense that the year could be years past or years future.

Time moves differently on these islands, though, so this seems right. The extreme imbalance of the light and darkness, the peculiar lack of trees, and the constant press of sea and wind have started to re-shape me. I want to ask the others about it, but no one in the crew speaks to me unless it's for business. The nature of my position is that I belong to Jack, as if I am an extension of his eyes and ears.

"I've come for the job," she says. "For your film."

The woman from the peatfire readings stands in front of me.

I'm first tier, technically doing the interviews unless he wants to follow-up. Meanwhile, he sits at a table to my left with a pot of tea and a stack of pages he's alternately scowling at or scrawling on.

"Name?"

"Margaret. You may call me Margaret." She pronounces these words as she's bestowing a gift upon me, and I don't feel able to ask for her surname. She has the same small smile that she had at the pub.

Jack looks up at the sound of her voice. I see him notice her voice and her figure. She's not wrapped in the layers that our crew still favors. Instead, she wears a simple black cotton t-shirt, jeans, and low hiking boots. Her only concession to the weather is a red scarf.

"We met," I manage to say.

"Yes. More than once."

I'm sure she's wrong. I'd have remembered her if we'd met repeatedly. "No, at the pub. I've only been here a few days and . . ."

She looks past me then. Smiling.

"And who have we here?" Jack asks.

His voice is slick and charming, and I know already that he'll offer her a job. Margaret will be the face and voice speaking of the sea. It seems fitting. She makes me think of the ocean, or maybe I'm simply smitten. The way she moves feels too fluid for land.

". . . with Isabel."

I look up, realizing that I've been lost in my thoughts. "What?"

"Of course," Jack says, speaking right over me. "These days one can never be too sure. Some men would treat a woman wrong, take advantage. You're smart to be cautious of strangers, but"--he drops an arm around my shoulders companionably--"Isabel will vouch for me."

"He is a talented filmmaker," I reply dutifully.

"And a gentleman." He squeezes me slightly as he says it.

I nod. I can't say he is--or isn't. Silence seems more like

truth. Somehow lying to *her* seems wrong.

We settle at the table where Jack was working, and the server takes this as a cue to check in on us. In short order, another pot of tea is en route to us.

Margaret's hands wrap around the tea cup as if she's afraid it might suddenly fall or shatter at her touch. She drinks carefully, and I worry that I've truly slipped into some other world for a moment. Perhaps this is what a psychotic break is like. I keep finding dead men, and I'm attributing odd traits to a perfectly lovely Scottish woman.

"Since you're hear for the seals, have you heard of selchies? Or of the Finfolk?" she asks.

Jack tenses. "This is a scientific film."

"Ah." Margaret pushes her teacup away. "I thought you were asking after local commentary."

"On tourism, maybe the impact of the fisheries. Not fairy tales. Do you know about the seal watching tours or the fisheries? Or--"

At this Margaret's smile slips a little. "The fisheries get angry at the seals for hunting fish, as if they should know that *those* fish are reserved for humans. Trap the fish in tiny spaces--" Her lips press as she cuts herself off. Inhales. Exhales. The smile returns. "I have no need to speak of them. There is nothing to be said that will change man's greed."

"Well, then, tourism? Or some sort of encounter with the seals?"

"An encounter with the seals," she echoes. Her hands curl around her teacup again. This time her fingers are too far forward, as if she intends to lift it with only her palms.

Without thinking I pull the cup forward by its base, resettling it in her hands.

She startles at the gesture, staring at me again as if *I* am some curious thing.

Trying not to shake and spill the hot liquid on her, I carefully pour Margaret's tea before I say, "I thought 'Selchie' was the Orcadian word for pinnipeds, seals."

I am rewarded with a smile. I'd do a lot more than pour tea for such a look. Margaret may not be carrying the moon inside her skin as I thought when I was too far into my whisky, but she is remarkably alluring.

Jack makes a small face, but he doesn't pursue the topic. I have no doubt that Margaret would feature in stills for the film, a human touch for the scientific project. It sells. Footage of seals isn't enough. Tourists in Southern California can walk up to the colony at La Jolla and take selfies with them. Until we'd come here, I'd questioned the logic of the project. Who *hasn't* seen a pinniped up close?

"Tell us," Jack relents.

"Here, on the islands," Margaret says, "there are selchies, seal-folk, and there are Finfolk. The Finfolk, like many fey things, steal away mortals. They are cruel and hurtful."

"Humans or Finfolk?" Jack interjects.

"Yes." Margaret's gaze drifts to the windows, and I can see in her the same longing I feel when I stand at the edge of the sea.

"The selchies," she adds, "are not cruel. By nature, they are seals. Harmless. Playful. They come ashore, and they shed their pelts so they might meet the humans they see from afar."

She turns to meet Jack's gaze and then mine. "They see you watching them. They see you with your cameras and your curiosities, and so they come to you."

Despite all of the reading I've done on pinnipeds the last month, this is new to me. The words pluck at something I've heard since we arrived in Scotland: a warning in a song in a pub one night, one of those folksy lamenting tunes that go beautifully with another glass of Scotland's finest drink.

"You cannot understand the seals if you don't know of the Finfolk and the selchies," Margaret warns.

"I'm sold." Jack leans back in his seat and claps his hands together. "We'll want you standing at the water when you talk. Intersplice your story with footage of the pinnipeds. This can work."

He's scribbling notes now.

"Isa, get her information." He's up and moving. "I'll call Ned. We'll want"--he glances at her, and she's no longer a woman but a subject behind a lens even though his hands lack the camera in this moment--"hair loose. There's always a breeze, so that natural thing."

He glances at me briefly. "Talk to Carrie."

"Cheri," I interject.

He waves my correction away. "The costume girl. Talk to her about wardrobe. She can't wear *that*."

And then he leaves, lost to any measure of civility now that his mind is on the project. This, too, is part of my job. I handle the hurt feelings. I explain his "creative genius." I turn to Margaret prepared to do my due diligence, but she's staring out the window again.

"He's doesn't mean to insult you."

Margaret stares at me in confusion. "There was insult?"

I exhale in relief. "Not intentionally. He's very focused."

She nods.

"Can I get information?" I ask. "Your mobile number?"

Margaret stands. "I am not one for being indoors. Walk with me, Isabel."

And once again she moves with such speed and grace that I wonder if she runs in her free time. I am stone sober today, but I still struggle to keep pace. It does not occur to me to ask her to slow or to refuse to follow her.

We walk quickly, me trailing her slightly, until she stops

as suddenly as she had begun. At the water. At the precise spot where I found Jason a few days ago. Warily, I look around for evidence that he was here, a washed-up credit card or shoe. There is nothing.

"Nature sets things right," she tells me.

I nod mutely.

"Shall I tell you of the selchie and of the Finman?" she asks softly.

"Sure." I don't see any reason not to listen, and there are several good reasons to indulge her.

"You don't believe then?"

I laugh. "In fairy tale creatures? No. I'm from the middle of nowhere, but that doesn't make me a fool."

Margaret glances at me without turning, so she looking at me from the corner of her eye. "So, do you think me a fool, Isabel? An island 'lassie' as your man would call me." Her own musical voice grows harsh, as if she's using the clunky accent Jason affected. "A wee island fool willing to be used to sell your film?"

"No." I swallow with difficulty. "He's not my man, either. He's my *employer*."

"Fine. You still do not believe the things I tell you, though?" Margaret sounds angry now, as if I've insulted her.

"I don't question what you believe, but--"

"I believe in truth," Margaret insists. "The things I see. The things I touch with my hands."

"Me, too," I agree.

"Then you'll want to hear about the selchie and the Finman. They weren't from the same place, but they wanted the same things." Margaret's voice rises and falls, as if heartbeat and the breath and the sea all aligned at once. Her voice was all of them, pulling my lungs to motion as she pulled the waves to her. It was foolish, and fanciful, but I would swear on my father's grave that she was somehow controlling all of it.

"The people forget that the selchies aren't as kind as the stories say. They forget that water folk are kin to the fey things that live in the isles," Margaret sing-speaks. "The Finfolk, though, if they are remembered at all, are known to be man-stealers. No one forgets their cruelty."

"But *both* are cruel? And . . . steal people?"

"They're fey," Margaret answers with a half-shrug, as of that's an answer. Maybe, to her, it is. "What they wanted, they took. What they needed, they stole. Who among us doesn't want to do the same?"

I don't reply. What is there is to say?

"Do not ever lie to me, Isabel." Margaret reaches up and cups the side of my face. "I am not so different from the sea. My anger is damning."

I'm not sure what the right reaction is in that moment, but I'm fairly certain that mine is far from wise.

"Come to my hotel?"

Margaret shakes her head. "I am not much for buildings. Even when a pretty woman will be there to greet me. I came inside once today. For you. Another day, though."

THE NEXT NIGHT I'm in front of the hotel where we're all staying when Jack comes outside for a smoke. He startles at seeing me there. After a moment, he lights a cigarette, takes a long drag, and says, "You're not at the bar."

I shrug. There's no polite way of telling my boss that I decided that I ought to stop drinking entirely because I've almost doubled my up close and personal contact with corpses in the past week.

"Did Mitchell say anything about a trip?"

"No . . . ?"

Jack scowls. "I wanted him to research the fairy tales that woman was talking about."

"Margaret."

He glances at me, motioning the hand holding the cigarette as if reeling a reply from me.

"Her name is Margaret."

"Right." He smokes silently for several moments before saying, "I don't need an assistant."

"Are you firing me, Jack?"

"No, I'm just pointing out the obvious. You knew that when I hired you, right?" He is hazy with the halo of smoke around his head. "It's more of a liking someone to handle details and any other needs I have. I have needs, Isabel."

"Sex wasn't in the contract."

He shrugs. "True, but if it's not offered, I won't keep you on payroll. That's not a secret, Isabel."

As much as I want to argue, claim insult, I don't feel like lying. I've started to think I lie to protect other people, avoid conflict, as much as to get my way. I don't actually care about conflict, and my way is not what I thought it was. I glance over at Jack and admit, "I figured I'd have a few drinks and let you take me to your room when you got around to it."

"But?"

"I don't care about the job enough any more." It feels good to be so honest with him, to not feel so trapped. After a pause, I add, "And you're not as handsome as you think."

He stares at me in shock.

"Success didn't change your looks or the flab at your middle or your horrible manners." I know better, but I keep on talking. "You're rude, and if you weren't famous, you'd never get laid without paying for it. And truthfully, I'm not enough of a whore these days to trade sex for a paycheck."

Jack's quiet for several minutes before saying, "You're fired, Isabel. Find your own way back to L.A. And you can pay for the rest of your trip if you stay past tomorrow's check-out."

He walks away, dropping his cigarette on the ground where it smolders.

I stomp on it before I collect it and toss it in the rubbish bin. Rain or not, that's an asshole move. He's not too good to care about the environment. Litter, especially in an area where rain is constant, makes its way to the sea. He's adding poison to the sea where the creatures he supposedly adores live and eat. Rage fills me. I want to scream at him, to make *him* pick it up.

"Fuckhead," I mutter.

Melodic laughter drifts from behind me. I know it's her before I turn. Margaret. Something of the sea is in her every sound and move.

"Who offended you this time?" she asks.

"My boss." I pause and correct myself, "My *ex*-boss now. He fired me because I don't want to sleep with him."

Margaret stares at me. And I am afraid. There is something feral in her that I'd not seen until now, and I can't decide if I should run or cling to her.

"It's okay. I shouldn't have said--"

"Filth." Margaret glances behind us, to the closed door. "I try to correct them, to make them understand. They destroy everything they touch with their filthy ways."

"I'm sorry . . . ?"

Margaret looks at me, her eyes brighter than seems possible. "You don't understand, Isabel. I thought you were different, but human women never understand either."

"Human . . .?"

She makes a gesture like she is cutting the air. "You will not have relations with him."

"Right. That's why I'm fired."

Margaret nods. "I shall fix this as well."

"My being fired?"

Her attention snaps to me. "His offense."

I WAKE several days later to the sound of someone hammering on my door. My resolve to surrender booze fell apart after I was fired, and I ended up on a bender of the most pitiful sort. I am alone in my room with a bunch of empty bottles and food wrappers. Obviously, I've left the room at *some* point as not all of the food was stuff I had here when I started drinking.

On the other side of the door is Margaret. Behind her is Jack.

"I won't go on the boat with men alone." She crosses her arms. "He says I must, but unless you are there, I shall not. I signed *nothing*."

"It'll cost you," I tell Jack. "Hotel tab. *All* of it."

I know the project is behind schedule. He's lost a researcher, and he's lost me. I can't imagine he knew exactly how much I did for him--actual tasks, that is, even though I refused the one he'd apparently hired me to do.

"No plane ticket," he says.

I shrug. I'm not sure when I want to leave—or if I will. I've fallen a bit in love with Orkney.

"Fine. Hotel bill in full for another week. Downstairs. Five minutes." He walks away.

Margaret lingers. She reaches out and strokes my cheek. Then she's gone, too.

"Pay my bill, or I'm not getting on the boat," I call.

He says nothing, but fifteen minutes later, I'm standing at the front desk as he prepays another week's lodging.

For reasons unknown to anyone but Jason, we are to go out onto the sea in a rigid inflatable boat. These "rib" contraptions seem sketchy to me, but half the tour companies in the islands and over in the Hebrides use them. I guess I'd rather trust the locals than my land-loving fears. Honestly, I'd have climbed aboard a Minke whale if it meant seeing Margaret.

When we set out, the small boat holds a captain, the camera man, Jack, Margaret, and me. The captain watches Margaret carefully, and unless my eyes deceived me, he made the sign of the cross when she boarded the craft.

"I have great respect for the sea," he tells me in an overly loud voice. "Those things that live in it are why these islands thrive. They protected us from the Norsemen in years gone by, and they protect us now."

Margaret smiles at him. "Indeed."

Jack rolls his eyes, not that she sees, but I do. Maybe he's right to doubt in the stories of the island, but there's a long space between doubt and mockery. I don't believe in selchies, or lindwurms, or faeries, or any number of things I hear of in the tales here, but I realize as well that we all believe in things that seem a touch far-fetched if we put them out on the table in front of strangers. That's what she's doing. For his film. For me. I wasn't sure *how* it was for me, but I got the sense that it was in some way that only Margaret knew.

"Once . . . a selchie lay with a Finman," she begins once we are far from land.

The camera's eye is trained on her, as is mine. The boat's captain does not look back at her, at any of us. He's not in the frame of the film.

There is only Margaret and the sea.

"Their child, a girl, grew up with the need to bring mortals into the sea," she continues. "She offered them like gifts, tithes to the waves. She culled the herd of men that came to the edges of the sea. It was not enough. Never enough."

Jason, to my side, opens his mouth like he's about to object.

"The men were cruel, and the women weak. Too afraid to shed blood." She glances at me, smiles, and leans forward to tug Jason into the frame of the film. "The daughter of the sea found a way when she could, culling them as a shepherd with a flock."

Margaret stands and pulls Jack to his feet. The boat shifts, but the captain keeps us steady. Maybe that's easy, but I'm terrified.

She leans in and kisses Jack.

And I am no longer thinking of anything but this, but him touching her.

Steadily, as if it's nothing, she reaches up and chokes him. He flails, trying to pull away, clawing at her wrists and fore-arms, kicking.

"What the--"

"Don't stop filming," I whisper. There is no other way to believe this. I'm not sure why I want to, but a tiny sliver of logic reminds me that there were two other dead men I've seen lately. Men I have wondered if I killed.

The camera man drops his camera and leaps overboard. The captain does not look behind us. I, however, cannot look away. She chokes Jack, kisses him, cradles him as he goes limp, and when she stops kissing him, he is dead.

Margaret sighs, and I am certain that her sigh is why the winds have begun to churn the sea. Suddenly, the waters seem more like the edge of a storm than the calm sea of an hour ago.

"If he were pure, he would've survived. I'd have tasted goodness, and he would've lived." Margaret meets my gaze. "Three for sacrifice."

"You . . . KILLED THEM."

"Did I, Isabel?" Margaret's voice is a whisper of waves, so slight that I barely hear her even as I am next to her.

"You did. The camera. You killed Jack *on camera*." I point at the camera, which is sideways at the bottom of the boat. "It's on there. Proof."

"Maybe."

"You killed *all* of them. The men. The ones I found." I sound a bit manic, but I thought I thought I'd murdered a few men again.

It happens, you know?

"I thought it was me," I whisper.

"Perhaps it was." She motions me to the camera.

I debate between watching and letting it record. It's the only proof I have. I left the shore in a boat with a captain and three people. Two others are dead—because the cameraman won't survive that cold water.

"Come with me, or they'll send you to prison," Margaret points out calmly, voice still a murmured whisper.

"I'm innocent."

She shakes her head. "No. You chose them. Each dead man. You *chose* him. I paid your dowry."

I pick up the camera, stop the recording, and watch it. There is no proof. Margaret's face is never in the frame. I try to back it up, to see earlier footage of her telling a tale. The cameraman must've done something wrong in his fear. None of it is there.

Margaret opens a rucksack, pulls out a fur, and strips. She

stands bare naked for a moment and says, "Come with me, Isabel."

She clutches the fur to her and jumps into the water.

I scan the waves, for her and for the missing camera man, but all I find is a seal.

"Are you going?" the captain asks, finally glancing back at me but steadfastly not looking over the edge of the boat. "I'm headed to shore, miss, so if you're going . . ."

I look back into the waves, and I am faced with the same beautiful woman I've found fascinating. The only significant difference is that she's blue now and as she moves I see a tail fin.

"What . . . this is . . .Is that a costume?"

Margaret laughs, and the sound is the lure of the sea. She is the voice that drowns sailors, that crashes ships on rocks, that invites a woman to her doom.

Still blue, Margaret shifts so she's floating on her back, bare breasts breaking the surface of the water like a mermaid. When my gaze lifts from her chest to her face, she says, "You are not afraid, Isabel. Not of death or blood. And you are not happy. Do you want to be happy?"

I glance at the men, think of the recording, of my empty life, of the fate that will await me on land. There is no hope on shore. I'm not sure if death or life awaits me if I agree, but I see no other answer. I leap overboard, and in moments, I feel Margaret's arms wrap around me. Her bare skin against my layers of clothes and jacket.

Together, we sink into the sea.

Days later, the boat is found, drifting. Empty but for a camera. The crew attaches a tow rope.

Silently, the fishermen haul the boat to shore.

After they dock, their captain lifts the camera from the boat. After a few moments, the men start playing the footage. The captain watches as one man is tossed overboard by a woman's hand. The camera drops. Another splash.

"You . . . killed them," a woman's voice says in the recording.

"You did. The camera. You killed Jack *on camera*. It's on there. Proof."

"You killed *all* of them. The men. The ones I found. I thought it was me."

There are pauses as if she's speaking to someone, but no other voice is recorded.

Finally, the same woman says, "I'm innocent."

Another splash, and then nothing but the sounds of the sea.

On the whole of the recording, there is only the sea and the voice of one woman, a drunken one that they'd all heard at the pub more than once. No one knew her, only that she'd come with the filmmakers, and like them, she'd vanished.

"Toss it in the rubbish bin," the man closest to him says. "The sea took them. Her, too, from the sound of it."

Murmured prayers and gestures ripple over the crew. Not a man there has a family without a tale of someone lost to a storm. Death was the price paid for a life drawn from the waves. The sea gave, but the sea demanded tithing.

"Better strangers than our own," one of the fisherman says.

A seal watches them as they discard the camera, and then a fin--that several of them will swear was blue--flashes in the waves as the seal departs.

END

Fall is upon us as I sit in my stolen cottage and plan. Should I survive my next few months, I'd rather not dangle from a noose in the center of town. If my soon-to-be husband does not kill me, I have to hope that the citizens of Prudence will spare me. Some folks frown upon murder, and if I get caught, I'll hang for it.

While I'm not planning on dying or getting caught, I know that both are possible. I've been tossed in various jails, one dungeon, and even had one whipping—which is, truly, more than anyone needs. I worry over the questions that will come when my husband-to-be sees the lash scars on my back, but I have a plan for that, too. I always have a plan at this point in my life. I've managed twenty-seven years in a world that is not kind to women, and I've lived ten of those on my own. Given the choice, I'd never be in a village like Prudence, but the devil I seek is on his way here. So, I ponder both my defense and his death, and I pray to any gods that still listen that all will be well.

"I was a fool," Mother whispers from behind me. She

haunts me wherever I go. My ship. The stolen cottage. Taverns in far flung ports. The woman is inescapable.

"No one blames you," I mutter the lie without looking up from my tinctures and herbs.

Mother had outwitted death, and I have the great fortune of having her at my side as she knitted spectral scarves and shrouds at all hours of the day and night. We've spent ten months this way, and although she no longer shrieks at me, we both know that she is with me because I am to blame.

"My poor babies," she wails, her lament sending icy air cascading through the cottage.

She does not, of course, include me in her wails. I am not yet dead, and even if I die, I doubt that she'll mourn me. Mother haunts me. She jabs at me with knitting needles as though the ghostly things could pierce me. In my idle hours, I wonder if they will once I'm dead, too. An eternity with her wailing and stabbing me sounds like my personal hell.

The sky grows darker as I read my sister's last letter. Again. There are no clues left to find in the paper so creased that slight holes are wearing in it from my reading and re-reading the damning words.

Dear Adelaide,

Mother seems not to realize that the captain who has offered for me is the same man who offered for Lucy last winter. Her vision is long gone, but it is not so simple as that. Hayes is poisoning her, spoonfuls of laudanum in her tea, and I cannot get her to believe me. She's drifting away, and I cannot help but think that he must have given her this same thing when he was asking for Lucy's hand. He tells me he'll stop if I go with him quietly and willingly. What else can I do?

Sister, he is not without charm. When he takes my

hand, it feels as if I am already sinning. My soul is at risk with one such as him. The virtue I've held on to is but a memory already.

His ship, the Fitcher's Bird, is a magnificent thing, but unlike you, I fear the sea. I fear being on the ship with no escape, and if he has already wed our Lucy, where is she? I believe the worst, Adelaide, but I cannot let him destroy Mother. I go to my sin, and undoubtedly, to my wretched end.

Find me, sister.

Yours,

Biddy

By the time I'd read the letter, my mother had passed on to her eternal unrest and both of my beloved sisters had vanished. I'd been caught up with work, delayed by a storm at sea, and though my work was what paid for their linens and gowns, I'd had a duty to look after them in other ways, too. No father or brother. I was all they had. The care and protection of their needs was my burden for a third of my lifetime so far.

And I failed them.

Both Lucretia and Bridgette are lost to me—because of him. I was away too long, and my mother was too trusting. Lucy had married the pious Reverend Hayes in the winter, and by the following autumn, Bridgette had married the honorable Captain Hayes.

They were the same man.

I consoled myself that if they were dead, my sisters would either take shifts appeasing my mother or they would come to me with answers. Neither has happened, so I have to think they might yet live.

I have come to Prudence to try a bolder plan than is strictly wise. Hayes is the devil who owns this cottage, and here, I will ensnare him. He is a man who collects brides, including both of my sisters. Through a liberal application of coins and the occasion blade, I discovered that the village of Prudence is the devil's haven. He retreats here to a community of people so pious that they've doubled back around the edge again to reach sinfulness. The citizens of Prudence are holier-than-thou, and they accept Hayes as one of their own. The devil was born here, so they discount whispers of his heinous deeds. They dismiss word of his depravity as the slings and arrows of the damned tossed at the righteous.

He is a defiler, a liar, and a murderer. He is, in sum, a devil among men.

Before the moon grows full again, I will marry this devil. I will be his bride whether or not he consents. It is the penance my mother and I both think I deserve. After all, if I'd turned down that last job, I wouldn't have been at sea so long that my sister's letter was unanswered. It is that letter that damns us all.

"I was a fool," Mother whispers from behind me. "I trusted you, Adelaide. I was wrong."

"Go look for Biddy," I urge her again, but her knitting needles clack louder, faster, and I am left grateful that she cannot end my life with her ghastly needles.

As Mother glares at me and knits her latest shroud, a lovely thing in what looks like sea-blue angora, I review the plans in my mind. I must marry a devil, and once wed, I must learn of my sisters' fate. And then, in the way of many a dissatisfied bride, I shall murder him quietly.

Or violently if all goes as I dream.

I examine the compressed herbs and assorted weapons I've gathered: Foxglove, belladonna leaves, castor seeds, and one precious vial of rattlesnake venom. Once they are all ready, I will sew the tiny packets folded into wax leaves within the thickest fabrics of my dresses. I will carry the means of murdering the man with me in every dress. I will wear his death in folded pieces of poison over my heart.

It is not my way. I prefer the honesty of bullets, but an innocent bride does not carry a gun or sword. She brings a trousseau. And thus, each day, I wear a skirt hemmed with weapons, and I learned how to pretend to be a maiden again. Hidden in the seam of the newly-made merkin I have procured to wear for my wedding night is a small glass vial of blood. I have practiced in order to be most thorough in my ruse.

Given my choice, I'd be back in familiar chaps and a good corset, sword in one hand, gun in the other, and cussing with the spirit that sparks a brawl far more often than my sainted dead mother should ever know. Instead, I'm trapped with my mother's ghost in a daub and wood cottage that has a layer of dust over even the holy book. No man of good intent would leave that book under a thick layer of dust. My sisters were to be wed and bedded, by a good man, expecting to be brought here to the village of Prudence. They should've had babes in arms and been thinking of the next by now. Instead, they married the same man, and they never arrived here.

My associate Blue-Eyed Bill swears he saw Biddy in a port a few months back. When last the devil's ship was spotted, a woman was lashed onto the masthead of a ship like a garish totem. Tatters of dress and tendrils of fire-red hair made my sources strongly suspect that the corpse on the ship was my baby sister.

Dead.

Bridgette is dead.

The man who'd offered for her, Captain Hayes, was no more a God-fearing man than I am a milkmaid. He postures now as a noble, a captain in His Majesty's Navy, and he moves from village to village seeking a wife. Does he wed and murder them?

There are no bodies lashed to his ship's prow when they're in port, but sailors tell tales. Hayes spreads his money around at taverns and shops, makes donations to churches, and while it might not buy the devil a ticket through the pearly gates, it buys him sympathy as he shares some version of the same sad tale in village after village. Widowed. God-fearing. Lonely. The villagers offer up their maids for him to pick his next victim. Six villages. Six wives, including both of my sisters.

I look at my map. I can see his pattern now. He'll search villages for a wife, claim that he'll have a home for her, but then he'll come here. Alone. I don't know where the wives are sent, but I'll find out.

This time, he'll find me waiting.

I LOOK BACK at the parchment I've been drafting and read the first of many letters I've created for a defense after my eventual arrest. One can hope my future husband shall die easily, but I find that I need more. I want everything. Every coin and cloth, every ship or cottage, even the firewood leaning against a tree. All of it. That, however, means I must plan to explain my reasons for claiming his assets—and explain in a town run by men who must have some clue as to the true nature of the devil Hayes.

To the Good Citizens of Prudence,

I was born to good people, raised with good values, and did intend to live a good and righteous life. It is my hope that upon finishing my tale, you will vote to acquit me. I am beset by a devil, and I fear for my very soul.

In the spring, I found that the man I'd planned to cleave to was engaged in impure activities. He has taken wives before me, and those wives have perished. Such wickedness in this man! I did seek out and speak to several ministers, prayed to hope for a sign from Our Father above, and I did even consult with the schoolmistress for advise [sic] on this matter. Mistress Anne counselled me at great lengths, and if you consult the enclosed [Item 1, evidentiary supplement] you will see that I attempted to turn her wisdom to deed. Alas! The devil that plagues this village outwitted me. I am to sea with him, and I fear that I shall go the way of my dear departed sisters.

In trembling regards,

Adelaide Barbon

Sister to Lucretia and Bridgette

THERE IS much truth in my words, as is the way of compelling lies. What I have failed to explain, of course, is that I sought the devil. The second letter, the supplement, is trickier.

Item 1, Evidentiary Supplement:

Dear Reverend Mister Kramp,

I am writing to seek employment in your household as a laydies maid or cook. Please consider me for a position in your household, sir, as I fear devils will have their ways with me if I do not flee this village.

Sincerely and in holy fears,

Adelaide Barbon

I will need to mail it to Nox, and then have it returned with a rejection.

Nox,
    Rejection letter back to me. Regrets and prayers.
Return it with my letter enclosed.
    Addy

I lean over my desk and consider how many letters a proper defense requires. How much evidence must I accumulate in order to be thought innocent? It's a sort of madness perhaps, but I'm not really a go-down-with-the-ship sort of fighter. Not that I wouldn't. If I have to die in order to avenge my sisters, I will. If I have to sink Captain Hayes' whole crew, I will. But, I do like to plan for the best, and a widow's cottage in a meadow outside a small village seems like the retirement plan I hope to use one day.

Of course, I also plan to take the man's ship, stolen riches, and--if I'm able--his very soul. Vengeance, as the good men say, is the domain of a woman wronged, and I have been wronged. Bridgette and Lucy were the innocent ones, the daughters who had a fine dowry and a soft laugh. I earned that dowry, so they would be safe.

Mother experimentally jabs at the letter.

"The devil will get his due," I assure her.

"My poor babies," she wails.

Waiting might make me as maudlin as her. Perhaps, I might admit that the other reason I have begun to draft these letters is simply that I am not suited for patience. Had I been the sort of woman to enjoy letters and stitches, I wouldn't have been much use as a mercenary or pirate. I was, however, my father's daughter in this. When he passed during my sixteenth year, Nox took me to sea, and at the side of the man I trusted most in this world or the next, I learned the sea.

In ports, I learned of love, liquor, and licentiousness. I learned to gamble. I learned to duel. But neither my mother nor the man who had become my most trusted and beloved companion could teach me to be patient.

"Dead. Like your father. Like me. Everyone dead," Mother wails.

I do not point out that I'm quite living, as it never benefits anyone to argue with wailing women. Or dead ones. Or my mother. She was a stampede in motion at her most elegant, and now that she is free of society, she's only become more difficult.

I hold the letters I've written up to the evening light. They look more recent than they ought to look and not nearly tear-stained enough. Honestly, the holier-than-thou men who run the village of Prudence are about as bright as the sky on a New Moon. Nonetheless, if I am to continue to be free, I must learn to seem meek. I dip the feathered end of my quill into my tea and shake it over the pages. Tea will create prettier stains than tears.

I am, of course, as meek as a whore at dock, but I cannot avenge my sisters if I am jailed again. And honestly, the last of the lice from my most recent stay in His Majesty's care are finally gone, so I'd rather not resume such quarters. The village of Prudence sits only a half day's ride from the docks, and the Fitcher's Bird will dock here this month.

It would serve my needs best if the captain thought I was innocent, vulnerable, and susceptible to sin. The captain has a type. I am not it, of course, but I have been studying the man long enough to learn how to mimic it.

He likes girls. Not women, but girls.

He prefers the daughters of poor men. The more desperate, the better.

He prefers the sort who are dreamers. The more trusting, the better.

He prefers no brothers who might come after him. The more isolated, the better.

He was not expecting an angry sister.

I have no idea where he takes them, but I have theories that he earns a fair penny for their souls. If I had tears left to shed, I'd stain every page with them. As it is, I spent mine when he destroyed my sisters.

———

I HAVE PAID for the cottage's thorough cleaning. My bright hair has been bound and hidden under a scarf. My preferred long-knife is lashed to my knee in a modified holster. It limits my knee's bend and gives me a limp that makes me ever-so-slightly more vulnerable.

Night as fallen when I hear movement outside the cabin. Not creatures, but man. Do I play the innocent in case it's the captain or do I prepare to defend myself? I've been assaulted in the past. I didn't care for it.

A tap at the window is followed by a loud whisper, "Addy?"

Nox stands outside, his skin as dark as the shadows he uses for cover. His clothes are likely darker still.

I motion toward the door and pace toward it.

In our business—the sort best hired in dim taverns—his ability to move with stealth is a highly prized skill. Neither of us will ever be greeted in fine homes; we are limited by his skin and my failure to behave as a proper woman. If that life was appealing, we might mourn, but Nox and I were made for better lives, for open seas and loyal bonds.

When I jerk open the door, I have to work hard to sound irritated. "What are you doing here?"

"Brought your letter, Addy."

If I step forward, he's going to brush his lips over my forehead. My height makes such things possible.

"They're dead!" Mother calls to him.

His smile is a slash of white in the shadows. I've never met anyone else who lived on a ship and managed to keep his teeth so bright. He tells the gullible that he made a bargain with Old Scratch for those pearly white teeth. Of course, I tell my own lies. We are a well-matched team, Nox and I.

"I don't need you to come," I mutter.

"I hear that your mother is still with you." Nox smiles again. My lies never do work on him. I think it's because he loves me. He claims it's because the sea taught him to hear truths.

"She could go look for my sisters," I call loudly.

Mother ignores me.

"Trembly and Mick are signed on the man's ship," Nox says.

"That was the plan," I remind him.

"I thought you'd want to know in case you were worrying that sweet head of yours," he says mildly.

I snort.

But Nox is here with me, a fresh bottle of liquor in hand, and I admit that what he doesn't say in words is often as important as all the rest. He was worried, and he knows me well enough to know I'm terrible at waiting.

So, I open the door and motion him in. I've never turned him away when he's come to my door, and he's never turned me away. Sometimes, I swear, we're no different than any old married pair.

"He'll dock tomorrow, Addy. We could just kill him." His objections to my plan have been vast and frequent. Murder is easier. Murder meets my objectives. Murder is safer.

Nox and I settle in at the small fire I've built in the hearth. As he settles back on the wretchedly uncomfortable floral settee in the room, I wonder at the thoughts that he's not sharing.

"What if Biddy is alive?" I ask.

"Addy . . ."

"A woman with red hair. That's all they saw." I pull out the cork and drink. "I'm a red-haired woman. My bones would look no different. Same as with the whore we met in Belfast. Or the one over in . . . that city with all the well-fed rats."

I hold out the bottle.

Nox accepts it and sighs. It is the sigh of a man who's known me in all my moods, my hopes and my violences. It is the sigh of a man who will likely be standing at my side at some gallows in our future. Some day between now and then, we'll wed.

Not that a marriage between pirates is legal.

Not that a marriage between races is legal.

And not, most truly, that I think we'll find a wee hamlet and become crofters.

But someday, we'll die back-to-back or dangling side-by-side from the hangman's nooses. It makes a woman think about exchanging rings.

"Biddy's not alive," he says softly after a few swigs of whatever liquor is in the bottle.

Mother appears at his words, a shrieking cold harridan if

ever there was one. Nox shakes his head, but he does not respond to my late mother. Neither of us are that mad.

"Well, I need to know for sure, don't I?" I reach for the bottle. "And if I marry the bastard, I'll lay claim to all his things when he dies."

The look Nox gives me is filled with disapproval. Not the possessiveness of so-called nobles over their daft wives. Not the doubt of merchants when their wives make suggestions. Nox looks at me with a kind of worry that makes me pronounce, "And we'll use it to plan our wedding. If I'm lucky, I'll rescue Biddy, and she'll be there."

He laughs as he always does when I speak of our inevitable wedding. "My blushing bride, the pirate's widow."

"Pirate and widow," I say. "Thank you kindly for remembering my achievements." I stand and curtsy. "Businesswoman, Nox, and my business is filling my coffers."

"This one isn't business," he reminds.

"Not only business," I amend.

"The boys are there. Just . . . try to be safe, Addy." Nox stares at me like I am precious. It's a look I've only ever seen him give the sea herself.

I don't want to lie, though, so I stand and offer him my hand. His hand in mine, I lead him to the bed where I will trick my sisters' murderer. It's not enough, but I hope he hears my unspoken words, too, tonight.

WHEN MORNING COMES CLOSER, Nox kisses me and slips into the last of the night's shadows. Someday, no one will think askance at skin not matching skin, or women taking lovers, or any number of things that so-called civility finds troubling in our age. For now, both Nox and I risk lashes—or worse—for the same things we do on ship. The sea only judges whether or not one can survive her wrath. The laws of the land are not for us.

Land laws, power and religion's laws, and their worry over propriety has allowed a devil to take my sisters away.

When evening comes, I've aired the cabin, so no scent of liquor or lovemaking will ruin my lies. I feel stronger with my letters carried away in Nox's trusted hands, and I feel purer somehow for having spent the night with him.

The devil arrives at sundown, and I would be remiss if I did not note here that he is exactly as I expected. No more. No less. If I survive, it will be a sign that there is yet a god who hath not forsaken me.

"Be bold," Mother urges from the shadows.

Hayes is tall, easily a hand or more taller than I am—and I am an uncommonly tall woman, seeing eye-to-eye with most men.

"I was not expecting a guest," he says.

I curtsy. Bow my head. Hide my initial rush of hatred. "My father said you spoke to him about my hand?" I lift my voice to indicate doubt and fear. "He sent me here when he passed on."

"I'm sorry for your loss, Miss . . .?"

"Adelaide, sir." I lift my gaze briefly. "I'm called Adelaide."

"What if I'd found another wife, Miss Adelaide?" He studies me, as if he'll find a detail to spark his memory. He clearly doubts my story, and in this, he is right.

I wait. I do not squirm overly much, but I remind myself that my character would be anxious, so I wring my hands together. I'm counting on the fact that he's met dozens of girls, young women innocent and hopeful. I am a face in a sea of faces, a woman he could not recall because there is nothing particularly special about me. I've played at such acts in the past when a job required it. This time, though, the stakes are higher.

"I've cleaned." I motion at the cottage, pointing out that I am useful. "And gathered wood so as to build a fire for you. I spent some time in town, praying of course."

He nods, but I know it is in response to my implied warning that I have witnesses who know I am here, people expecting to see me with him. I've planned my trap, and for the moment, he must either accept me or cast me out. Murdering me is not going to go unnoticed; the good men of Prudence know I'm here. For the moment, his options are limited.

"And where will you sleep, Miss Adelaide?" he asks after a long pause.

I cringe a little, and it's not fake. The thought of touching this devil fills me with revulsion. I've done worse things, but not many.

"Until we're wed, I'll sleep there." I point at the pallet I've made by the fire. It's not soft, but I'll likely sleep fitfully anyhow with him in the cottage.

"I've been to sea for months." He appraises me as if to see if I'm worth the time. I know instantly that he's assaulted women before.

I straighten to my full height and stare at him boldly. "Perhaps you should marry me quickly then, so I can go with you next time."

Hayes gives me a small smile and says, "That seems like an excellent plan. I've been looking for a good, dutiful wife."

WITHIN TWO DAYS, I am accompanying Hayes to his ship, Fitcher's Bird. It takes a moment to remember that I am pretending to be a land dweller, and that I ought to be teetering on the deck more than I am. I clutch his arm.

He summons a man to marry us, and I know that the ceremony is not binding in the least. I'd wondered how many women he'd wed and how he accomplished it, but I see now that it's a simple deceit. The ceremony is not binding. There is no authority in a random crew member mumbling words over us, and I'd wager that he can't read the Bible he holds carefully in his hand like it might become a serpent.

I resist the urge to remark on their sin in lying over a Bible. Starting a fight now would serve to undermine the rest. I briefly meet Trembly's eyes and then Mick's. The men stand apart from one another, ready to aid me when I act. Their swords are mine, and as I look around at Hayes' crew, I am grateful to have two of my men here on what might be a suicide mission.

I startle when I meet a third set of eyes. Nox. He glances at me, but then resumes fixing a sail with a forearm sized tear in it. He's a deft hand with a needle, and despite the mockery of stitching as tidily as he can, I'd trust his work over even the seamstresses that stitch royal garments. The trick is in the stitching. Nox uses a waxed hemp rope and a zigzag pattern. I'm not convinced he ought to be patching Hayes' sails, but if we set to sea, I'll be grateful for it.

"Are we going home?" I ask quietly.

Hayes smiles, and if not for the man's character, I could see how he might seem attractive. As it is, I'd rather kiss an angry walrus.

His crew seems to be restraining laughter or barking laughs that I cannot grasp.

"We're going to take a quick trip," he says, tucking my hand into the bend of his arm.

"Perhaps I could wait at the cottage. I have no clothing or—"

"No need," Hayes cuts in.

He leads me to a room, the captain's quarters I assume, and closes us in. He has a ring with two keys. One is used to lock the door. I tell myself I've survived worse, but any pretense of gentility is absent as he disrobes me.

I know we are here to claim his marital right, but when he's interrupted by a banging on his door, I sag in relief. Teeth marks mar my belly, and I am fighting the need to vomit from his harsh kiss.

"Captain!" a man yells, thumping the door again. "The guards are here."

Hayes glares at me as he stands and fastens his trousers. It's easy to weep and appear vulnerable under his hands. No acting required.

He stares at me. "You will stay here."

Mutely I nod.

"If you leave my quarters, I am not responsible for your fate." He opens a wall-mounted cabinet. In it are six nosegays, little bound bouquets that Mother still calls tussie-mussies. The flowers are rotted and covered with what I know to be blood. The white ribbons are splotched with red. There are three other bouquet holders, and one with fresh flowers.

He hands me the fresh, white flowers. "If you exit, these must be in your hand. Perhaps, it will protect you if the men see your bridal flowers."

I swallow, knowing that my own sisters' blood stains two of those bouquets, but I nod.

"I'll have guests for dinner," he says. "We'll eat here. You'll tend my needs."

I say nothing.

"These are loyal men, wife." He stares at me. "You will treat them as if they are your husbands as well."

"Surely, you don't mean—"

"Being at sea is lonely," he says. "I keep my crew loyal."

There were horrors I'd feared, but this? This is worse. I would that I could kill him a thousand times. When Hayes leaves, I wipe my tears.

"My baby," Mother wails as she joins me.

I'm caught with no words when I realize that she means me. My mother mourns my sisters, not me. She cares about them, not me.

"He must die, Adelaide." Mother's temper fills the room with such chill that frost blossoms on the wall. "I want him to die."

"He will." I meet her spectral gaze, and in this moment, we have a rare understanding. We are in perfect accord.

By the witching hour that night, I've poisoned the man. Not fatally. I'm hopeful that I will find answers, but until I do, he may survive a bit longer. I slipped a bit of dried this and that into his ale. Not the first or the second mug, but after I was sure he was not likely to taste it.

The three others he'd brought laughing to his quarters, those men I killed. No man there touched me, but they gave such lascivious looks that I couldn't still my need for vengeance. His most loyal are dead on the floor. I set the stage, of course, suggesting that the ale smelled wrong. I blushed and tolerated the leers and forced kisses, but the rest? The rest I stopped with a few pellets of poison.

They laughed. What else could I do? I made a choice

informed by knowing what they intended to do with the innocent wife I am pretending to be. I cannot imagine the fates my sisters faced. No, I could. I shall not. To think of it is to kill Hayes on the floor where he's sprawled.

I take the key from Hayes' unconscious body after I've taken the tussie-mussie and stored it somewhere safe. Whatever message it was to convey to his crew, I wouldn't do it. It's shoved behind a set of books. I cover myself with one of his cloaks, hiding my telltale red hair and womanly face. It's a lousy disguise, but I'm hoping that I can have enough stealth to find clues without being seen.

I have a sliver of time before he wakes, and I'll not waste it. I take a short sword of his, a pair of pistols, and the holster. Being armed makes me feel better than I've felt in two days. I whisper a prayer that I will find answers and be done with this ruse, and I leave the room.

With a gleeful pause, I lock the door. Hayes can stay tucked away with the corpses of the other devils I've dispatched.

In the corridor, I listen at doors and open a few of them. I creep through shadows and seek out my own men.

Trembly is the first I find.

"Horrible man," he says. "Vile crew."

I muffle my snort of agreement. "Tell me things."

"Room below deck. Stays locked. Only his special ones can get the key." Trembly cringes. "Heard a scream there when I was boarding, Addy."

I can't decide if I have hope or horror at what that scream could mean. Based on their treatment of me, I could not fathom what horrors hid behind locked doors.

"Where?"

Trembly points, explains twists and turns.

"Get Nox and Mick."

He nods.

"Be subtle, Trem. If you kill anyone, put them to sea."

A look came into his eyes. Trembly—and the rest of my men—weren't the villains that Hayes had gathered. No man who served under me or Nox was a mindless brute. We tolerated no prejudice. We forgave no senseless torments. That did not mean, of course, that they were gentlemen. Some people appreciated violence, and as long as they followed my rules on when and how to release that need, we were at peace with it.

"Rules?" he asks.

"Don't ruin my mission," I say each word clearly.

"Of course!" he says, and we both hear his glee in being let off his tethers. Trembly is often at the edge of difficult to control. Mick is, too. I know that Nox chose them because of that. If they perish, we would not suffer their loss as we would with others. Such is the life of those who work with a band of killers. We are loyal to our own, but we know them for what they are.

I step around Trembly and followed the directions he gave me. I have hopes that the key on the ring will open that door.

When I reach the room, I find a man there.

"What are you doing?"

"I'm lost," I say in my meekest voice.

"Captain let you loose for the ship to have already?" The man leers at me, and I am sickened. Again. It's not his leer but his words.

Captain Hayes is not the only devil aboard this ship. I take the knife that I've hidden under my stolen cloak and plunge it into his throat. Blood spills on his hands as he tries to cover the wound, but I step around him and open the door he guarded.

Inside five women cringe. Two look back at me from

defeated faces. One doesn't even glance my way. Three of the five are strangers. The others . . . look at me as if I might be an illusion. My sisters are not dead. The red-haired woman that was tied to the ship was another unfortunate soul. I will still avenge her. Hayes must atone, and I am still determined to be the instrument of his doom.

"Mother said you'd come," Lucy says softly.

Mother's ghost appears and grins. I can't lie and say she looks lovely, but the vengeance-fueled ghost of my mother looks pleased.

"My babies!" She gazes at me and says, "Now, kill him. Kill them all."

"Mother knows best," Biddy murmurs.

At that, Lucy and Biddy exchange a smile. No one mentions that she was the one that consented to their faux marriages to this devil of a man. No one mentions that her guilt has tethered her to us.

"My babies," she sighs and opens her arms.

A yell from above deck makes everyone pause, and Mother howls in what I suspect might be a frightful cry of glee.

"Addy!" Mick calls as he comes careening into the room. "Trem gave the sign, and the Morrígan is fast approaching."

"Nox?"

Mick gives me the look most of the crew would: the one that says my other half is headed my way. If not for the fact that they'd give him the selfsame look, I'd scowl at Mick. He glances at me, tosses a long gun toward me, and grins. "Trem said you weren't carrying a rifle."

Then he's gone and I'm left with three strangers, my sisters, and my dead mother—none of whom are able to fight. The five wives are weary, under-nourished, abused, and one appears pregnant. My mother, despite her rage and knitting needles, is a ghost. They are mine to protect today.

I lead them back to the captain's quarters.

There, the wives help me drag the corpses into the hall. Afterward, they settle in the room with the unconscious captain.

"Shoot him if you want," I tell them, and I give Biddy my rifle.

"If we don't shoot him . . .?" Lucy asks.

"I'll see that he suffers." My answer is low, but I am rewarded by smiles from the collection of women. "I'll be back or my man, Nox, will."

They lock the door behind me, and I join my crew in the take-over of Fitcher's Bird. I thought the mission to discover my sisters' fate would take longer. I thought they were dead. So, it is with a lighter heart that I lift my sword and gun and work my way to Nox.

"They're alive," I call to him.

"Good." He cuts down a man. Typically, we are not so bloodthirsty. Nox is more of a gentle creature than I am.

A few moments and another man down, and Nox asks, "Are you . . .well?"

"Yes." I know the question he's trying to ask. Nox was with me after my assault during a rough battle with one of His Majesty's Naval Vessels. It was a toss-up as to which of us had more nightmares afterwards.

We fight our way to overcoming all of the Fitcher's Bird's crew, and I stride across the deck with my head held high. Nox has gone to collect the captain and the women. My sisters know him, and they will trust him.

"Your captain fell for a ruse," I say. "If you are innocent, you will have options."

They begin to announce innocence, and they defend one

another. A devil vouching for another of his kind serves no purpose. I wait for the jury to join me.

Voices still when the five wives are at my side.

Nox and my men—which include several women with their hair shorn and blouses loose—stand with weapons in hand.

Hayes stands on wobbly legs. He glares at me, and I smile. "I seem to have lost my bouquet."

Biddy takes one and hands it to me. Dried blood on dead flowers. The women start tossing bloodied corpses into the sea, and I wait. I know what they seek. They've seen this done.

Hayes watches in silence as they chum the water with their dead assailants.

The crew only reacts when, finally, Lucy points at a living man and says, "Him."

Trembly looks at me. I nod, and the man is tossed to roiling sea where fins slash the surface in their frenzy. If my crew wasn't attentive and armed, the guilty might revolt. They beg, and they wait. One man charges me, apparently hoping for a quicker end.

One-by-one, the wives pronounce judgment on the men. Those who visited their locked prison are given to the sea, food for the sharks that have gathered. By the end, there are ten men left onboard who are found innocent.

Hayes, however, each woman cuts once. He is bleeding profusely when we tie him to a rope and lower him to the water. As we sail toward Prudence, to the cottage that I now own, we let him flounder atop the water, not sink, not drown, but dragged along the water for sharks to tear and sea to batter.

My crew and I will build onto the cottage that is ours now.

We widows will winter there. We shall heal. We'll plan and rest. Come spring, we'll sail, but my work is done.

Never let it be said that we did not give the devil his due.

AUTHOR'S NOTE on "The Devil's Due" (2019):

I have a shelf of pirate history, as well as quite a few shelves of folklore and women's history. "The Devil's Due" is a result of that mix.

Last year, I read *Dead Girls* (Bolin; a NEW YORK TIMES NOTABLE BOOK OF 2018), and it got me thinking about this folktale. It's not a new thought. My story "The Maiden Thief" and my 2020 novel, *Pretty Broken Things* (an Audible Original), both explore what it means to be the wife of a killer. The latter is a thriller novel, and the former a fantasy story. Both are about facing the idea that you had intimacy with a man who kills and abuses women—and what you do with that information.

In "The Devil's Due" Addy is a pirate, a woman on a mission, and she's still able to love and care about family. We can be all things. . . even when the ghost of your mother is wailing at you.

The source stories for the folktale start with the devil, who has married three sisters over a span of time. In these tales, each girl was given a token that the devil can use to verify if she broke his rules. In some of this tale type (Bluebeard, Fitcher's Bird) they are at a castle or manor. The tussie-mussie, white dress, egg is stained by blood, and so the villainous man knows she's opened the forbidden door. In some, she dies, is imprisoned, or is rescued by her brothers/father/the town. In a few, she rescues her sisters.

These tales remind us that women need rescue, and/or

they must be objects under men's control. They tell us curiosity results in disaster (Pandora, for example, but there are many more).

We still fetishize the death of women in thrillers, action films, and literature. Writing against that is a kind of power. I think we are more powerful if we are alive and speaking, that our stories matter more than as "character" development for male heroes. So, I tend to write "women who dare" in almost every text I write. We dare to be bold. We dare not to stay broken. We dare to be our own hero and tell our own tales.

"NOT UNLIKE A CHILD"

The door opened with a drawn-out shriek of objecting springs and rusting metal. I had bones out to dry, mostly ribs and a few femurs. Only family came calling in the holler, though. One of my aunties was due to stop by and check on me soon, so I couldn't be too fussed by it. The tea leaves had warned of a guest.

A part of me hoped it was a salesman or some other lost man. I had need of a man. Not to keep, mind you, but they did have theirs uses.

Instead of a knock, or even a polite *how-dee*, Auntie Imogene walked into the house and scraped her shoes over the wire hedgehog that sat on the floor. Family knew to use it, or I'd put vinegar in their tea. Men-folks in my family don't drink tea, so they thought they could avoid my temper. After I added laxatives to a pie last Memorial Day, they realized that they best scrape their boots, too. I couldn't stand disorder or filth in my home.

"What're you baking?" Auntie Imogene sniffed, drawing the air in like a pig scenting a corpse.

She paid no mind to the bones. No one did. They knew I

had need of bones—and more than a few of them delivered me a carcass for my work. We all had skills. Mine was revealing the stories in the bones. Some people could see a branch or a stone, and they'd know how to release the story inside it. What I did was like that but with bones.

Aunt Imogene couldn't care much less about my work. Food was what caught her attention. Imogene had always had an unfortunate nose and a body like a wire frame. No matter how much she ate, that body was changeless. The only thing that changed was her last name. She always took back the family name between husbands. Imogene was on her forth husband, but he'd pass, too. They all did, and each one died and left her hoard of wealth a little bit bigger.

"Pineapple cookies." I motioned to the counter where the little moons sat. The dough was cut out with the same fluted glass I always used, and in the middle was a fat spoonful of pineapple mix. A cookie that big was reserved for long visits.

I hated long visits with family, but there was a way of telling truths in the mountains. Things here got done well, done right the first time, and that took a bit of jibber-jabber. I 'spect it was a case of knowing the rules. People talk like mountain folk are unfriendly. That's a lie. We just have our ways, and those that don't follow them aren't going to like the results.

Auntie Imogene nodded. She pulled up a chair, at ease in the way of family.

"Good to know you expected me."

Expected was not the same as liked—which we both knew. I'd seen her visit, and I'd baked. Sugar always helped a bitter pill go down easier, and her words were always pills.

Sometimes the burning need to hex Auntie Imogene was like a kidney stone. It would hurt if it passed, but you still wanted to get it out of you. The hexing urge built until I had to let it go or place it—and I was never sure I could place it.

If I hexed her, Auntie Imogene would undoubtedly do something creatively unpleasant. She specialized in things like yeast infections, vomiting fits, and migraines, but she'd veer into insect infestations if her mood was right. Once she'd placed a small mammal hex on my kitchen. Possums, skunks, raccoons, rabbits, and squirrels all felt irresistible urges to come calling.

She watched me, eyes narrowed, as I decided if it was worth risking another episode of incurable crotch itch or a few weeks as a skunk nanny.

"Well?" she prompted, eyes fixed on me like a viper in a foul mood.

I let go. The energy I was summoning to hex her pig-snouted face fizzled.

"Fresh pot for you," I muttered, looking away and gesturing at the flowered tea pot on the table.

My family might be—most of us—mountain poor, but we set a generous table for guests. And Auntie Imogene *was* a guest, whether she thought so or not. Technically, the house, like the rest of the mountain, was owned by the eldest of the family. It got complicated a few years back. Juniper and Gin were twins. Uncle Catalpa might've been older, too, but he hadn't been sober since '03. This was, practically speaking, *my house.*

"No man yet?" Auntie Imogene looked around, as if expecting a pair of boots to materialize.

"Not that I've noticed." I moved a few cookies onto a plate and set in on the table. "Haven't been in the shed for a while, though. Hard to say."

"You're a pip, Annabella." Auntie Imogene drew a cookie

onto her napkin, using her fake nails like red-lacquered tongs. "Sometimes, you remind me of Philomena."

I poured her tea and waited. She never brought up my mother without reason. No one did. Abby and I were raised by Gin and Juniper, Mama's cousin's, and by Auntie Imogen. They never spoke ill of Mama, but I knew they thought it. Mama got swindled. She lost a bunch of money—and her freedom.

And all that she had to show for a life of grubbing was me and my sister.

I stirred honey into my tea, added more until it was sweeter than it ought to be but maybe enough sweet would leak into my mood.

"I don't need this anymore, so I thought I'd pass it on," she finally said, opening her satchel-sized handbag and drawing out a book wrapped in butcher's paper.

She watched as I unwrapped Mama's copy of *Der Lange Verborgene Freund*, the grimoire that I'd thought my sister burned.

I stroked the cover. "How. . .?"

Auntie Imogene shrugged. "Magic is a start, Annabella, but there are words, tinctures, spells. Margin notes by most of the family. I wasn't going to let Abby burn up the things that kept generations of our family safe."

I stroked the aged and burned cover. It was more than a book. Mother's copy had loose pages that had been folded inside. Those pages were *everything*, and I knew that my prayers had been answered.

"What if you need something?" I cradled the book, wanting to rush off and read every loose page my family had slid into the book.

"I'm done with husbands once Gerry dies. I'll have all I need, then."

"Is he sick?"

She gave me the look that has quelled many an awkward question over the years. Gerry wasn't sick, but he would be. Auntie Imogene's husbands only ever lasted five or six years. They all had a "use by" date.

Knowing how to harness nature cured a lot of stress in this world.

"You wanted a child," she said quietly. "It's for the good. Summon you a man or whatever other way you want to get one. The family needs new children."

"Abby has—"

"Abigail has all but cut us out. It happens." Auntie Imogene's voice made me grateful that women do not turn on other women in our family. If not for *that* law, my sister would be as dead as most of my uncles.

"Maybe her youngest will be family, but I can't be sure. And everyone else just has sons." Aunt Imogene said 'sons' like the word was dirty, but that was just because the gift only went to girls.

"We need a guarantee," Auntie Imogene stressed. "It's time for you to do your duty."

I nodded. We were a family of traditions, and try as I might, I was failing in my duties as a Meadows. I tried men on for usefulness, even a few that had children already. I didn't intend to keep them. I just needed their seed, but my womb never took. I'd had a few miscarriages, but I was too much like my Mama, I guess, broken inside.

"I do want a baby."

"So have one." Auntie Imogene shrugged. "Use a Fetch. Make it up right, and your baby will grow with it. If you keep the Fetch fed, you'll be fine, and you'll have a baby for the family."

I've only ever wanted to be a mother. Some women dream

of offices, of contracts, of careers. I have no objection to that, but I dreamed of a baby. I prayed for a baby. I bled for a baby. I laid with men--even ones I hated—to try to make a life.

I always failed.

Every Meadows woman has a role in this family. Some, like Imogene, add to our wealth, and others are fertile as sows. A few tend towards an ethical absence; they know where the bodies are buried. Me? I haven't seemed good at *any* of it.

I traced the faded cover of the grimoire with my fingertips. Everything would change now. I'd be more than a bone carver. I'd be a mother. Useful. Creator of my own child.

\#

I read, prepared myself, and waited. I considered calling my sister, but she wasn't a believer these days. I made an offering to the wood, sorted the innards for signs and then gathered the bones that would be useful in my work. A Fetch, a double for the real baby, required both know-how and a list of pieces.

In Appalachia, the ground often has "root gold." Now, those that don't know any better will harvest ginseng roots, and then they'll sell them for up to a thousand dollars a pound. It's the only kind of gold we have in our mountains.

If times were tough enough, I'd harvest the root to sell.

Right now, however, I dug it up for other reasons. Auntie Imogene suggested I use a Fetch, and she wasn't wrong. A great many things can be hidden in the woods, and a Fetch is easier than most. I figured I'd make it and leave it in the woods once I had my real baby.

I followed the guidance on my mother's handwritten notes from between the pages of the book on *"How to invite life into the womb."*

First, I had to make the shape of it. So, I put up my gloves, galoshes, and gathered my basket and trowels. I thought about the risks, the traditions, and the way things sometimes just echo. The trouble with a Fetch is in the feeding and care of it.

Not unlike a child, if I'm truthful about it.

A child, though, will be a helper, a comfort. She'll be there one day when I am old, and I cannot get the things I need for my work. She'll give me meaning—and love. A Fetch will be different, a burden I must accept as the cost of my child.

The Fetch won't have feelings. So, as long as I give it food, there should be no other cost. Truth being what it was, I often had things I could feed a Fetch. I might not know where the bodies are buried in my woods, but I know what to do with the ones I encounter. They tell their stories in the bones.

Under my hands and knives, their secrets slip out of them. In the end the bones are art. Building a Fetch is somewhat the same. With my work, I start with death. With the Fetch, I'll need to do the same.

I thought about Auntie Imogene's wisdom. Luring in men and trying to fill my womb had never worked. So, this was the only way to be a mother. I found the instructions in the book, and I thought about her words: "If you keep it fed, you'll be fine."

I stitched up a new, hand-stitched, fresh-cleaned peanut bag. I'd carry the burlap sack to fill with bone and meat and root I harvested under the New Moon, and then I added the words of life on a tiny burnt piece of paper. I checked and rechecked, and I followed every rule. There would be no mistake.

When my cycle came to me, I squatted over the earthen womb where the Fetch was waiting.

Then I watched the moon. I drank my teas. I waited until the right time, and I invited Uncle Gerry to take a walk with me.

"Imogene thinks you don't like me," he said. "The women in this family sure are something."

I didn't say much. I pushed him to the ground beside my hidden Fetch. And under the moon, wearing nothing but my muck boots and herbs, I invited his seed—which he freely offered--into my barren womb.

Then I watered the soil with his blood.

"You must feed the Fetch," my Auntie Imogene had told me.

No different than a baby, not really. Sometimes it took a little witchery to have one. Sometimes they grow up different from what a mother hopes. My sister Abby rejected the family more and more. She tossed around words that cut, calling us social-a-paths, which was another way to say murderers.

But nature is a cycle. The fallen trees nourished the land. It wasn't wrong to follow the code of the earth.

Abby had made her kids the regular way, and they weren't raised on the mountain. I wasn't sure if any of them could do witchery as a result. No matter the number of times Aunt Imogene married, there were no daughters. Mama was never getting out of the hospital-prison. That left me. I was a traditional woman in this.

A Meadows Woman.

I looked down at my uncle as he bled into the soil. He'd been married to Imogene for three years already, so he was nearing his death anyhow.

"Thank you," I said as I closed Gerry's eyes.

I drew the symbols on his cheeks and chest. Then I felt my womb quicken, and I knew that life had been brought from the darkness. My womb would carry the next Meadows' daughter.

Before I left the spot where life had started, I took an ax and set to work on Gerry's body. Men weren't so different from deer or hogs, really. When they were done prancing and chuffing, strutting and grunting, they were just meat and marrow.

I drained my Fetch's food all into the soil, then I took the pieces I'd need for my workings. Afterwards, I carried the sack of bones I'd kept home to clean. And in nine months, the seed that had been sewn in my womb, the child tied to the Fetch was born.

Aunt Imogene was there at the birth, even Abby was there. Juniper and Gin came to deliver the blessing. Uncle Catalpa showed up for the naming.

Imogene looked at my daughter, and then she looked at me.

"The child looks a bit like Gerry in the chin," Auntie Imogene whispered.

My uncle, who was as likely as not my real father, pronounced, "I shall call this child Clear Meadows."

The way he said it sounded more like "Clear" than "Claire," but it was hard to tell. We called her Clear.

They left me to rest, taking Clear to clean and adore.

I got up from my birthing bed, walked into the wood with birth blood in a jar. Before I could offer it up, I was struck down by pains. I laid on the ground, and I had my second labor.

I knew he wasn't a real babe, but there he was, small and misshapen and on the earth between my bloody thighs. He looked so real, so human. The placenta spilled down, and I offered the placenta to the Fetch. He shrieked, even when I gave it to him like a breast.

So, I held the Fetch to my breast.

"Clancy," I whispered to the misshapen little thing. I know I wasn't to name it, but I did. I named the creature and took it home.

When I saw Clear in the cradle, I swear she reached for the small bloody monster, so I put him the cradle, too.

\#

Feeding Clear and Clancy was a challenge—and I wanted to give them everything. Aunt Imogene was being unpleasant, claiming that I took Gerry as if she was going to let him live. At least he served a purpose. My family was afraid to get between us, which was fair. Imogene was deadly on the best of days.

So I decided to help myself. I borrowed Uncle Catalpa's caddy and decided to go off the mountain in search of money. The trunk and the back seat were full of things that barely worked or had been forgotten in the shed.

I found an antique store and swayed my hips as I led that man to my borrowed car.

The man wasn't looking at my cherry pitter or my milk jug, though. He was fixated on a sternum I'd left in the trunk. It happens.

"Do you have more?" he asked.

Clear was squalling her seat. Being too far from Clancy made her scream, but Clancy didn't do so well around people. I kept him in my guest room most of the time, although Aunt Imogene thought I ought to leave him in the woods not long after the birth. I couldn't, and keeping him in the shed seemed wrong somehow. So, I kept the Fetch in the house.

That was another issue Imogene was having with me.

But if Clancy died, Clear would, too. That was the way of it with Fetches, so I kept him at home as if he was a person. Maybe that was why he and Clear bonded. I wasn't sure. All I knew was that my daughter had grown shrill while that man stared at a bone in my trunk like it was valuable.

"More what?" I asked the man.

"Scrimshaw." The man pointed at the sternum I'd been

working on. That particular sternum had been Gerry's. I guess it makes sense that Gerry had found a way to support Clear. Witchery meant he'd had to fertilize Clancy's earth womb, but this was his way to look after Clear. I saw that in an instant. He was helping his daughter, and I was grateful to him. Like I said, Gerry had been useful at the end of his life.

"That was Gerry's," I said, and something of my feelings in that moment must have been in my voice because that antique's man offered me a whole lot of cash for Gerry's bone.

He put on gloves when he touched it.

That was the day I started selling my bone carvings. I said they came from a relative who'd left them in a steamer trunk in the house. I called that relative Gerry because Mr. Martin wanted to know about my relative who'd brought me the scrimshaw.

That was also the day I drove Clear and me over to the library and got out books on scrimshaw. A lot of scrimshaw came from sperm whales, but mostly, scrimshaw is simply carved bone. Men on ships carved beautiful pieces onto their canvases of whale bone, ivory, and baleen. I like bones. They always felt special to me. I whittled on them because I hated to hurt the trees. I shaped them because bones have stories, and no one listens much to the dead. My family never told me much about the bodies or parts of bodies they brought to my house, just carcasses because they thought I needed bones or because they didn't have time to toss them into mine shafts or the strip mines.

And I wanted to know them, know their stories, so I carved them.

But suddenly, the things I did to protect the holler were things that turned into money for me, Clear, and Clancy.

I even got the internet up at the house and took classes to get me a degree. Maybe it was time to move into town, just while Clear went to school. It was that or Clancy and me would be on the mountain alone.

"Mama will take care of you," I swore to both of them.

Now, I know Clancy might not be *real* like Clear, but he was special in another way. He wouldn't leave me like she would. I could see it now—without needing to read the tea leaves. A Fetch doesn't leave its maker. Clancy was mine forever.

First, though, I needed a home and a place off the mountain so Clear had a future.

I smiled, and I simpered. I spread my legs for Mr. Martin at the antique store every few months. It was enough at first, but in time, the children needed things I couldn't afford on lies and lying down under a rutting man.

So, when my Clear turned twelve years old, I packed up my house, and I married Martin.

\#

At our new home Clear was still called Clear Meadows by me and my family, but Martin called her Claire. He was my husband for two whole years. I might've lasted longer, but Clear spoke of Clancy.

Two years was enough. For two years, Clancy had been up there on his own, and none of us were happy about it. I couldn't risk Clancy dying, so I left him in my house instead of in the woods. He was safer, and he had food. Clancy was kept locked up safe.

Clear got to crying over it one night, missing him like she did. That changed everything. I couldn't blame her.

"Who's Clancy?" Martin asked. "Claire said there's a boy living in the house on the holler. Are you stepping out on me, Annabella?"

Now, I'd always known our time was limited. Meadows women weren't good at husbands. Mama had sacrificed hers, and I'd sacrificed Auntie Imogene's last one. Gin and Juniper had cast theirs into the pit together, and when Uncle Catalpa heard of it, he simply plowed them under. There were a lot of bones in the strip mines.

Everyone knew Martin would die, even though it was about to be a surprise to him.

"Let me explain," I begged. "Come with me."

We drove the car up the mountain in the dark that night while Clear slept. Fourteen years of my life as a mother to Clear and Clancy had me excited at the thought of us altogether again. Uncle Catalpa and Auntie Imogene looked in on Clancy these last two years, but it wasn't the same. I saw it in his eyes when I visited.

He didn't say as much. Fetches don't speak, but I felt the rage in his eyes when I visited. And Clear said she heard him whisper things that scared her.

I paused at the door, scraped my feet on the hedgehog, and turned to Martin. "It's probably best if you move slowly. Clancy has moods."

Martin didn't scrape his boots, so his feet were leaving mud on my floor with every step. "Who is Clancy, Annabella?"

His voice was loud, and I knew before the night was out that I'd be widow.

Clancy came out of the shadows. He smiled with a flash of teeth, and then he met my gaze.

"For you."

He was on Martin that moment, but he was careful. My Clancy had grown graceful over the years. We practiced on small animals, and as Clancy grew, we moved on to the larger ones. The year before I'd married Martin, Clancy had ended a mountain lion. I was as proud of him as if he'd been a real person.

Maybe that was because he was the spitting image of Clear.

I figured it was a Fetch thing, the way they looked so alike.

Clancy had his hands around Martin's throat and was shaking him. There was a little blood, but not much. When he dropped my late husband on the ground at my feet, I almost forgot that he wasn't my real child.

He moved his lips like he was speaking, and I saw the word "mama" there.

"What a good creature," I praised.

Clancy snuffled the air and walked over to the door. I knew that he was hoping to find my daughter.

"Clear isn't with me."

I couldn't endure the look of pain in his eyes, so I steeled myself and pointed at Martin. "Grab that. I'll get the tools."

We walked into the wood, as we had in other years with other offerings. Clancy dropped Martin on the spot. It was where we drained the offerings. It was how I kept my Clancy and Clear alive.

Clancy sat on a log and watched. He couldn't help with this. Nourishing my children was my duty. I cut the body at the joints, and then I removed the bones I'd need. Those, I set aside.

The next part was the hardest. Clancy had grown stubborn with time.

I cut out Martin's heart and held it out. "if you don't eat, you'll die."

He shook his head.

"Clear will die," I added when he still refused. "Do you want that?"

Clancy wept, and he choked, but he ate Martin's heart. Later, he'd vomit. That was normal, though.

He was, after all, not really human.

"CHANGING GUARDS: A GRAVEMINDER PREQUEL STORY"

Alicia met William Montgomery at the mouth of the tunnel. The peculiarity of her inability to enter the tunnel was no stranger than the fact that anyone could transverse it, but it still felt odd to her. Once, more than a century ago, she'd believed the preachers with their beautiful sermons. She'd trusted them when they told her that death was the end, that a fiery pit waited for those who sinned, and that peace was an option for those who lived a good and righteous life. Then the dead woke, and she'd found out that death was not the end.

"Alicia." William stepped into her world, the land of the dead. He was the only living man who could do so right now. There'd been others, including her own husband, but they were gone. Another would replace William, as he'd replaced those before him, but for now, there was only him.

She said nothing. It pained her to hear an old man's voice coming from his lips. Years ago, he'd caused a flutter in her heart every time he entered the land of the dead. Of course, the fact that he was still alive made him more alluring than most everyone here.

He held out a bag, and she tried not to see the wrinkles on his hand. It always seemed wrong to see the Undertaker grow old when she was frozen at the same age.

"I brought a few surprises." William's expression was the same bold one that he'd worn as a young man, and Alicia knew without asking that the bag he passed over to her contained items sure to upset Charles. She didn't pressure William to cross the old bastard as she had a few decades ago when William had first become the Undertaker, but that didn't mean that the temptation had passed—only that her affection for William had grown.

A little shiver of excitement rippled over her as she peered into the bag. Inside was a thin book on homemade explosives, a bunch of wire, assorted gadgets she couldn't identify, and various packages wrapped and labeled with only numbers.

"There's a key to the numbers in the book," William said.

"Not that I don't appreciate it, but what gives?"

"Just thought I'd settle up and buy myself a little credit." He walked toward her little corner of the land of the dead with the comfort of someone who'd trod this path more times than either of them probably liked.

Alicia fell in step with him.

In the alleyways of the old wooden buildings, her boys waited and watched. Milt and Mickey were nearest, but a good half dozen more were scattered about the area, standing guard and keeping order. The streets of the land of the dead weren't always safe . . . truth be told, they were rarely safe. Any illusion of an afterlife filled with sweet cherubs and fields of flowers had been shattered long before Alicia died, but sometimes she regretted the loss of those idealized fancies. She supposed, sometimes when she was feeling a bit more hopeful, that those things might exist beyond this land. Most of the time, though, she wasn't given to hopeful musings. The fact was that this world was a strange one, and she had no way of knowing if what came next would be better or worse. Here at least she occupied a singular position: she was the only Graveminder who had not moved on after her death. Out there, presumably, her long gone husband waited, but the idea of facing him after she'd killed him was reason enough to stay where she was.

"Alicia?" William voice interrupted her reverie. "Are you well?"

She forced a smile. "Well enough."

He nodded. "Understandable." His grandfatherly face wrinkled with lines as he frowned. "Does the love for your partner change after you pass?"

There was no question as to which partner he meant. Every Undertaker had a Graveminder, a woman who could lead the Hungry Dead to this world. He lived as her partner, her guard, and often her lover. They were a pair, bound together more surely than any marriage contract. It made living a life with anyone else nearly impossible. William had done it, but only because both his wife and his Graveminder accepted the inevitable division of his heart. Alicia couldn't have done so. She'd have gleefully murdered anyone who took her Conner's attention away from her for even a moment.

"Course it does," she lied. "It's just a part of the contract, William, but even if not, your Graveminder won't ask to stay here in this world. She'll move on like all the rest."

"Except you," he amended quietly.

After years of steadfast refusal to talk about who she was and what she was, she'd given in recently. William knew what most of the Undertakers before him hadn't: she was a Graveminder, same as his beloved Maylene. She'd served Death in her life, minding the dead, keeping them in their rightful place, just as the women before her and after her. Telling him was probably why it was on her mind too much of late. Her life was long since over, and any hope she had of a peaceful afterlife was quashed by the reality of the land of the dead.

"Soon, my son . . ." William's words dwindled, and he steadfastly didn't look her way. He'd been almost fifty when he had his son and heir, Byron.

William had delayed for a long time on passing on his duties, not by choice, but because his Graveminder asked it of him. William would do anything for her. It was why he'd carried on his duty long after he should've passed it on to Byron.

William cleared his throat and said, "I've been talking to Maylene about telling the kids about the contract. It would be easier if I knew that you were . . . amenable to rolling my credits on to him."

"You know better," she chided him. "He has to find his way here just as you did. It's the way of it. I can't offer him any special consideration any more than I did when you were young and stumbling around here."

William nodded, and they walked the next few blocks in silence. He'd needed to ask, and she'd needed to refuse. The transition as the Undertaker prepared for death was always hard. The question of the passing on of the duties of Undertaker was raised by every generation. Some focused on the "what next" question, as if being in *this* land of the dead gave her special insight into what happened in the next plane. It didn't, and she told them as much. The other, *harder* questions were the sort she expected of William. They were also the sort she couldn't quite answer.

A warning whistle from her left made her stop and shove William to the ground.

She felt the sharp sting of the bullet a moment after she'd heard the warning from one of the boys.

"Damn it." The bullet grazed her shoulder, tearing through her jacket and bloodying her skin.

The Undertaker stood, gun in hand, eyes scanning the shadows where the shooter could hide.

Milt arrived a few moments later. He exchanged a nod with William, and then both men turned on her.

"What were you thinking?" Milt snarled. He pulled his shirt off and wadded it into a ball that he pressed to her shoulder.

"William could've been hit." She knocked Milt's hand away, but kept the shirt. Now that it was already bloodied, there was no sense in trying to use it for clothing. She'd buy him a new one and add this to the always-growing pile of rags they kept. Infection wasn't a problem once you were dead, but bullets still hurt, and blood still stained. Some things were truths regardless of the world around you.

"Thank you," William murmured as he slipped an arm around her. She didn't need his protection, any of theirs actually. Death could only truly kill her twice.

And although the old bastard had done just that over a century ago, he wasn't likely to kill her now that she was here, and no one else in the land of the dead had the power to cause a second passing. In the land of the living, everyone can kill. Bullets, animals, illnesses, the causes of death were myriad and omnipresent. In the land of the dead, there was only one person who could end a life. The rest of them had to settle with taking a person out of commission for a few days.

Still, she wasn't going to rehash it with the boys—or the Undertaker—again. They were always surly when she got shot. It was far less hassle to let them have their moment of worry.

"One of Charles' people?" Milt asked. "I didn't think there was any trouble brewing right now."

"Look into it." Alicia hoped so, as the pleasure of another quarrel with him would be welcome, but it seemed unlikely. Charles usually didn't do anything underhanded. With them, the exchange of gunfire was more a matter of habit than of maliciousness. He found it a necessary evil, a thing that helped remind her that she was under his domain, and she tended to resort to it because . . . well, because it simply made her feel better. Some women took up needlework, and some took up arms.

OVER THE NEXT FEW WEEKS, Alicia threw herself into creating the explosives that she'd sought. It wasn't that she had any particular need for them, but they were *new*. New was a rare and valued commodity in the land of the dead. She did what she could to stave off boredom, but after so long in the land of the dead, excitement was harder to come by than she'd like. Her sole source of dangerous thrills was provoking Charles.

After what she considered sufficient experimentation, Alicia bribed a delivery boy to take an innocuous looking box to Charles' house. She timed it on a day when he was busy with a few quarrels she'd set to brewing in the Depression Era section of the city. They were often the easiest to rile. Their steadfast desire to live in houses that resembled shanties seemed tied to some sort of religious theory about Purgatory and completing penance. For the most part, those citizens weren't even people who'd lived during the Great Depression, but Charles allowed them their peculiarity—and Alicia leverage it for distractions time and again.

Milt and Boyd stood on either side of her as they waited to "field test" the explosives they'd made. They weren't scientists, and no one on their employ had made homemade explosives before now, so they weren't entire sure of the ratio. Their small-scale tests were successful, so they'd used that as the basis.

"Do you think it's big enough to even hear it?" Milt asked.

Alicia shrugged.

"Maybe there will be a vibration," Boyd suggested. "Dynamite shakes the ground. This is like dynamite, so—"

His words were abruptly cut off by a deafening *boom!* Dust and debris scattered outward as a wall crumbled. It was a much, much larger explosion than they'd planned.

"Shit, boss!" Milt muttered.

Immediately, a crowd began to gather.

"Move," she ordered Boyd and Milt. "*Now.*"

She'd never done something quite this . . . extreme. Charles wouldn't hurt her, not really. She counted on that. It enabled her to poke and prod at him in a way no other resident of the land of the dead would dare. Her people weren't impervious though.

"Get moving before he gets home and sees . . ." She glanced back as the second floor of his beautiful mansion started to slope toward the ground.

"Holy fuck," someone nearby muttered.

Gazes were turning to her. There was no doubt who was responsible. No one else would be foolhardy enough to blow up Charles' new parlor. Alicia strode through the crowd, hoping that she hadn't finally gone too far.

She glanced back as that second floor section of wall came crashing down.

"Faster," she urged her people.

WHEN CHARLES RETURNED to his home to find flames, debris, and dust, he shook his head, but said nothing. What was there to say? Alicia, no doubt, had either been irritated by something he'd done or was in a mood again. Sometimes he thought he'd be lost when she finally moved on to join her own Undertaker. Right now, fear and guilt kept her here—in the land of the dead that he ruled. Eventually, she'd realize that she should go.

Ward, his right-hand man, muttered a curse that included the oft-uttered phrase "damn Barrow woman."

"It's unexpected," Charles said.

Ward snorted, but didn't engage in an argument. He was respectful of Charles' strange friendship with the dead Grave-minder even though he had told Charles years ago that he thought it was twelve shades of stupid. Charles, for his part, respected both Ward's loyalty which resulted in his opinion of Alicia *and* his willingness to mostly keep silent on that opinion. He was a good man.

"How much shall I repair?" Charles mused. He liked to let the destruction she wrought stand, but in this case, there would have to be repairs made. He couldn't have his house collapse or allow a gaping hole in it. The repairs would give focus to some of his citizens, and the reminder that he was unpredictable served his purposes too.

He visualized the building once more intact, and with that thought, the walls were replaced. The rubble from the original walls remained—both inside and outside the building. It was a concession to both his practicality and Alicia's destruction.

"Hire some workers, Ward. That part of the house was due to be remodeled anyhow. Have them submit designs and teams, and I'll pick among them." Charles made sure his voice carried, and then he smothered the smile their excited murmurs evoked. He might not be able to relieve all of his citizens' unhappiness, but he saw no reason that being dead should have to equate to being miserable.

CHARLES WAS sure that he had more than enough patience to manage the Land of the Dead. He'd been doing it since before the humans had built proper cities over on the mortal side. Dealing with emotions was an altogether different situation. The peculiar nature of his domain was that every era in history existed within the reaches of the Land of the Dead. Boomtowns and modern cities vied for attention within the space of several blocks. The inhabitants of each area were all sure that the way the world had looked during each of their lives was how it *should* be.

And Charles had the unenviable job of keeping order among the lot of them.

For the past week, he'd been concentrating on the tedium of just that—instead of going to Alicia's General Store and demanding answers. She'd come when she was ready. Until then, he'd concentrate on the business of the dead, including choosing a new design for the section of his home that she'd destroyed.

"Sir?" Ward stood in the doorway of the study; the steady man was as patient as the statues that sat in the alcoves of the room.

Charles rubbed his eyes again. "Did I have an appointment?"

"Of a sort." Irritation flickered over Ward's expression so briefly that Charles wouldn't have noticed if they hadn't spent the past two centuries together. Only one person evoked such irritation in his right-hand man.

Charles rolled up the blueprints on his desk. "I gather Ms. Barrow is finally here?"

A curt nod from Ward answered the question without Ward himself having to find polite words.

"Where is she?" Charles asked.

Ward hesitated before admitting, "The west parlor. . ." He paused, cleared his throat, and amended, "The *remains* of the west parlor, sir."

Charles' smile became a laugh. "How long has she been there?"

"She did not have an appointment, sir." Ward stared directly at his boss. "She decimated the parlor, and today, she arrived wearing boots with . . . *dung* on them again. The foyer will need scrubbed, and the new rug"—Ward let out a pained sigh—"will need laundering. There is nowhere more suited for that woman than the ruins she created."

"I see." Charles stood and came around the desk. "So . . . she's been waiting a while then."

"She doesn't get *more* difficult with waiting," Ward muttered.

Charles walked toward his valet-bodyguard-friend. He clapped Ward on the shoulder. "I trust that the chairs that are *not* in the room will arrive not long after I do."

"Of course." Ward gestured for Charles to precede him down the hall. "Would you like full tea?"

"I suspect a bit of whiskey will be more useful." Charles didn't admit that the weight of the day slid from his shoulders as he left Ward behind and headed to the ruined part of the house, and Ward, likewise, didn't remark on the fact that he knew exactly how much Charles didn't admit.

Alicia might be the one dead person who always irritated Ward, but she was also the only person in the Land of the Dead who surprised Charles. If she ever decided to get over her anger and fear and move on to a better realm, Charles feared he'd be inconsolable. They weren't friends in any traditional sense, but she was valuable to him in the way he had rarely known.

ALICIA SAT in the center of a debris-strewn room. One knee was pulled up to her chest, and the other leg was extended in front of her. She didn't like sitting in the dirt, but it wouldn't make her jeans much filthier than they already were. The old bastard had left her in a chairless room for over an hour. Idly, she studied the space she'd been forced to occupy while she waited for *him* to decide he was done making her stew.

Never get tired of showing me who's really in charge, do you?

She had to admit that the punishment was fitting this time: her boys had detonated the charges that resulted in the debris around her. *It was just business.* She grinned. Charles might be the law, but she had become more than adept at provoking him—and getting results on a few key reform areas.

Alicia tensed at the sound of footsteps behind her. Without turning around, she knew the old bastard had arrived. No one else walked with that same cadence. He moved across the stone floor with music in his footfall. She wasn't sure he even noticed the song in his step. She did. After over a century of dealing with him in the land of the dead— and a few years more when she was still alive—she knew Charles better than she knew any person alive or dead.

Despite her best efforts, her spine stiffened, and her every nerve was on alert. It wasn't that she was frightened. *Much.* It was simple caution. He was the one person—*thing*—here that could end her existence. The land of the dead was his, absolutely and completely. That was why there had been no competition to setting up her business: no one crossed the old bastard.

Except me and mine.

"Alicia," he murmured. "Lovely to see you, as always, my dear."

She still didn't turn around. She wiped her hands on her jeans, but she didn't rise.

"I would've had lunch prepared if I'd known we had an appointment." Charles stood just behind her. "Perhaps you'd care for a drink since you're here."

Finally, Alicia looked over her shoulder at him. She patted the dirty floor beside her. "Have a seat, Charlie. It's quite cozy here."

"Ah, yes." He looked around. His gaze slid over the charred bits of wood and tile. He frowned as he spotted a painting that had been made unrecognizable by the blast. "I liked the room a bit more before you left that little package here."

"The explosives are a new item," she said softly, drawing his gaze back to her. "We made it ourselves, and I didn't realize how much damage it would do."

Charles didn't smile, not quite, but his expression softened. "That almost sounded like an apology, Alicia."

She shrugged. "Near to one as I'll get."

"Thank you," he murmured.

Alicia nodded. They couldn't exchange civilities as well in public, but here behind closed doors she knew she'd make more progress with Charles if she tried to be cordial. She wasn't sure if she'd ever admit that she preferred their civility to the hostility they needed to embrace if there were witnesses, but the rare quiet conversations she shared with

Death these days reminded her of long gone times, back when she was alive and only visiting this realm.

"William's getting old," she said as politely as possible. "The boys and I notice it more and more each time he comes in to the General Store. He isn't as careful around town as an Undertaker needs to be." She paused, weighing the words as carefully as she ever did when the subject of the Undertaker and Graveminder came up. "It's time to replace him."

Charles frowned. His relationship with the Undertaker—as with every Undertaker before William—was contentious. They were both adversaries and allies, both dedicated to the one human woman who could move between the land of the dead and the living world. The complicated relationship didn't mean Charles disliked William or wished ill on him. Alicia understood that as she hadn't years ago when her husband, Conner, was the Undertaker.

"He'd not that old," Charles objected. "It was only a moment ago that he became—"

"It's been *decades*, Charlie," she interrupted.

His sense of time was skewed at best, and she'd realized several Undertakers back that it was up to her to help Charles notice when time had passed. Being the embodiment of Death made for a peculiar relationship with time. She'd taken it upon herself to be loyal to the calling she'd embraced when she'd been alive. She might be dead, but she *was* still a Graveminder.

She watched as Charles paced away from her. He stooped and lifted a handful of rubble. Silently, he let the powder slip through his fingers. She knew it would take only a thought to turn the white chalky dust and bits of rubble into a wall again. He wouldn't though. Whatever she destroyed, he left broken. That, too, was on the long list of topics best not pondered. He'd done only enough repair work to keep the building intact, and now he was auditioning designers to repair and renovate his home.

While they waited in silence—her on the floor and him surveying the destruction—Charles' personal assistant, guard, and all-around pain in Alicia's ass came in with a tray. On it were glasses, an ice bucket, and decanter. Behind Ward were lackeys with chairs and a small table, as well as two men with brooms. In minutes, they'd cleared a space, arranged the furniture, and left the drinks.

Ward looked to Charles, ignoring her as if she weren't visible to him, and at Charles' nod, he departed again.

Alicia and Charles sipped their drinks in silence, a companionable peaceful habit that she knew they wouldn't admit to cherishing.

"I've not met the new Graveminder yet," Charles admitted somberly after he finished his drink. "After the way things went when I met Ella . . ." His words faded, but they weren't necessary. The unprecedented actions of the young girl who was to replace Maylene Barrow had led to this awkward situation. Ella Mae had committed suicide, determined to hasten her journey to the land of the dead, and the current Graveminder had decided to hide the truth from the girl who would replace Ella. William, by extension, had hidden that same information from the next Undertaker. Neither Byron nor Rebekkah knew of the land of the dead. It was well past time for that to change.

And Alicia was going to make sure it happened.

"William is weary," Alicia pointed out. "He's vulnerable every time he comes here. If you don't act, I will."

She didn't specify how she'd act, but Charles knew—as did William. The Undertaker and Death were both too worried over the current Graveminder. Maylene was hiding her replacement, letting the girl wander outside Claysville, utterly unaware of her duties. It was well past time for the changing of the guard, and even though Alicia's descendent was cosseting the next Graveminder, Alicia wouldn't be.

"Insist he bring the boy to meet you, or I'll force the matter," she announced.

CHARLES SAT in the destroyed parlor long after Alicia had left. Alicia's ability to offer to kill William bothered him. He wanted to think that her willingness to kill was a result of having been here in the land of the dead where shooting, stabbing, strangling, or any variety of heinous acts only resulted in temporary death. He wondered sometimes, though, what she'd have been like had she not been trapped in Claysville because of the contract he'd made with her long-gone ancestor.

The only person who could kill the already dead was him, and that was an act he rarely took. He didn't want to do it now either. Minding the dead wasn't quite the same as taking their lives. He found the curious spark of the living rather intoxicating. Every Graveminder was special to him, not just because they were living but because, through them, Charles knew the world of the living. None were as special as the first Graveminder. He'd been in love with Abigail; it was why the contract was created. Love for her had made him unable to deny her anything. The result was a gap between the living and the dead, and the inhabitants of Claysville were still paying for that. There, the dead didn't always stay dead, and it was all because Charles couldn't say "no" to a living woman who looked at him fondly and said, "Please, Charles?"

Unfortunately, that very same weakness for his Graveminders meant that he was at odds with their living partners.

There was no love lost between William Montgomery and the ruler of the land of the dead. That did not mean, however, that Charles was keen to commit murder. The death of the Undertaker would cause the subsequent death of the Grave-minder. The peculiar bargain Charles had made with their predecessors centuries ago meant that the mortality of the two was entwined.

Reluctantly, Charles admitted that Alicia was probably right. He sipped the remainder of Alicia's drink in silence. It was as close to actual contact with her that he ever got.

He was still sitting there when Ward returned some time later.

"I need to see Maylene and William," Charles told them. "It's time that I meet the next generation. The new Grave-minder and Undertaker need to be brought back to Claysville so they can be ready to assume their duties."

"LOVE HURTS: A WICKED LOVELY STORY"

Set after the Wicked Lovely series

Irial looked at the letters that had been delivered to the current house in Huntsdale. He stood in the doorway, exposed in his bare feet and bare chest. Spring, fortunately, was a true and reliable event the past few years. If anything, the former Dark King was wondering if the season had come a touch early this year. Trees were erupting in new growth, and the ground seemed speckled with flowers. If not for the curious, hand-delivered package, he'd be debating popping over to Winter's abode and asking for a last frost, just a brief freezing before the Summer Queen had her way with nature.

Not that he minded an early summer, of course, simply that he *was* the embodiment of Discord. Stirring a minor tiff over the greenery seemed the right path. It had, in fact, been his plan. Now, though, he couldn't focus. In his hand was what appeared to be the key to his unraveling. Yellowed pages were covered in protective sheaths. It was the word on the top that left him, the man who had led the Court of Nightmares and Monsters, terrified.

Da

Dadaih.

Athair.

Father.

Irial was the embodiment of chaos, of discord. He'd fought, slain, and even died. He'd loved and lost—more than once. His first love, Niall, abandoned him for many centuries. His next love, Thelma, left and died without their even reuniting. The third love, Leslie, had risked death to leave him.

Dadaih.

The script went from childish to mature. The sophistication of the words changed, and the tone grew cold.

Father.

With a jolt, Irial realized that the door was still open. Still, he stood at the threshold of his home, a house he shared with the current Dark King, and read. Flowers bloomed outside, and the sky was clear. Somehow, Irial felt as if a storm was about to erupt. Sadly, his was not a court of nature, as the Winter Court and Summer Court were. He could not send storms free to vent his feelings. All he could do was draw shadows to his skin.

Da.

Irial read that one word in all its forms repeatedly. He didn't need to read the pages that were stacked in the other envelope to know that sender's name. Thelma was the only of the three people he'd loved who had died. She was gone.

And between leaving me and dying, she had my child.

Niall stood in the grand lobby of the Benedum Center, appreciating the now-familiar chandeliers of theater. In the latter part of the 1900s, it had been a concert hall of a different sort. He'd seen both Prince and Bob Marley there in the '80s. These days, it housed both opera and ballet, and as much as *some* faeries mocked his fondness for both, the current Dark King knew that anyone who doubted the appeal of opera simply hadn't been paying attention. It was often terribly tragic stuff, rife with manipulation, murder, and mayhem. Any faery worth his salt would like theatre.

Luckily, even the fey like the Hounds, who might not understand his love of *this* type of art, appreciated arts and music in general. Even better, Leslie shared his interest. Typically, Irial did, too.

Tonight, they had planned to see *Faust,* a French opera of the medieval scholar who makes an ill-fated deal with a devil. Niall had, not so secretly, always wondered if Méphistophélès was inspired by Irial. An unwise bargain with a "devil" who is clever . . . the idea seemed rather more fitting than a mortal dealing with the fey, and although Irial never owned up to it, Niall recalled the years the courts all gathered in Germany. Goethe met fey creatures.

Of that, Niall was certain.

But the devil in question, Irial, had made excuses to miss the opera tonight. Worse yet, he'd done so badly. Now, Niall was left trying to convince Leslie that all was well—an illusion neither she nor he believed.

A glass of wine. A smile. A stroll under beautiful chandeliers that sparkled in the high-ceilinged lobby that was filled with mortals and more than a few fey things. It should've been lovely.

"You look beautiful," he told his date again.

"And you look handsome," Leslie replied.

This is when Irial would've made an inappropriate remark, fished for praise, or simply kissed one of them. His absence rankled. The lights all seemed to dim at once as shadows swarmed to Niall like a ripple of midnight seeping into the evening.

Leslie's hand tightened on his arm, and Niall sent his emotions like a nourishing elixir toward the rest of his court. Some of his faeries perched in nooks in the high ceiling, and others languished in the room, dressed in human guises, pretending to be nothing more than ruffians amongst the gentry in their fine dresses. It was far from the theatre of the past, where everyone was bedecked in gems and formal attire, but it was still very much a crowd where those who *have* wanted to be clear that they were superior.

Or maybe they were as smitten by the grand spectacle of the opera as he was. His box seat was not a statement of status. It was simply a space where he could have privacy. No one not *with* him was in the box. The idea of reserving only a few seats in the box seemed odd. Privacy mattered.

He and Leslie made their way to the Dark Court's seasonal box and took their seats.

She was silent, uncharacteristically so, but he was attempting to respect that. They were never awkward, with or without Irial at their sides, but tonight things were tense in a palpable way. Irial had asked Niall to excuse him, had put Niall in the position of misleading Leslie. There was no good answer, so Niall had chosen evasiveness as his solution to the mess.

Leslie vibrated with tension at his side. The lights dimmed, and he thought that the moment of risk was over. Then she leaned closer.

"He's not ill?"

And as much as Niall wished he could lie, he could not do so. "No."

"Injured?"

As much as he did not want the former Dark King to be ill, he could not help the flicker that came over him in that moment. "Not yet."

Leslie smiled wanly.

"I don't understand either," Niall admitted. "He's avoiding me."

The show began, and with every tear that trickled down Leslie's cheek, Niall thought about strangling Irial. Avoiding *him* Niall could forgive. Avoiding her? There was no excuse that Niall could imagine accepting.

After the show, Niall and Leslie walked to the street, and there a steed waited. It was a living creature, one that had the heart of a wild steed but chose to serve as Leslie's personal guard. Not quite a horse, not exactly a car, it was a member of the Hunt, but was riderless and technically remained so. Leslie was not a Hound, so she couldn't be its rider—and the steed tolerated no other unless Leslie was there, too. Tonight, it wore the illusion of being a fire-red convertible.

Leslie caressed the side of the car, much the way one greets a beloved pet. The fact that this particular "pet" was a monstrous beast with fire glimmering where eyes ought to be was immaterial. She was beloved by the whole of the Dark Court.

"He'll explain, or we'll *make* him," Niall swore to her as he walked around to the passenger seat.

The engine roared when Leslie's hands touched the steering wheel. She didn't steer, not really. The steed carried her home or wherever else she wanted, as if it were a car. And Niall chose not to linger long on the thought that this once-mortal woman had tamed a steed so thoroughly that it functioned as her car—and seemed quite content to do so.

When they reached the apartment where she lived—in a building he'd recently and stealthily bought when the landlord was causing her anxiety—Leslie stayed in the car, as it purred loudly enough to mimic a fine engine. She stroked the dashboard and steering wheel. After a moment she announced, "I'll handle Irial."

And Niall wasn't fool enough to argue. If anything, he was certain that when he returned from his trip the issue would be resolved. Leslie wasn't meek, and she'd become downright formidable these last few years.

"Should I warn him?" Niall asked lightly.

"Not unless you want to get caught in the crossfire." Leslie stepped out of the car. "I won't have him ruin our night, though. Join me?"

If Méphistophélès were a woman, she'd be no more tempting than Leslie as she held out a hand. Niall would give her his soul, his vow, whatever she wanted. He was certain Irial would, too.

"Forever," Niall told Leslie as he took her hand.

And she smiled with a sweet darkness that made him wonder how he could have earned such love.

The weekend would come, and they would confront the secretive faery they both loved. Whatever Irial was hiding was something they could figure out together. First, Niall would attend to business, and Leslie to her classes.

IRIAL WAS NO CLOSER to knowing what to do about the news of his child than the day he'd learned the news. Niall was away, and Leslie should be in class. Irial had counted on that time to figure it all out.

The doors to the study opened with a thunderous noise.

"You're avoiding me." Leslie stood in the doorway to the library after flinging open the doors in a burst of temper. Her once-blonde hair had become increasingly shadow-dark over the last three years, finally reaching the black of the ink that Rabbit had once tattooed in her skin.

College would end soon, and their lives would change. Irial wasn't sure how—and he was afraid to ask.

What if she wants to move away?

He did not stand. "What do you mean?"

"The opera?"

"Ah." Irial nodded. "You weren't alone, though."

She sighed. "Is it because you are feeling guilty?"

Irial shrugged. Guilt? Perhaps. He'd unknowingly abandoned a child—and he was hiding it from both Niall and Leslie. He paused. "Aren't you to be in classes today?"

Leslie scowled. "I couldn't concentrate." She stared at him. "You promised not to meddle. I know there aren't threats like there used to be. Bananach is dead. Ren is . . . "

"Apparently missing," Irial filled in helpfully.

She'd never asked, and he'd never volunteered an answer on that particular situation. Ren had threatened Leslie, *their* Leslie, in order to draw out the faeries who loved her. They'd been drawn out, and when they had, Niall had removed the threat to their shadow girl.

"I don't want you to meddle, but if you do . . . don't avoid me afterward," she ordered.

One of the abyss guardians—sentient shadows that were typically only tied to the Dark King or his consort—slithered over to encase Leslie.

"Hello, sweetie," she whispered to the shadow-wrought

creature as she came into the room and pulled the door behind her.

The soft snick of the door catching was loud in the still of the room, and Irial felt strangely like prey for a moment.

"I don't only need you when there's trouble," she announced. "Don't you understand that?"

Mutely, Irial nodded. The shadows glided back to the walls as if they'd only ever been the ordinary shadows any lamp or shelf would cast.

After a moment, Leslie crossed her arms and held his gaze. "What are you hiding?"

"Hiding?" Irial echoed. The sight of her, the sheer force of her mortal self striding through the house of monsters, left him longing.

"I know you, Irial," Leslie said.

"That you do, shadow girl." Truth be told, he'd slaughter near every being in the world at her whim. Leslie's very existence was a balsam on a soul that felt increasingly shredded these last few decades. Denying her was physically painful.

Of course, seeing her today ripped at his heart more than he expected. Thinking about her inevitable death seemed impossible now that he was thinking of Thelma, and tangled into that was the thought of a child. His child.

Half-fey children lived much longer than mortals, but not as long as faeries. Would he want that? Would Leslie? Would Niall?

A child would be complicated, but the thought of watching his own daughter or son grow up made Irial struggle to breath. He had never had that, and according to the letters he'd received, he should have. The closest he'd come was the half-fey children that Gabriel had sired. He was an "uncle" of sorts to many halflings, but the thought of his own child suddenly filled him with longing.

As she walked toward Irial, her footsteps were muffled by the overly thick burgundy and gold rug. Shadows puddled where she stepped as if to soak up some sort of magic in her very touch.

"I do not ask you to be my tiger on a leash," Leslie explained softly.

"Mmmm."

She paused, despite the catch in her breathing and the widening of her eyes. The control she had made him certain that she could rule a nation of pirates . . . or monsters. Leslie was not immune to his allure, but if he didn't know better, he might think she was.

The sound of her breathing, of her trying not to run to him, was enough to make him have to resist leaning forward. For all of his centuries of living, only one other mortal had made him feel so oddly *human*. That was over a century before Leslie had been born, and he still wondered if he ought to mention it to her.

Niall knew. Gabriel had known. The only others who remembered his brief relationship were fey of his court, those who would not share his secret—even with Leslie.

"You're staring," she teased, voice breathless as he felt.

"As are you."

"It's been three weeks since I saw you. Staring is sort of inevitable."

"Ah, and here I worried you were immune by now," he kept his voice teasing, but they both knew that he could not lie.

It *was* a fear—one of many these days. The gazes of others, fey and mortal, still raked over him. From thistle-skinned creatures of the Dark Court to the Scrimshaw Sisters of the Winter Court to the vine-bedecked Summer Girls, faeries watched him as if he was every dream they had. Although he knew Leslie wanted him, she could—and did—leave for weeks.

Niall did the same. It made Irial prone to waves of melancholy. If those who loved him didn't long for every moment with him, was he . . . lacking?

"Immune? To you?" Leslie laughed softly. "We both know that's impossible. Staring would be just as unavoidable if I'd seen you last week. I always want to see you, Iri. That's part of love."

"I *do* love you," he assured her.

There was a question in her words, though, one he was trying to avoid answering. Telling her she had his heart didn't seem to be enough this time. Niall had delivered Irial's excuses to Leslie, but neither of them believed him. The difference, of course, was that Niall was more tolerant of Irial's tendency toward secrecy. They lived together more peacefully than he'd hoped possible because they both kept more than a few boxes of secrets hidden away.

Leslie had no such patience.

She stood in front of Irial now, her knees not quite touching his, and he had to resist the dual urges to reach out and to run away. "But you could've come with Niall last week. Perhaps *I* am not irresistible these days . . . ?"

"He told you that I wasn't able to come," Irial hedged.

"He *told* me a bunch of excuses, and I'm not so innocent as to believe them. Lies are lies, Iri, even when they are delivered by someone who knows how to distract me." Leslie caressed his face. "Why don't *you* tell me you weren't able to come, Irial? Say those words to me."

The half-accusing, half-angry tone in her words made his resolve falter. He couldn't lie outright, and those words were a lie.

"I would say them if I could," he admitted. "I chose not to visit."

Leslie withdrew her hand, leaving him wishing he could lean closer, but too proud to do so. "Because? Tell me, Irial. Is it because of threatening my landlord? He offered to extend my lease suddenly. And there was some error, apparently. I no longer owe back rent. Are you feeling guilty?"

The former king leaned away, more to resist his own temptations than anything else.

"I know you can't help yourself sometimes," Leslie allowed.

"If I have meddled, I'm certain it was justified." He'd far rather discuss his supposed sins than his actual ones. Then, at least, he could be truthful with her. He hadn't avoided her from guilt, so there was no harm in owning whatever she thought him guilty of this time.

His reasons for avoiding her were harder to discuss.

Once, almost four years ago, they were bound together by blood and ink. Her emotions were the food that sustained him, the wine that intoxicated him, but their bond changed him even as it nourished him. She'd severed all but the barest thread of their connection, setting him adrift in the world, feeling like a strange new version of himself. Back then, Irial had been willing to give up everything . . . except her. Now, he was facing the possibility of losing her. It was an intolerable fate.

"You're *hiding* something," she announced.

"Trying."

"Failing." She reached out again, hand not quite touching him but near enough to make him feel like a hapless insect drawn to destruction.

"Don't ask me why I didn't visit," he half-begged, half-ordered. "Tell me how to atone for this meddling you say I did."

He'd ruled the monsters that were only spoken of in whispers, but for the second time in his life, a human girl held power over him.

"You didn't do it, did you?"

Irial shrugged. There was no harm in being held accountable for what Niall had likely done. From all of his years in the Summer Court, Niall carried an impulsiveness that sometimes made him unable to use caution or common sense—and those outside the Dark Court thought Irial guilty of many an ill-thought out act that was Niall's doing.

"So. . . not you."

"I didn't say that, love. I am guilty of all manner of things. I simply asked which has you in this mood." He lit a cigarette, pulling the smoke into his lungs with the comfort of a man who will never weaken or die from the poisonous stuff. It was a pleasant perk of being fey.

"No. I can feel your emotions, Irial. It's not the same as before, but it's growing stronger the past few months." Leslie spoke carefully as if she were weighing the words, sliding invisible fingers over the tendrils that flowed between their bodies again. "When I . . . cut the ties, it was like a ghost that passed by me sometimes, but now, it's like I can feel you more and more every month."

"Not enough to know whether I'm truly guilty, though."

"True," she murmured.

He caught her hand and pressed it to his cheek. "Does that help?"

Leslie laughed before saying, "Touching you always *helps*, but it doesn't always make you easier to read."

She caressed his face for a moment before settling onto his lap. There was no doubt in her, no insecurity as there had been when he'd first seen her. Back then she was a broken doll hiding her fears behind a false bravado. She'd survived an assault that left her screaming inside and trying desperately to pretend she was untouched by the pain. She'd been everything he needed for a conduit to feed the Dark Court: all but destroyed but still fierce inside.

For the past several years, the Dark Court had been her home. The monsters she'd saved would willingly kill or die for her. Admittedly, they'd also willingly kill for a cookie, but they wouldn't *die* for just anyone. They'd donned glamours and cheered her every victory while she was at university. They'd been planning a party for her upcoming graduation that even Irial thought might be a bit over the top, but he wasn't their king anymore and their current king would agree to any excess if he thought it would please Leslie.

"Niall's away," Irial said, trying to remember that she wasn't only his, not now.

"I know. I saw him last week. *He* isn't avoiding me." She slid her hand from Irial's cheek to his throat. "I'm here to see you, Iri. You can't hide from me if I'm in here with you."

Possessiveness flared at the thought of a few uninterrupted days with her. He ground his unfinished cigarette. No amount of time with Leslie was ever enough, could ever be enough. She was too mortal, too fleeting, and fate had a horrible habit of stealing those he loved.

As Leslie twined her arms around him and pulled him into a kiss, Irial stopped thinking. She was here now, touching him, and that was more than he'd ever expected when they'd first been bonded. Ink exchanges were often fatal, so by the time he realized he loved her, he'd expected her to die. When she severed their bond, it held a likelihood of killing her. When he'd been poisoned, he hadn't even had time to see her before he slipped into a comatose state. So to be kissing her several years later was . . . whatever came *after* miracles.

And like all miracles, he couldn't even quite believe this was real. He'd been the thing that led the worst of Faerie's monsters for over a millennium, the embodiment of Discord for the past few years, and his greatest fear was losing the two people he loved.

He'd done so once. Twice. Three times. Centuries ago, he'd lost the faery he now shared his home with, and then he lost the mortal he'd loved, and then he'd lost Leslie briefly, and then he'd died.

Dying ended up being a temporary state, but he felt the finiteness of life since that unfortunate event.

Losing a loved one always hurt, but with Niall and Leslie, they were still alive even when they weren't *his*. He'd been separated, partly, from them when he died. That, too, was bearable. Death of a loved one, on the other hand, was a far uglier thing. He'd gone through it once, and he'd thought the madness of losing the only other mortal he'd loved would break him. He wouldn't do it again.

"You must *never* die," he whispered to the woman in his arms.

Leslie smiled, kissed him again, but she made no such promises.

Mortals age. They die. And Leslie thought she was mortal still. He hoped she was wrong, but he wasn't sure. The thought that *he* might be wrong made him pull her tighter to him. "Never. Ever. Leave. Me."

Not long after, both of them half-drunk of kisses, Leslie watched Irial decided what and how much he could still misdirect her. It was a lie, but he had been king of the Dark Court for literal centuries. He was good at lying by way of omission, misdirection, and other subterfuge.

"I need answers," she nudged.

From the comfort of the sofa, Leslie watched the centuries' old faery pace as he acted only slightly older than the boys at university. Faeries age slower than mortals, and Irial had been a creature of self-indulgence so long that he reacted to restrictions, rules, or confusions with a mix of temper and embarrassment.

"Time to talk," she announced.

"Fine." He sulked—and she tried not to laugh. Learning to live with the Dark Court meant learning that the monsters were often not as scary as people thought, and not nearly as scary as they pretended. At least it seemed that way to her.

Certainly, after the battle between the courts in which Bananach died, Leslie could admit that there was a violence to them that she rarely saw.

"I graduate in a few weeks," she nudged. "Is *that* what has you upset?"

"No." Irial poured himself a drink.

Lightly she said, "Sometimes I swear you have single-malt bottles in every room."

He grinned, drank, and refilled his glass. "I usually do, but *this* is the study. What sort of study lacks liquor? Or books? Or a comfortable sofa?"

As Leslie was stretched out on said sofa, she wasn't likely to argue. "Fair enough."

He shook the glass. "Drink?"

Leslie shook her head. She was legal now, but she didn't often drink. "My liver isn't as eternal as yours."

His face darkened.

"Is *that* what this is all about?" Leslie stared at him. "My lack of eternity?"

"Perhaps." Irial downed his drink. "I dislike how easily and quickly mortals die."

"I'm here right now." She stood, hands on her hips, but regretfully not terribly intimidating. "I'm in my *second* decade of life, Iri. Second."

"And unless something changes, you only have a handful left. Not even a century." His voice grew louder, not quite yelling but far louder than normal speech.

Leslie took a step back. He was far from perfect, but it wasn't like him to yell. He was calm, sardonic, charming, and a million other things. He could be irritating, and on a few occasions, she'd seen him seem cold or cruel when he and Niall were at odds.

Never to her, though.

"Something else is going on." She stepped toward him, approaching as if he were a feral animal that might flee.

"I don't know if I can do this again," he said quietly. He bowed his head.

"Do *what?*" Leslie reached out, and he withdrew further.

"Love someone who is going to die," he admitted.

As pieces started to click together, she stared, mouth agape.

Again.

He was afraid to love someone again who would die. Foolishly, she'd assumed there had only been Niall. He'd lived for centuries, though. No one was sure how many. He was older than Keenan, the reigning Winter King and former Summer King, and Keenan was over nine hundred years old.

"A human?" she asked.

At first, Irial simply stared at her. Then he gave a nod.

"I had no idea," she said, as gently as she could.

Irial shrugged. "I don't discuss her."

Leslie felt like her heart would break as his wave of sorrow washed over her. The ties that bound them were still fragile things, but even the edge of his grief brought tears to her eyes. Once, before them, Irial had loved deeply. Not Niall. Not her. A stranger. The thought of it made her understand his attempts to withdraw from her. What was confusing was why now? Why did he feel so much fear now when she had always been mortal?

"How old was she?"

Irial smiled sadly. "Young when we met. Older than you, but times were different then." He took Leslie's hand in his. "You are very different people. . . and I've lived longer than I can fathom. Do not feel jealous, love."

Leslie kissed him gently. "I am *well* aware that I am not the first woman in your life, Iri."

He nodded, and they were together quietly for a moment longer.

Then, sheepishly, she admitted, "I just figured that you hadn't *loved* any of them."

He lit a cigarette and paced. His energy, the sheer emotional chaos that rode in his expression, reminded her that while he was gentler with her, he was still something of a caged tiger.

"I almost started a war over her," he said quietly. "When I lost her, I wondered why I ought not start it anyhow."

There was little that she could do. His withdrawal and her healing connection to him— Leslie had to wonder if it was all connected.

"I am not good at grieving," Irial said lightly, as if she had forgotten how devastating grief could be.

Leslie thought back to Niall when he'd been grieving.

She walked into the room to find Niall holding a fire

poker which he'd just tried to shove into Seth's eye. There was a madness there that she'd not ever seen before, but struggled to forget. Inside one of the two faeries she loved was a darkness that was more unstable than Irial's calculated coldness.

"You are not this person," Leslie told Niall.

He dropped the poker to the warehouse floor when he saw her.

Slowly, carefully, Leslie walked farther into the room. Niall's skin sizzled from gripping the poker, and Seth's face was burned. The smell was unsettling, but not as much as the lost look on Niall's face.

She stepped in front of the cage that held Seth, the beloved of the Summer King and friend to Niall until today.

"Niall? You don't really want to hurt yourself . . . or him."

Niall looked lost, as if his very world had vanished. He stared at her. "Seth Sees things. He knew and . . . He knew that Irial . . ."

"I heard what happened." Leslie approached Niall with her hand outstretched, as if she could touch him and heal him with it. She understood as no one in the world did. Irial wasn't the sort of person who could be replaced, who could be lost without a ravine in the middle of her heart. She knew what Niall felt because she felt it too.

"Ash called me. Donia called me. . . . You sent for me. Do you remember that, Niall? You sent Hounds."

"I didn't want to tell you," he whispered.

"I'm here." Leslie looked over her shoulder.

Behind her, a Hound stood in the open doorway. She wasn't sure if he was there for her safety or Niall's. It was all the same though. The court—and it was her court, too—was in pain. They were grieving, and their new king was unraveling.

"I am here with my court," she assured Niall. "I am here

with you . . . because you needed me. They need me to be here with you."

She took Niall's uninjured hand in hers, careful not to look at the burned flesh on the other hand, and used the only words she was sure would matter just then: "Irial wouldn't want you to hurt. You know that."

Leslie remembered that sorrow, how it had nearly destroyed the entire Dark Court.

Her own grief was less horrifying in its results, but she would never forget that utter terror that washed over her at the thought of never again touching or laughing with Irial.

She reached out and caressed his cheek. "You're in pain, and I understand."

He stared at her.

"I lost *you* once, Irial. In all the world, there is no one like you, and you were dead. . . and I love Niall as fully as I love you, and *he* was grieving." She felt tears escape her eyes. "Do you think I don't understand your fear?"

SEVERAL HOURS LATER, Leslie lifted her head from his chest and stared at him. "Are you okay?"

At some point in their lovemaking, Irial felt a tear slip from his face to hers, and he hoped she hadn't noticed. He hadn't *wept*, but in the moment of union, he was overwhelmed.

"Mmm." He pulled her down and kissed her, enjoying the sheer novelty of trusting a woman enough to have her on top of him.

She'd gotten far too able to read between his words, so his default with her was typically distraction. It was an excellent plan, if he did say so himself. Kissing Leslie was high on his list of favorite pastimes, alongside touching Leslie and making love with Leslie. Luckily for him, she didn't seem to object.

When she pulled away for real finally, she kissed both of his cheeks and his forehead affectionately before straightening back to a seated position and saying, "I'm never sure if I should be offended that you think I'm that easy to sidetrack. It doesn't work on Niall either, by the way."

Irial shrugged as best he was able with her on top of him and offered her his most innocent look. "You're the one who closed the door and attacked me."

She pressed her lips together and narrowed her gaze. "That's your summary of our day?"

"You made accusations, and we talked. Then you seduced me—after insisting I ought not meddle. So I was merely *not* meddling in your obvious plans to seduce me," Irial continued with the closest approximation of innocence he could muster.

"You might be delusional."

"I've been accused of far worse." Absently, he traced the tattoo of his eyes and the wings that still graced her back. He could feel the inky tendrils that once bound them snaking out to answer his touch.

"It's healing," she said. "The tattoo is almost healed."

"I know."

"That's why I feel you." She leaned back so his hand was tighter against the tattoo. The smoky threads that had stretched out to meet his touch tightened like vines grabbing his hand. The sensation rocked through him, burning along pathways that she'd once yanked out in her—quite justified—anger and fear.

He shivered, the wash of emotions that he felt from Leslie catching him off guard and bringing his own tangled mess of emotions surging to the surface. "Steady, love."

She didn't listen, though. She reached back and held his

hand to her skin. He could've jerked away, but . . . he also *couldn't*. She could read his feelings as if he were a book open before her. He wouldn't reject her and risk her turning away from him.

Once Irial and Niall had been gancanaghs, addictive to mortals. When Niall became Dark King and Irial became the embodiment of Discord, they were no longer addictive. Irial had wondered more than a few times over the past few years if fate had a sense of humor. Leslie could stay away from them, but they both craved her nearness the way junkies craved their drugs.

"You're afraid," Leslie murmured, her voice heavy with shock.

Instead of speaking, Irial let her taste his emotions.

"It didn't used to work this way." Her voice was wonder-filled then. "You're worried that I'll leave, that I'm hurt, that I'll die, and . . ." She paused and closed her eyes. She bit her lip, and then opened her eyes and looked directly at him. "You love me more than before. When we were connected, you didn't love me like this."

"I loved you then," he objected weakly.

"Not *this* much." She studied him in silence for a long moment before adding, "You let down a wall, unwillingly, and it scares you."

At that, Irial came to his feet and had the unexpected urge to don his trousers, as if clothing would somehow shield him. After tugging clothes onto his bottom half, he walked away to pour himself a drink. It was bad enough that he had to deal with Niall's ability to read his every emotion; adding Leslie to the mix meant that he would have no walls left to shelter him. Sometimes a faery simply didn't want to have his heart laid bare on the table.

"Come to New Orleans?" he asked Leslie, turning to face her once more.

"New Orleans?"

The former Dark King nodded. "Once, a century or so ago, I lived there."

She smiled, and in a drawl far too like his own, said, "Of course you did."

ONE OF THE Hounds pounded on the door. It was not Gabriel, who had been lost to the same forces that had nearly taken Irial, but one of his brothers who rumbled through their home with the same sense of force and thunder.

"The rest of the boxes from the buildings that were flooded are here," he announced as he shoved the door open.

Irial started, "Good, but—"

"Leslie!" Cam grinned at seeing her. He held his arms wide open to hug her.

"Cam," she said, not rising.

Irial pinched the bridge of his nose. "Cameron, close your damn eyes before I pluck them out and feed them to you."

The massive man frowned. "Why?"

"Because I'm naked, Cam," Leslie said, visibly trying not to laugh at either Cam's confusion or Irial's frustration. Her gaze floated between them, and the shadows from the floor zig-zagged toward her.

Cam closed his eyes quickly. He nodded, and eyes still tightly closed, he fumbled for the door. In the process, he knocked a painting from the wall and set a floor lamp to rocking precariously.

Abruptly, he paused and turned back, frowning. Without

opening his eyes, he asked, "How come you're not naked then, king? I mean, Discord. Err, Irial?"

"Because I have already pulled my trousers on, Cam," Irial said with exaggerated patience. Cam was a fine Hound. He simply lacked the common sense of an average goose.

Leslie giggled.

Cam waved in her general direction—still not opening his eyes—and said, "Good to see you . . ." He paused and amended quickly. "Umm, not that I could *see* you."

Irial sighed again. "Goodbye, Cameron!"

And Leslie's giggles turned into belly laughs as Irial watched. This, this moment, was what she deserved: happiness. He wasn't sure how to make sure she always had it, but he wanted to do so. He didn't want any distance, any secrets between them.

When she stopped, Irial blurted out his great secret: "I think I had a child."

Leslie stared at him.

"I don't know if I meddled in your life, but if I did, I'm sure I had a reason," he added to fill the silence.

After a long minute of staring in silence, Leslie said, "I think I need clothes for this conversation. You do, too."

She tossed his shirt at him, and all Irial could do was think that an event in his past was about to destroy his present happiness. He had no idea that Leslie would react this way. "Before you," he added quickly. "The child was before you were ever even alive, shadow girl."

"Oh, Irial! I'm not angry. I just find all of that"—she gestured at him—"a bit distracting, and I need to focus, especially if I am going to need to buy baby supplies."

The wave of relief that rolled over him was palpable.

Leslie trailed her fingers down his bare chest and pause at

his trouser buttons. "Nothing will make me reject you, Iri. Nothing. Don't you realize that yet?"

He exhaled loudly, fears he'd not yet named falling away briefly. He still needed to tell Niall. Hell, he still needed to decide if he'd look up his descendants in person if they existed. One disaster at a time, though. A man doesn't discover children and lost years with them every day.

He pulled his shirt on and watched Leslie dress. It never ceased to amaze him that even the act of dressing was enticing with her. He'd forgotten that charm in the centuries between Niall and Thelma, and the decades between Thelma and Leslie. With most people he'd had in his bed, his interest was only held in the disrobing. Once the present was unwrapped, his interest faded quickly and inevitably.

With Leslie, Irial was as enchanted by her dressing as with the way she covered her mouth as if to keep the giggles from escaping. He could paint her on every canvas he found, and still he wouldn't grow tired of studying her. It was unsettling after so many years of solitude. Now, he had her and Niall in his home, and he felt unmoored.

Once she was dressed, she stood in front of him and said, "Spill."

"Once, many years ago, there was a girl. Human. Unusual." Irial smiled remembering Thelma. "She was bookish when most women were focused on husbands and homes."

Leslie nodded.

"I came near to starting a war. There were people seeking her, and—"

"Irial." Leslie gave him the sort of look that came from knowing him better than most people could imagine. "What people?"

"Influential ones," he hedged.

"Influential as in . . . mafia or as in rich parent or politicians or . . . ?"

"Politicians of a sort." He turned away, hand on the glass door knob to open the door and flee. Admitting who Thelma was, who had pursued her, would add complications he'd rather she could avoid. In as casual a voice as he could summon, he said, "Let's not talk about that. What matters is that I protected her, and I did so because I was developing a fondness. Who *they* were is not the point."

Behind him, Leslie put a hand on his back, stilling him, stopping him. "Are you asking me not to ask who pursued her?"

He nodded. Without looking back at her, Irial added, "He didn't deserve her. He wasn't going to love her as I did. Sometimes . . . I am impulsive."

Leslie's arms slid around him, and she kissed his back. "You're an absolute fool when you love." She squeezed. "And I am grateful for it. As is Niall. I suspect your missing love was, too."

Irial hoped so. The day he'd decided to pursue Thelma was as clear as if it had been that morning. The downside of near immortal lives was that he couldn't always keep track of time. That day, though, was one he hadn't forgotten.

Gabriel's steed shifted into a handsome horse-drawn carriage, one fit for nobility or the American equivalent of it.

"Well come on then." Gabriel climbed aboard and took the reins, although they weren't technically necessary with the bond between Hound and steed.

"No horseless carriage then?" Irial teased.

"Bah."

The new mode of transportation irritated Gabriel for reasons that seemed to be primarily a matter of loving his steed in its natural equine-like form. Irial, unlike a lot of faeries, was fascinated by technological advances. He'd even had several images of himself made in the last few decades, including a daguerreotype and a tintype. In time, Irial intended to own several horseless carriages as well. What was the point in immortality if one continued to live as if it were centuries past?

"Without being seen," Irial ordered.

Gabriel gave him another raised brow look, but said nothing.

"I don't want her to feel stalked," Irial explained.

Ignoring Gabriel's snort, Irial continued, "I simply need to move to the house in the city for a short time."

"And the Hunt?"

"It's not as if you cannot fetch me if needs be," Irial stated.

"Or we can come with you, Irial." The rumbling in Gabriel's voice clarified that even as he pretended to be suggesting the answer, he was actually demanding it.

"Fine. You can come, too."

As the steed swept by the girl who was walking toward the city, Irial wished he could pull her to him. It was foolish. A wise man would vacate the city, ignore the mortal, stay as far from the quarrel between Beira and Keenan as he could. This one, though, had looked right at him.

"I ought to leave the state," Irial said aloud.

"Are you going to do so?"

"No."

"I'm not going to lecture you, Iri." Gabriel grinned, all teeth and menace, and added, "You're more use when you're not pouting."

"I don't . . ." Irial made a crude gesture at his closest friend and added, "I am not pouting, Gabe. I am simply enjoying a vibrant city, filled with music and distractions. A favorite city, as you know."

Gabriel laughed.

Prostitution was newly legal in New Orleans now. The Crescent City was the first city to legalize it in this country, and the Dark Court enjoyed the profits of that law. His fey fed on darker emotions, and the so-called Storyville District added to the court's already-deep coffers.

"She might simply be a distraction," Irial claimed, careful to phrase his words in such a way that they were not a statement of absolutes. *Lying, after all, was not possible for a faery.*

"Or a way to cope with your guilt," Gabriel added.

"Or boredom," Irial admitted.

Or something else. He didn't say that aloud though. *Far better to think of guilt or boredom as motivators.*

Irial smiled. Thelma—much like Niall before her and Leslie after her—was far from boring. Irial, if he did say so himself, had excellent taste.

"I treasured her," he said. "And she hid my child."

LATER THAT AFTERNOON, Leslie and Irial rode to the airport in the company of assorted Hounds. There was something about feeling so cherished that never grew old for her. The massive fey creatures, looking for all the world like a multicultural biker gang, escorted them to the ticket counters.

Cam carried the small bags that she and Irial had packed. In truth, she was surprised that Irial had agreed to pack things. He had the ridiculous habit of believing that a credit card and a whim would suffice when it came to most clothes. His suits, of course, were tailored, but things like jeans or shirts were a matter of little concern.

"No time for stores?" she asked.

"I need all the time to research," Irial murmured, not even looking up from the latest of the letters he'd retrieved from a locked fireproof box and slipped into his Italian leather satchel.

The pages were yellowed, ink faded, but each letter was in a protective sleeve, as if a careful librarian had stored them. Leslie wanted to read them, to know his every secret, but her life with Irial and Niall worked because she had the ability to be patient—and the ability to be brash. She knew the two men well enough to know which trait she needed, and right now, the living embodiment of Discord needed her support and her patience.

They checked their bags, cleared security, and went to stand at a gate. The Hounds, of course, still stood like fierce guards around them. The difference was that no one saw them now. However, in that way of such fey things, they radiated a kind of terror that meant no one came near Irial.

"You really want us to stay here?" Cam asked.

Irial lifted his eyes, met Cam's gaze, and nodded once. To anyone looking their way, it would appear as if he nodded to himself upon reading something pertinent.

"King's not going to approve," another Hound muttered.

"Does Niall know?" Leslie asked, even though she knew exactly what Irial would say.

Or not say.

Irial lifted a shoulder in a small shrug.

Leslie texted: "With Iri. Airport. NOLA. Love."

Then she looked at Irial, back at the Hounds, and said, "Go."

"Leslie?" Cam asked in apparent confusion.

"We need a little time to ourselves," she said, leaning into Irial even with the metal arm rest jabbing into her side. "Just us."

To a bystander, she seemed to be talking to Irial, but the Hounds knew what she was saying. They—like most of the

Dark Court—acted as if she were their queen. No one really pressed the matter, and she was cautious not to issue orders. Today, though, she was taking advantage of their obedience to her.

"Just the two of us," she repeated with emphasis.

Irial lifted his gaze, looked around at the fey creatures that were standing there watching over them. Hounds were stronger than many faeries, but this much steel had to be unpleasant for some of them.

"Begone," Irial ordered.

They rolled through the airport boarding areas, an invisible wave of discomfort that the observant could track simply by noting the ripple of fear and anxiety that the passengers' faces showed. Even seasoned businesspeople seemed suddenly ill-at-ease. The trick for those without the Sight was to notice waves of joy, or fear, or chills that seemed to roll across a crowd or street. That was often the result of passing faeries.

Once they were gone, and Leslie saw no other lurking faeries in the area, she turned to Irial and gently prompted, "Tell me what's happening."

Silently, he slipped the letter back into his case.

"A very long time ago, Thelma asked me not to seek her out. She was mortal, and I was not," he paused and smiled. "*Am* not. Will never be. I knew she lived a long life because I looked her up from time to time."

He leaned forward.

"I gave her a vow. In fact I gave her"—he laughed as if there was a joke she hadn't heard—"quite a number of them. The first before we acknowledged that she knew what I was, but the last vow . . . I never saw her again after it. Never spoke."

All traces of laughter were gone, and Leslie felt waves of loss assail her.

"And so I never knew, and she never sent word. I don't know how she could've, but if she had . . . I'd have known my daughter."

Leslie stared at him. "She intentionally hid your child from you?"

"I don't know," he whispered.

Leslie reached over and took his hand. There weren't a lot of words. Being a woman meant that her child—if she had one —would not be a secret. One notices such things. For men, though, the fear that a child out there might be yours, that you might never know, was a real possibility.

"She lived in New Orleans?"

He nodded. "A long time ago, I was there, and she was there, and we met, and . . . if things had been different . . ." Irial shook his head and simply noted, "I would have liked to know my daughter."

They sat in silence, Leslie feeling his emotions and trying to send calm his way, until the plane boarded. They remained the same on the flight to the city at the mouth of the Mississippi River. She'd never been there, although it was on her list of places to see, but not like this.

By the time they landed, Leslie no longer worried that Irial's sorrow would drown her. So she asked, "What year?"

He looked her way.

"When did you know her?" Leslie clarified.

"We last spoke at the turn of the century."

"Which one?" Leslie kept her voice pitched low.

"In the 1800s, love," he said. "She's dust and ash now. Gone from me."

Irial stared at her so intently that Leslie worried that he was about to become inappropriately affectionate—not that she ever minded, but ending up naked in the middle of a deplaning crowd would be awkward.

"You must never die," he said, not even trying to be quiet. "I couldn't live without you. Swear it."

A nearby older couple looked at them curiously.

"Love . . ." Leslie started.

Irial pulled her to him and kissed her breath away. They were still both dressed when he released her, but the aisle was filled with people who were waiting for the doors to open.

"Newlyweds?" a woman asked.

Leslie leaned against Irial and said, "Close."

Behind her, he was holding her hips in his hands now, as if to keep her from flying or pull her closer to his affections. His fingers tightened, and she was suddenly more than ready to be off the plane and in the French Quarter hotel he'd booked.

"Niall's madness would be two-fold if you died," Irial whispered. "Mine would rival his, *exceed* it, demolish the world."

"I am right here." She covered his hands with hers and glanced over her shoulder at him. "Healthy. Yours. I *love* you."

He nodded, but he looked far from convinced. "Mortals die in a blink. Like mayflies and falling stars. You expire so soon."

When they'd left the plane and were walking from the gate to baggage, Leslie kept her hand in his.

"Do we even know I'm still mortal?" she asked.

She hated to bring up the ink exchange, but she was—quite literally—the only mortal who had survived it. No one expected her to live. Irial had hoped, but even he had thought she'd perish. "It's grown back, roots in my flesh, tendrils stretching to you."

"I'm not sure. Maybe it will tie your life to mine. That was the initial intent." Irial shrugged. "But you burned it, severed it, so I have no idea what it means."

This time Leslie shrugged. "So, love, you may be stuck with me for centuries."

She didn't mention her fears that she had grown less emotional again because of it. What was different now was that she had still chosen to be involved with both Niall and Irial when she was clear-minded. They were what she wanted, and who could blame her? After being loved by them, how could she go back to dating mortals? Being loved by the former Dark King and the current Dark King had taught her that she needed a partner—or partners—who were a little bit feral.

The way she'd handled the monsters she'd met because of them convinced her that she had a spine that was wrought of whatever was stronger than steel. Leslie was able to find the monster in herself when those she loved were threatened, and because of them, she learned that although love can be scary, it can also be empowering.

They'd encouraged her to go to university, respected her desire to not accept their money, and not because they thought she would change her mind but because they'd have done the same. In a stubborn ass contest between the three of them, she wasn't sure who'd win. The only real difference was that Niall attempted to avoid conflicts whereas Irial thrived on it.

MILES AWAY IN NEW JERSEY, Niall was ready for a long, peaceful weekend—one that didn't require a suit or manners. He loosened his tie and looked at his mobile. In the assorted messages from Seth, Chela, and Donia was one that stood out: "With Iri. Airport. NOLA. Love."

The text Leslie had sent a few hours ago had plenty of information, but no actual answers. The Dark King lit a cigarette and pondered. He'd never understood the appeal of drawing burning toxins into his body as much as he did now. The Dark King, the whole of the Dark Court, was made for poison.

Shadows from the coming evening crouched at his sides, drawn to whatever strange thing made him a king. Shadows ought not move on their own, but they did. None so often as the abyss guardians that traveled from one shadow to another anywhere in the world. Right now, the same guardians that had touched Leslie earlier that day were now slithering along his arms. He could sense her skin as they did so; the taste of her sweat and perfume lingered in these shadows.

She was safer than most anywhere if she was with Irial.

On the other hand, the man was now the embodiment of Discord. He'd protect Leslie, but that didn't mean he was making wise choices in general—at least not wise by Niall's standards.

For all that was right in his life, Niall was unable to have a single month without drama. This time—hell, a *lot* of times—it originated in the faery who had bequeathed the court to him. Niall stood in the hotel lobby where he'd finished up sorting out the accounting discrepancies at the two new Atlantic City casinos the Dark Court financed. For all his comfort with the dark, Niall preferred when vices were controlled.

Irial's voice, from when they'd first met, came echoing over the years: *You like them. Mortals, that is. Genuinely* like *them.*

Some things were unchanged. Irial wasn't prone to liking humans. He'd bedded his share, but genuine fondness for them was as rare as a blizzard in the Mojave. It could happen, but now that the last Winter Queen had been replaced, it was unlikely.

He looked again at the text Leslie had sent a few hours ago: "With Iri. Airport. NOLA. Love."

He could reply, but getting answers when Discord was involved was as likely as turning coal to diamonds. It could happen, but not without a degree of pressure that Niall was unwilling to apply via another person.

Niall glanced at the time. By now, they were on the ground. *Why?* That was the real question. Of all the cities in the world, that was one of the few Irial avoided. That hadn't always been the case. Niall remembered seeing him there, thinking that it was a city positively designed for the Dark Court. Back then, Niall had been advisor to the Summer King, and Keenan had toted the court there in pursuit of a potential Summer Queen—one who'd vanished.

He called Irial. Once. Twice. Tried Leslie's number, too.

Then he did what any sane Dark King did when Discord was not easily located: he booked a trip of his own. His, however, was a bit more primal than steel tubes hurtling through the air as if by magic.

"Chela?" He spoke the word into the air, the shadow slithered across the ground, and the word moved at the speed of darkness. He ought to call her by her title, but he'd known her too long for that. Before her, her mate—Gabriel—had led the Hunt, but upon his death, Chela assumed the mantle.

"Gabriela," Niall added, using the title out of respect.

Then he ordered a coffee. There was no way to keep up with Irial in New Orleans of all places and catch a bit of much needed sleep. Coffee was the best solution. Again. Some days, Niall wondered if he'd have flat-out refused the crown if he knew how little rest there would be.

Before an hour had passed, Niall could feel them: The Hunt rode. The earth itself seemed to quake, as if the soil would shake loose the dead. The weight of the fear that rolled out before them made the very air heavier, thicker, as if moving was impossible. Several mortals in the street shivered. The roll of terror that surrounded the Hunt made more than a few passing mortals look to the sky as if a storm rode overhead.

"We come," the voices echoed. No mortal ear would hear. No human eye could see.

Chela and the Hounds never moved at a saunter.

When they arrived, Chela did not get off her steed, Alba, who appeared to be a massive lion currently. Chela's shifted shapes the way some people changed clothes. Alba expressed his feelings with his shape. Since Gabriel's death, Alba was often leonine, feral and ready to hunt anything that threatened Chela—or looked as if it could.

None of the steeds were in car form. Instead, they looked like a deadly menagerie: an oversized lion snarled next to a lizard-like beast; something that resembled a dragon paced next to a chimera; and scattered among them all were skeletal horses and emaciated red dogs. Atop the steeds were equally fierce Hounds.

The leader, Chela, dipped her chin. It was the closest to a bow that most Hounds offered. They weren't strangers to the etiquette of court, but they weren't *subjects* of any court either—and Chela was keen on reminding him of that truth. They stayed because she chose to stay. The fears they roused by their very presence were nourishing to the Dark Court. The terror that rolled off their skins was like the finest wine. And they, not shockingly, liked to be appreciated.

"Home?" The Hound paused and grinned. "Or has the old King done something troubling again?"

Niall walked up to her and said, "I don't know, but I need to go find out."

Chela grinned. "Where to?"

"New Orleans."

Her pause would've escaped his notice if several of the Hounds accompanying her hadn't frozen, too. For one extended moment, they all seemed to stop moving, as if time itself had held its breath. Then, with a falsely casual expression, Chela said, "Sure. We haven't been there in ages. A little bayou excursion sounds good." She motioned him toward her. "We'll drop you at the house and go—"

"The house?"

Several Hounds exchanged glances.

"In the Garden District . . .? I thought Iri would be at the house," Chela said haltingly.

"*What* house?" Niall rubbed his temples and lit another cigarette. At some point, Niall figured he might know all the secrets the last Dark King held, but some days he suspected that was impossible.

"You visited," a Hound said.

"The court *owns* that house?" Niall clarified. He remembered. It was an ostentatious Garden District mansion, but he'd assumed that Irial had merely rented it as most courts did in most cities.

More shuffling and their glances went everywhere but him. Niall couldn't order them to obey him. The Hounds only obeyed Chela.

"Sentimental reasons," Chela offered. "We all do things for reasons other than logic, don't we?" She glanced at the steed that kept pace with her, riderless still.

The steed that had belonged to Gabriel had remained in the form of a giant black horse with a reptilian head. It flashed pit-viper fangs at Niall, not in threat but in a smile of sorts.

Aside from Chela, the steed had only allowed him, Irial, and Leslie to ride. Niall suspected the Winter Queen could, but she simply visited the nameless creature from time-to-time.

Chela could order it to shift or choose a new master, but she had done neither.

"Why do I feel like there is more you could tell me?" Niall asked.

"Because you're not as dim as I once believed." Chela watched as Gabriel's steed stomped over to him.

A rush of sheer exhilaration rolled over Niall as the beast nickered through those pit-viper fangs and tossed its head.

"I'm coming," he murmured. With a leap he was astride, and the steed was already tensed for motion.

"New Orleans," Chela said as soon as he was mostly, but not quite, seated.

And the world blurred in a way that was both dizzying and beautiful.

Leslie said nothing as Irial opened a door to a house that seemed more haunted than anywhere she'd been. If a building could be melancholy, it would be this one. The building was in immaculate condition, the marble floors inside the door gleamed as if they'd been polished that morning. The tall wooden balusters lining the upper floor had the patina of hands gliding over them often. The Turkish rugs seemed as bright as if they were new.

But as she followed Irial into the house, she saw that every room was filled with sheet draped furniture. No one lived here. Irial pulled a few sheets away, revealing books that were still open to assorted pages on end tables. An empty tea cup sat next to a pair of hundred-year-old glasses.

And Irial looked into corners as if his memory and will alone could summon a body from the past.

Faeries were magical creatures, capable of any manner of impossible things, but not returning faces from the past or making ghost breathe again. The look of sheer pain on Irial's face made Leslie wrap her arms around him. There were no words, but she could offer him comfort.

At first he said nothing, simply pulled her closer to his side like a child holding a stuffed toy. Then a few moments later, he said, "I loved her. I would've loved my child, too. I *do* even though I've never met her."

Leslie couldn't pretend to understand his pain, but she listened and she held him.

Then, they went to the dining room and uncovered a table that would seat a dozen guests. There, Irial spread out the letters and files he had, and they began to read.

WHEN NIALL ARRIVED, the last thing he expected to see was what looked like a midnight study session. Containers of take-out, a bottle of wine, and the unmistakable scent of chicory coffee assailed him when he opened the door of the Garden District house he hadn't entered since the late 1800s.

"The door was unlocked," he said in lieu of a greeting.

Irial nodded. "I figured you'd be here sooner or later since she texted."

Leslie was more enthusiastic. She crossed the few feet between them and pulled him into her usual welcoming hug and kiss. Exhaustion fled in that moment. He was home—because home was wherever these two baffling creatures were.

Mutely, Irial kicked out a chair and resumed reading.

At Niall's querying look to Leslie, the calmest of the three, she sighed and quietly walked over and plunked her hand over the middle of the letter Irial was reading.

"Talk. To. Him."

Irial stood and paced across the room, where several bottles of whiskey had been hidden under another sheet. "Whisky? Gin?"

Niall nodded. He didn't simply grab Irial and kiss the answers out of him as he might if they were alone. Sometimes there was a wall that they kept around Leslie still—not that they lacked affection in front of her, but faeries who were well over a thousand years old could be more violent in their affection than he thought Leslie would understand.

"You're stalling," Leslie said.

Niall smothered a grin with a sudden need to cough.

"I have—had—a child," Irial announced as he handed Niall a beautiful crystal highball glass that would've hit the floor if not for Irial's reflexes. He handed the still-full glass back to Niall. "Thelma had a babe."

"Thelma? The young . . . the potential Summer Queen you spirited away?" Niall emptied his glass and stalked past Irial to refill it.

"The *what*?" Leslie asked. Her arms folded. "The people who were seeking her were faeries?"

Irial shrugged.

And Niall knew. He knew the secret that Irial hadn't shared back then. "You made the curse."

"True."

"Did you always know?" Niall stared at the faery he'd finally started to figure out the past handful of years.

Again Irial shrugged.

Niall half-fell into the chair Irial had offered when he'd arrived. "So you shagged the woman who would have been the Summer Queen if Keenan had found her, and she had your *child?*"

Again Irial shrugged.

"We suffered over a hundred more years of winter because you felt like *hiding the queen?*" Niall wanted to throttle him, simply squeeze until Irial had sense in him, but as such a thing was neither possible nor wise—and the events were all in the past—he simply stared at Irial.

AFTER A FEW MOMENTS, Irial stood and walked away. Niall wasn't wrong, and Irial was sure that from the outside it probably seemed like a heinous thing he'd done. It wasn't that simple, though.

Thelma was special.

He didn't risk the wrath of both Summer and Winter casually. Admittedly, such a thing wasn't out of character for him, but he wasn't foolish.

Except when it comes to love.

He turned the door knob, feeling a sharp edge of the glass knob, a memento from when he'd thrown a few things in anger. Just inside the room, Irial paused. The last time he stood here was the day after Thelma left. The room had still smelled of her perfume. Her sheets had smelled the same.

He'd brought her beignets and coffee, as they had shared the first time they had a meal together, and for the first time in centuries, Irial was truly happy. He had been well aware of her mortality, of the fact that loving her as he'd allowed himself to do could only end badly. He'd been equally aware that the then-weak Summer Court and the over-strong Winter Court would both have him skinned alive if they knew that the missing Summer Queen was nestled in his sheets.

What he hadn't know was that Thelma would leave so soon.

"You weren't trying to thwart Summer, were you?" Niall's voice came from the doorway to the room.

Irial had heard his steps, known that the first wave of anger would pass once Niall tasted Irial's feelings.

"Iri? I was rash," Niall said, not quite an apology, but they'd never been much for such words.

Irial shrugged. When he'd met Niall, Irial could taste every feeling, every glorious bit of desire, of hope, of joy. It was a skill unique to the Dark King. He romanced Niall, Thelma, Leslie, and then Niall again with the unfair ability to taste what they felt. He negotiated with kings and queens with that same gift. It had made him formidable. And still he lost more often than made sense. Sometimes knowledge—or love—was not enough to overcome fears or doubts.

"I hadn't planned to love her," Irial admitted, back still to Niall. "Or you. Or Leslie. I'm terrible at it, you know?"

"No," Niall corrected. "You are terrible at dealing with the fears that come with loving, not at *being* in love."

Irial walked over to the bathtub, a claw-footed indulgence that Thelma had thought the single most remarkable part of the house. . . other than books. She'd read the way most mortals breathed or slept, as if death himself would come if she went too long without words.

"I had a child," Irial repeated. The letters that had been delivered the week prior, the strange missives from the past that had been all addressed to him but never sent, had finally arrived a century late.

Irial turned to face Niall. "My daughter wrote to me, and Thelma saved each letter. She wrote, too."

Memories of the past crowded in as Irial tried to contain

the massive well of loss, of anger, of confusion that threatened to swallow him.

They stood, awkwardly in silence, until Leslie joined them. Her hand was shaking when she held up a letter.

"This was delivered to the house," she said. Before he could panic much at the thought of Leslie unprotected, she added, "Chela brought it to me."

Irial opened it and pulled out a single page of spidery handwriting.

Father,

I grew up hearing of you. I wrote letters as soon as I could write—at Mother's order. Mother wrote as well, but she often wept when she did. I don't know how things ended, but I know that she never married. As I grew older, never quite aging as children should, we moved a lot. We stayed clear of fey things, and she often spoke in terrified words of the Summer King . . . and of my father, a beautiful man who saved her.

What she failed to tell me, of course, was that the man who saved her was also the Dark King. I knew your name, but not what role you filled in that world. Had I known, I would not have written.

When the Summer King—the same faery that you saved my mother from—came to my door for my daughter, Moira, I tried to figure out how to find you. I discovered then that my beloved grandfather, a *good faery* in a sea of monsters, was the king of the worst of fey. Still I was prepared to reach you, but Moira died, and she left behind a child. No tale my mother told was enough for me to risk that love had blinded her, that you were as awful as I feared.

I believe you are already acquainted with your great granddaughter, Aislinn.

Ash is powerful enough that I thought about writing to you when she became fey.

At the least I wanted you to have the letters I wrote before I knew what you were. I decided that if you came to the house where I was conceived, I would tell you. Mother said you left the house boarded up because you could not bear to be there without her. Every so often, I would check to see if it stood empty. One of my granddaughter's faeries has been watching it for me—the whims of an old lady--so if you ever read this, I believe you've proven that Mother was right, that you loved her. If so, some day, if you would like, I would welcome the chance to meet you.

I have questions about my longevity that sooner or later I'll need to address with Ash. I was old (despite appearance and strength) when my own daughter was born, and I seem to age no further despite the passing of years. I've learned to appear to age, but often I simply moved. Now, though, I'd rather not leave Ash. Perhaps it is time for meeting.

your daughter,
Elena Foy

IRIAL HANDED the paper to Niall. "My daughter is alive."

As Niall and Leslie read, Irial knew when they understood the import of what the letter contained.

"Of all the people in the world, why did it have to be *her*?" Niall muttered.

"So the women in Ash's family were always the ones who would be the Summer Queen," Leslie pronounced. "Grams, Ash's mother, Ash."

"And Thelma," Niall added.

"Thelma had the Sight," Irial said. "She *saw* me, and she still chose me."

The three stood in silence as the sheer enormity of the thing settled on them. He was blood family to the Summer Queen. Aislinn Foy, the Summer Queen, was Thelma's great-granddaughter. *His* great-granddaughter. How in the name of all that he held sacred was he going to navigate that relationship? He couldn't fathom her taking that well.

Her partner, at least, tolerated him. He and Seth weren't *friends* precisely, but they had a relatively congenial acquaintance.

Then Irial grinned. "Wait till the whelp realizes you're his stepfather-in-law!"

"Not quite how that works," Niall pointed out.

But Irial was, in his heart of hearts, the embodiment of Discord. He wasn't going to do anything to hurt his daughter or great-granddaughter, of course, but his mind was already spinning on the possibilities of teasing Seth and on strengthening the alliance between Dark and Summer. It might not seem like *discord* or chaos, but it strengthened some court alliances, which necessarily weakened others.

"Shall we go out on the town to celebrate parenthood?" Irial draped an arm around both of his beloveds. The issue of Leslie's mortality still lingered as a fear, but that was a trouble for tomorrow.

"Stepdad. Stepmom. We have so many years to make up for with Elena," Irial said.

"I'm *not* her stepmom. She's Ash's *grandmother*," Leslie objected.

"I think I should start with a house," Irial mused. "This house. And a pony. Kids like ponies." He frowned. "Kelpie or steed?"

Niall and Leslie exchanged a look of horror that Irial pretended not to see.

"THINK of it as preparation for our little ones," Niall said.

Irial stopped. Leslie froze, but Niall could taste her hope, her joy at such thoughts.

"Come now," Niall said mildly. "Leslie said she wants children. Once she's finished with school and moves in—"

"She's moving in?" Irial said with raw hope. He stared at Leslie as if he'd just been granted a gift. "There will be *children*."

"Eventually," Leslie murmured.

"Oh, when Ani and Tish were tiny, I bought them this little toy shoppe in Philadelphia."

"No," Leslie said firmly. Her flood of amusement surged toward Niall, and undoubtedly to Irial, too, through their ink connection. Leslie folded her arms and announced, "Our children will not get their own stores."

"So just one store," Irial said. "We could do that."

"Not what—"

"We really ought to think about buying more property," Irial announced. "For Ash. For Elena. For Elena's half sisters and brothers."

In a faux whisper Leslie asked, "He does realize that Ash may not be as excited by this as he is, right?"

"Pish!" Irial gave them both big smacking kisses. "What

about water parks? How old do the children need to be before we buy that?"

"I'm not pregnant," Leslie reminded him.

Irial waved his hand, as if to brush the objection away. "When you're ready, love." He motioned toward the stairs. "For now, I shall dote on Elena and Ash. My girls."

They followed him down the steps, all but tumbling when he came to an abrupt halt. "They should have guards. Give me a moment to talk to Chela before--"

"They have guards," Niall reminded him. "Summer Queen. Her grandmother."

"More guards!" Irial went to see Chela.

Niall and Leslie stood in the house. He glanced at her. "Have you told him yet that you're moving in after graduation?"

"Not yet. He hasn't been visiting, and . . ." Her words faded, and she shrugged. "He'll figure it out when I stop leaving."

Not a single month without drama, but Niall loved them both. Petulant. Mercurial. All around maddening. Riddled with complications he couldn't imagine. They were everything he could want in life.

"Perhaps we should ask Seth to use that future-seeing of his about your mortality or semi-fey nature *before* Irial tells them he's Ash's great-grandfather," Niall suggested.

"Agreed," Leslie said with a laugh.

Then they went to join the new father to enjoy a rare, beautiful event in anyone's life: celebrating life and parenthood.

The End

"SUMMER BOUND: A WICKED LOVELY STORY"

Set after the Wicked Lovely series

Siobhan flinched as Tavish took another blow to the face from Tracie. Her Summer Court co-advisor, on the other hand, smiled joyously as he rarely did in public. Their makeshift gymnasium was filled with cool air and the soothing sounds of soft jazz. It had not been designed to encourage the fighting they were there to do.

Most of the others had left. Only Siobhan, Tracie, and Tavish were still there. Siobhan wanted to be left alone with him, and he'd demanded Tracie stay.

"Are you afraid of Siobhan?" Tracie taunted as she kicked out at him.

He caught her ankle. Blood already dotted his typically impeccable clothes, and strands of tinsel-like hair fell into his face. The plait that usually bound his silver hair tightly back had become loosened after several hours of training the small group.

"Not bad for a Summer Girl," Tavish said, shoving Tracie toward the ground before he sneered at Siobhan. "Unlike you, Siobhan. Unable to hit me?"

Siobhan winced. He was intentionally being a prick. Tracie, one of the few of the former Summer Girls who had become a guard, was ruthless, though. Kicks followed punches, and Tavish blocked almost all of them.

Unlike Siobhan, Tracie seemed to be making up for their centuries of semi-dizzy lust with bursts of rage. She had found her place as guard, and Siobhan felt pride in seeing one of her own flourish. They had never been competitors. The Summer Girls were bound by Summer, trapped by the Summer King, and they had a bond that was unbroken still—even as a number of their group left.

Tracie stayed. Eliza did, too. A few became solitary, and a few went to the High Court. Siobhan had stayed with the Summer Court, but not as a guard. She'd become an advisor, not interested in unnecessary violence after the fight between the courts had ended.

Not that Tavish cared.

"And here, I'd heard that the Summer Girls were only good for—"

Tracie's fists flew, and Siobhan watched as the other woman hit Tavish repeatedly and say, "I am not. a. Girl. Asshole."

"And you?" Tavish dodged Tracie's last blow and snaked out his leg to pull Siobhan off balance. She toppled to the ground in their makeshift gymnasium.

"What use are you, Siobhan?" he asked.

Siobhan glared at him as she launched to her feet. "Jerk. I serve Ash by advising her, and I learned enough to stay safe."

"Pay attention. If someone comes here, you're vulnerable," he said, as if forgetting the guards that kept watch over the doors—and the queen herself, who was as fierce as any faery in any court.

Several centuries of playing at foolishness made Siobhan instinctively pout. It wasn't an act that worked on Tavish anymore, though. His next punch was hard enough to knock her backwards.

"I'm not a guard, Tavish." Siobhan spread her feet to give herself a more stable stance and shot her fist forward with as much force as she could. Her punch wasn't enough to knock him backward, but it did distract him. "I don't like to hit anyone."

He was smiling, now. "Even me?"

Then, Tracie landed a solid blow across his throat. Tracie grinned. "I like hitting you, or anyone else I can."

Tavish coughed hard, hand to his throat, not far from the black sun tattoo there. No one knew exactly how or why it had been put there. With his stern expressions and tightly bound hair, he didn't seem the type for a tattoo on his throat, but one night over a lot of tequila, he'd told Siobhan that it was older than the then-king and had been applied when Miach, father to Keenan, ruled. That made it over nine hundred years old.

"Are you injured?" Siobhan asked

Rather than being upset, Tavish beamed at Tracie and said, "Well done."

"Thanks, boss." Tracie rolled her shoulders and asked, "Are we done?"

"You are," Tavish said.

Then he turned to look at Siobhan. His approving smile vanished. "You can stay. You need to be able to defend your-self. What if you're alone or with our queen and—"

"When am I ever alone?"

Tracie leaned up and kissed Tavish's cheek. It meant

nothing. Theirs was a court with little hesitation about affection. For a horrible moment, Siobhan hated Tracie for being the recipient of the approval she coveted. It was foolishness, but the more time she spent with him, the more his rare sweet words charmed her. She knew better. Faeries—especially Summer Court faeries—were notoriously fickle in their affection.

Far better to dream of a solitary, a Winter fey, a Dark fey. Not Tavish. Siobhan knew better.

She thought about all of the reasons he was precisely not what she should want. Tavish was the Summer Queen's advisor, head of the guard, and—as far as Siobhan knew—the oldest member of the court. And, Siobhan was the second advisor to the queen; she was expected to stand in opposition to Tavish's advice when necessary.

Tracie paused and kissed both of Siobhan's cheeks. Then she whispered, "Kick his ass."

Tavish made a sound of disbelief. Obviously, he'd heard. He didn't respect Siobhan in any way, as far as she could tell. How could he? She'd gone from frivolous member of the Summer King's harem, one of the many women who were wooed by him in his search for the queen, to the advisor to the Summer Queen.

"If you can land three solid blows—"

"No." Siobhan shook her head. "I've proven that I can hit you, Tavish. I'm not here for games. I come to these sessions to show support of you, but in this court, I advise. I do not like to fight."

"You are no longer some helpless mortal, Siobhan." Tavish raised his fists in a boxer's pose. "Or hapless plaything."

"Plaything?" she echoed. "Is that what you thought of me all these years?"

"You didn't even have the ambition to try to be queen."

He shrugged. "You chose his harem. Why would I think you more?"

"Because you know me," she said. In fact, Tavish knew her when she was mortal, when she refused the test to be Summer Queen, when she was sent by their king to seduce another king. He'd once been the faery she'd wept on when she was newly cursed.

"I was a spy for the king," she reminded him. "That's a fair bit more than hapless."

"But you were a seductress there, too." He stared at her. "You can't kiss your way out of every crisis. What if--"

"You'll never truly see me as an equal, will you?" she asked, although the question wasn't one he could answer. It was hard to recreate her identity when he knew her so well. He was the reminder of what had been. Of the original trio of power in the Summer Court, only Tavish remained. Niall was the Dark King, and Keenan was the Winter King. But Tavish remained—and they had centuries of history that meant he still saw her as someone who didn't matter.

All of which means that he's not going to form an attachment to me. Or even see me as a worthy advisor.

Siobhan met Tavish's cool gaze. "I am done for the day."

He frowned, but was silent for several moments as she gathered her things. The blood dripping from his cut lip seemed not to bother him, but Siobhan found it irritating— more so because she was not the cause.

"Is it wrong to want you to be safe?" he asked.

Despite logic, Siobhan paused. "I am safe, Tavish." She reached out to wipe the blood drop away.

Tavish caught her wrist. "No."

"You didn't used to mind my touch." Siobhan wasn't sure she'd ever been among his favorites, but they had memories over the years. Blurry ones, admittedly, but they'd enjoyed each other. "If all you think of me is as a seductress, perhaps—"

"You weren't an advisor to my queen then." Tavish squeezed her wrist, holding her in place. They stayed, caught in some silent battle for control until he asked, "Do you still visit the Dark? Do you still spend time in *their* court?"

And that was the trigger to her rage. She wrapped her leg around his knee and punched his shoulder with her free hand, using the push and pull of the combined motions to knock him to the ground.

"Do you doubt my loyalty? Or are you jealous?" she asked.

He tugged her forward, not releasing her wrist even as he fell, and she landed atop him. Chest-to-chest. Hip-to-hip. "My duty is to the Summer Court."

"Not an answer," she said, glaring down at him.

"Do you still warm the Dark King's sheets?" he asked.

She tugged her wrist free, hating that she could only do so because he allowed it. A part of her thought he was jealous, but such a thing wasn't normal for a Summer Court faery. If he was jealous, he was a fool. She had interest in exactly one faery—and unfortunately, he was the one who was currently insulting and rejecting her.

"I answer to the queen, Tavish. Not you."

THE NEXT DAY was no better. Tavish was already in a foul mood when Irial himself arrived at the loft where the advisors and queen of the Summer Court made their home. He stood in the doorway as if posing for cameras, dark eyes sparkling and a smile that could only lead to trouble.

The guards parted at Siobhan's nod.

"Irial," Siobhan greeted. She knew him well enough to know that the king who had become Chaos was not here without reason.

"May I enter?"

The guard at the door looked toward Tavish and Siobhan. It wasn't as if they could refuse him, not truly, but seeing him seemed to evoke unease in those who had been born fey.

"No," Tavish said, just as Siobhan said, "Yes."

Siobhan muttered a curse that had Irial laughing aloud. He strolled into the room.

"Lovely to see you, too." Irial was no longer the Dark King, and in truth, he had a unique status among their kind. As Chaos, he could not properly be refused welcome in any court. "It has been too long, lovely."

Siobhan gave him a look no one else could see, and his smile grew cunning. After his death, he'd managed to finagle resurrection as the embodiment of Chaos, and he had the unique position of also being the unofficial consort of the current Dark King.

"Irial. My regards to your better halves."

He laughed. "Oh, but if they are both my better halves, they've fulfilled all the good I could be. Does that leave me nothing but wickedness?"

"If memory serves, that always was a particular gift of yours." Siobhan stepped closer and allowed his familiar embrace, knowing well that he was harmless to her. No one who knew him would be surprised that he dipped her for a kiss.

While Irial's kiss was fairly chaste, it undoubtedly looked otherwise, and the wink he gave her made clear that he intended as much.

Siobhan bit back a smile as Tavish jerked her away from Irial.

"Why are you here?" Tavish asked. "I have no record of a meeting."

Irial grinned. "Niall kicked me out of the house for being 'absurdly cheerful,' so I thought I'd visit the other courts." He looked around expectantly. "Is the queen around? I'd like to pay my respects."

"On behalf of . . ." Tavish prompted.

"Chaos, it is what I am," Irial answered with a cheeriness that was slightly out of character. "Why else would I possibly be here?"

"Are you drunk?" Siobhan asked softly.

Irial laughed gleefully and said, "Not yet, my dear. A glass of Summer Wine wouldn't go amiss, though. Would you fetch me one?"

"Siobhan is not a cocktail maid. She is an advisor to Her Majesty, Aislinn, Queen of the Summer Court and—"

"I was asking you, Tavish." Irial looked at Siobhan's counterpart with an innocent smile that was about as convincing as kelpie claiming to be vegetarian. The innocence fled after a moment, and there instead was a faery to fear. Taunting. Powerful. Far too proud to back down, despite—or perhaps because of—centuries of encounters.

"Summer Wine is for those of our court." Tavish glared, eyes as black as Irial's now. The two could be brothers, opposing twins: Tavish spun-silver hair and Irial shadow-dark strands.

"I belong to all courts," Irial stated.

"Or none." Tavish held Irial's gaze and added, "Our queen is busy. One makes an appointment, requests a convenient time—"

"Are you refusing me access to the Summer Queen?"

"No."

"To the Summer Wine, then?" Irial taunted. "Are you

afraid I'll become drunken and difficult, Tavish? Afraid that I cannot control myself? Surely, you are not worried for my well-being."

"You are not of our court," Tavish said, not backing down at all. "Summer Wine is the drink of the court of light. You are a thing of shadows."

If Siobhan didn't know him so well, she would've missed the rage in his form and voice. Even then, however, she would not miss the accusations in his voice. The history between the courts was tense, and Tavish saw no beauty in the Dark.

But while the Dark Court was never a place of sparkling light and joyous laughter, Siobhan knew well that it wasn't evil. She had many fond memories of nights in black sheets with the shadows touching her skin. There was joy there, too, as in her own court.

She looked between the two faeries. Whatever grudges they had meant that this could turn ugly.

"Perhaps, we could—"

"Why would the Dark King want sunlight?" Tavish bit off, speaking over her.

"I am no longer the Dark King, old boy. Your liquid sunlight is no longer deadly to me." Irial held his arms wide. "Let us drink and be friends. I am no longer a creature that must fear sunlight."

"You are still him," Tavish said. "The past is unchanged. Call yourself something else, but you are still monstrous. I remember the countless nights Niall wept. I remember the laughter when my king was bound and weakened. You are still that monster."

"No forgiveness, then?"

Her co-advisor ignored the question and said only, "My queen is not without obligation. She may be indisposed or--"

"Come now, Tavish. I know Seth is not due back from

Faerie for several days." Irial's casual drawl barely disguised his growing temper. "And I am in rather immediate need of seeing Aislinn. You have no grounds to refuse me audience . . . or drink, for that matter. There are laws. Surely, you aren't going to ignore them, old boy."

"As you will," Tavish said.

Siobhan stared at Tavish. There was something off in the way he spoke the queen's name, the sheer weight of it was strange.

Irial caught her eye and looked at her as if daring her to speak.

When she didn't, he said, "Then will one of you please tell the queen that I request an audience, and"—he stared at Tavish then—"that I am here waiting? I will be here until she has the time to speak with me."

"I will wait with Irial," Siobhan offered. "Perhaps you could see if Aislinn is available. . .?"

"As you say." Tavish gave a curt nod and left.

His disdain could not be any more obvious if he screamed the words, and Siobhan wanted to follow him, to explain that she was not being disloyal to their court or queen. The queen herself welcomed Chaos to the table regularly. He might not be welcome at their revels, but Siobhan thought that might be as much the decision of the current Dark King as anything else.

Siobhan motioned for the guards to leave the room. "Wait outside the door. I am at no risk from him."

Once they departed, Irial's demeanor shifted. He wasn't as languid or seductive as he had once been with her, but he visibly relaxed. "You always were a clever one."

Siobhan glanced at him from the corner of her eye, emboldened by his trust, and said, "It may be presumptuous, but I do believe, after all this time, that I am safe in your presence."

"You always were. Well"—he gave her a wicked smile that once promised more—"as safe as you wanted to be. You're not as tame as some faeries."

She motioned to a seat, not taking up that thread, but Irial remained where he was. "Tavish seems increasingly stern. Is he considering a transition to the High Court? Niall has spoken to him of it, but would not reveal his thoughts. Should I press the queen on it? Despite what they think, I do not wish danger to your queen. I never have. If Tavish is not adept--"

"He is fine." Siobhan looked to where the silver haired faery had vanished. "Tavish is not without Summer's passion. He simply hides it well for reasons that are his own."

"So that's how it is." Irial plucked at a tendril of her hair. "Are you pining, love? Or are you helping him kindle that passion?"

She sighed. "I fear he sees me as a fool . . . or worse."

Siobhan pushed aside a drape of flowering vines, behind which was an inset bar. She gestured to the cut glass decanters and assorted bottles of wines, whiskies, and liqueurs. "We have drinks that are more to your usual interest."

"No. I want sunlight. I want to understand it." Irial walked over to stand next to her at the hidden sideboard and poured himself a generous drink of the liquid sunshine that was the drink of the Summer Court. His hand trembled slightly.

If Siobhan hadn't seen it herself, she'd never have believed it. Whatever his business with the queen, Irial was not nearly as calm as he pretended—or perhaps it was the fear of burning up if he was not, in fact, safe from the sunlight.

"Irial? Are you . . . well?"

"Shush, Siobhan. A little fear makes us alive," Irial whispered.

"The Dark King might think so, but you . . . are no longer that." Siobhan reached out and squeezed his arm. "If it does not endanger my queen, I am still your friend."

He nodded, and then a moment later, his grin returned. "Mustn't let your beau realize I'm not nearly as awful as he thinks . . . or perhaps we should."

"I care for him, Irial," she warned.

"I see, but"--he tilted his head and stared into the distance as if pondering-- "I'm afraid I'm about to upset Tavish's entire apple cart."

"His apple cart?" she echoed.

"I'm a father," he whispered. "I've come to share my news."

"With my queen? What . . . Leslie is with ch—"

"No. Not her. Not yet." He sighed, and Siobhan suddenly missed the shadows that used to undulate next to him when he was the Dark King.

"Irial . . ."

He took her hand as if they were, in fact, simply old friends, and in a way, she supposed that was as fitting a label as any for their history. Then he told her, "I have learned that I am a father, and I have a great-grandchild, too."

"And that child is of interest to this court," Siobhan filled in.

"Clever woman," he said.

"You do make me nervous."

"Chaos, love. It's what I am." He lifted his glass. "To family!"

And with that, the once-Dark King downed an entire glass of Summer Wine.

AISLINN PAUSED in her perusal of the latest reports. There were advisors, merchants, and managers employed to handle the court's business—as there had been for centuries--but the Summer Queen had taken a keen interest in the business of providing for her court.

Learning to control the full weight of unfettered summer wasn't as easy as she'd hoped—especially as a former human. The Summer Court was volatile by design, and the weight of so much power was still hard to control after several years. She'd taken up courses, managing the accounts, and a number of other hobbies to try to practice focus.

She'd taken courses at the college and read books on a variety of marketing and investing plans. These may not be the normal purview of faery queens, but Aislinn Foy had been mortal first. She would and often did let summer's essence fill her, and she did frolic as a proper Summer Queen should when the time was right—but she would also be a decision-making party when it came to her court's financial and business interests. Eternity was a very long time, and the practicalities of providing for a court could be expensive.

"Aislinn?" Tavish suddenly stood there, drawing her attention to him with the power of something greater than magic. He moved like moonlight sometimes, present suddenly and beautifully, and rather intense without realizing it. "My queen . . ."

"That look never seems to be a harbinger of joy, Tavish."

She stood and went to the faery who had been her guide and strength in her new role as queen. He'd become her family, as much as many of the faeries she counted on in her new life as a queen, but Tavish was more. He was the brother she had never had.

Embracing him, she asked, "What can I do to cheer you, brother? Summer isn't meant for such gloom."

Tavish had finally relented to her insistence on calling him "brother," but he only agreed to that if there were no witnesses. Hearing it—according to him—allowed her to let him know they were alone.

"Not gloom. Wishes of a bit of lightning to toss..."

Aislinn laughed and teased, "Shall I smite someone for you?"

"I would enjoy that," he said, lighter by a few degrees. "Alas, it would cause complications. You have a guest."

"With that expression, let me guess . . . Donia? Devlin? Irial?" She paused on the last name as Tavish nodded curtly.

"He is not our enemy, brother. Chaos is--"

"The self-same faery who once cursed this court." Tavish punched a section of wall. Here, without witnesses, he would reveal the side of himself that was more summerlike than anyone seemed to expect. Temper flared, and he glowed with a hot internal light.

Aislinn waited.

"Centuries, Ash. Centuries of futile searching, and he did not suffer. Our court. Our faeries. All of the mortals remade as faery. Keenan." He sighed. "You. So much pain, and for what?"

She reached out and squeezed his wrist. "I shall meet with him without you at my side. Go, find an outlet for this. Summer may rage, but we are a court of joy, brother."

"As you command."

"As you need," she corrected. There was little else she could say or do.

Tavish wasn't wrong, but she couldn't refuse Irial's visit. He was, these days, an entity that was welcome in all courts. The last embodiment of Chaos was only with the Dark, and that had led to hunger for power. Chaos had become War, and in doing so, Death had been summoned.

Aislinn had no desire to see such bloodshed again. She would have peace. Summer was for joy, for pleasure, for languid days and drunken mornings. Violence lurked, and she could feel that impulse. It was why she invited other regents to her table, broke bread and shared drinks with them as the long-dead Summer King Miach had done. Unity and balance were what let the world thrive.

"I will meet with Irial," she said. "The past is a thing we must set aside."

Tavish's expression made quite clear that he did not agree—but this was why her court was benefitted by her relative youth. Barely in her twenties, Aislinn had only a heartbeat of time in their world. No centuries' old grudges to sway her. No near-eternity of suppressed rage.

Tavish dipped his head in a bow. His calm exterior seemed as if it reformed like a great wall around the storm she knew he felt inside. "Ash?"

"Yes?"

"May I ask that we have a revel? I have needs that are interfering with my duties." Tavish held her gaze. "If I do not address them, I fear that working with Siobhan will be impossible soon."

If he were anyone else or perhaps if they were any other court, Aislinn would laugh, but this was the Summer Court. Pleasure was as much a joy as a duty.

"Of course! Seth will return soon and—"

"I would beg your leave that we do not wait that long." Tavish looked toward the room. "Seeing Irial embrace her did much to wear my last thread of control."

The Summer Queen nodded. Her advisor asked little for himself, so there was no chance she'd refuse. "You could speak to her, Tavish. I have no objection to my two advisors enjoying--"

"No. If she wasn't your advisor in opposition to me, perhaps . . ." Tavish frowned. "But this is the happiest she's been, Ash. I would not risk that to satisfy my own carnal interest in her."

Aislinn nodded. She already feared losing him to the High or Winter Court. If he could not find joy here, she would. There had to be a solution that meant keeping both of her advisors—and Tavish finding happiness. If not, she'd lose him.

———

AISLINN WATCHED the former Dark King walk into her aviary alone in surprise. Although Tavish hadn't mentioned anyone else, Aislinn had thought there must be someone else here with him. Leslie visited with Irial, typically, and though the two weren't as close as Aislinn would like, she wasn't sure what sort of thing would necessitate a visit from Irial alone. Dark Court business was a thing he absented himself from these days—at least ostensibly. No one who saw the way the former king watched Niall had any doubts of his allegiance.

Worry flooded Aislinn, and the weather around her reacted. A small storm cloud appeared as she asked, "Is Leslie well?"

"She is." Irial seemed unconcerned with the brief burst of rain that filled the room and drenched him. "As is Niall."

"Good." She waited, figuring out by now that there was no way to rush the fey when they were of a mind to stall.

"How are you?" Irial stared at her in a way that was wholly unfamiliar, as if he was studying her face for clues of . .

. something. Odder still, he approached her, instead of keeping his usual distance.

Vines sprung up, lashing together in a fence of sorts between them.

"Close enough," she said.

Irial simply stood there, leaning into the fence, pausing to sniff a flower that sprouted near him. "Tell me of your mother. Your grandmother. What were they like when you were younger?"

"My . . .what?"

"Your family." Irial made a careless gesture in the air. "Tell me of them."

"Why?"

"Is it so hard to believe I'm curious?" His tone was light, and his smile was hard to resist.

Aislinn tried to resist the answering smile she felt threatening. "Without a reason? Yes."

"I do not know you well enough." He lifted a shoulder in a shrug. There was something irrepressible about Irial—to the point that Seth had grown oddly fond of him and Aislinn couldn't help but find Irial charming.

"You're being peculiar." She gestured and a chair woven of ivy and flowers appeared as she sat.

"May I?" Irial held up a cigarette.

"Around my plants? No." With a flick of her hand, another such seat lifted next to Irial.

"Nerves," he said.

Aislinn paused. Although faeries—especially Irial—lied by omission and misdirection, they could not lie outright. Further, Irial sounded sincere.

"Are you well?" she asked.

He sat without replying. After a moment, Irial leaned forward. "Shall I tell you the grand news, my dear?"

At Aislinn's will, a table rose between them. Fashioned of tree branches twisted into an infinite loop of Celtic knots, it provided the illusion of a barrier. She'd been working on it as a meditation piece.

"May I call you 'dear'?"

"Irial—"

"Was there an affectionate name you would have liked as a child?" he continued as if she hadn't spoken. "Or a pet? There is a beautiful lioness that I saw when I was in—"

"Irial!"

"Mmm?" He stared at her in a way that she would almost call besotted, but for the fact that she knew without a doubt that he had never shown any genuine interest in her romantically.

"What are you here to tell me?"

"Oh," he said, "I'm a father."

"Leslie is—"

"No. A hundred or so years ago, I met a lovely woman. We had children, Aislinn." He looked both joyous and forlorn in a matter of moments. "I've forgotten for years, by my own design, as my Thelma was fated to be . . . well, you." He gestured around the room. "This."

"Your children's mother was mortal."

"Yes." He stared at her. "Thelma was a mortal."

"And she would have been the Summer Queen?" Aislinn echoed, trying to wrap her mind around whatever Irial was sharing. "If she'd have . . . and then I'd have . . . I would have been mortal."

"No, my dear." Irial met her gaze. "You were never truly mortal. Elena's father was fey. You've always been part-fey, a halfling like Ani and Tish—and your grandmother."

Irial leaned back in his vine-wrought chair and watched her expectantly, as she pieced together his statements to the conclusion he was implying. When she burst out laughing, flowers popping into existence throughout the loft, and several of the birds came zipping into the room.

"Oh! You almost had me!" Aislinn rarely felt so light-hearted around him. "Your expression. . . You are a master at lying without actual lies, Irial."

Irial, however, frowned.

She giggled. "That was so convincing. The whole set-up, walking in as if you were drunk and . . ."

She stood and stepped toward him. Leaning down, she brushed a kiss on his cheek. If he could play a prank on her, he could tolerate a token of affection.

"Was this Leslie's idea? Seth's?" she asked. "I can't imagine Niall having this sort of prankster urge."

Irial caught her hand as she started to step back. "Aislinn, I am serious. Many years ago, I met a woman, a fierce rebellious beautiful mortal, and I knew she was the one who could free summer."

Aislinn stared at him.

"I made that curse," Irial continued. "Over nine hundred years ago, I bound Keenan. There was a beautiful mortal girl, and—at that time—I thought it was clever to hide that sunlight in a family of women. Your family."

Aislinn pulled free of his grasp and sat back down gracelessly. No traces of her laughter remained. "No. Stop it. This isn't funny now--"

"Aislinn . . . I cannot lie outright. You know this." He paused, watched her intently as he added, "Centuries after my oh-so-clever curse, I met her. Thelma. Thelma Foy."

"You must be confused—"

"I am not. I see her in you now that I have my memories freed. Her courage and strength . . . She would be proud to see what you've achieved." Irial's expression was the same one he had when gazing at Niall or Leslie. He was as subtle as a brick through a window when it came to love. "I fell for Thelma, willing to damn the world if that was the cost."

"Foy is Grams maiden name, but . . ."

"She kept her mother's name. I had no name to give her." Irial met Aislinn's gaze. "I'd have married her, damned the world for her—and my daughter. After I'd lost Niall, I feared I'd never be loved again. Truly loved, not adored or admired or desired, but loved."

"Leslie and Niall love you." Aislinn stood and walked away from him, her back to him, wishing she could have Seth at her side.

"I don't deserve it, but I am grateful that they do," Irial said, tone still tender and open. "I would do anything for love. I learned that lesson when Niall left me. Had I known that I was cursing my own, I would never have cursed that long-ago mortal woman, Aislinn. I swear to you."

Aislinn nodded. She wasn't sure she could say the words she needed for the revelation he'd brought to her. What were the words? Did he want a pardon? Understanding?

"Thelma was desperate, you see, to avoid her fate." Irial's voice had grown softer still, tender as if she were a small child —and to him, she supposed she was. "I wanted to stay in Faerie, raise Elena there."

"So was my mother," Aislinn whispered. She glanced over her shoulder at him. "Desperate, I mean. She died to stay human."

Irial nodded. "I wish I could have known, could have saved her. I wish I could have raised Elena—and been there for Moira and for . . .you."

He walked closer and dropped to his knees before Aislinn. "I loved Elena when she was born, and I love her granddaughter, my great-granddaughter already. Instantly.

Family is precious, has always been precious to the Dark Court. You are my family, Aislinn. Let me into your life."

Aislinn stared down at the faery who had cursed her, who had cursed her mother and grandmother and great-grandmother—the faery who had loved her great-grandmother.

"You're my . . ." Aislinn's words fled. She couldn't even say the words.

"Great-grandfather," Irial finished, sounding reverent. "And I want to rebuild our family."

"I can't." She shook her head and backed away. Grandfathers weren't to look your age, or be sleeping with your friend. They were old and smoked pipes. They told rambling stories, and they had not cursed you. "I just . . . I can't . . ."

SIOBHAN CRINGED at the sudden storm that flashed over the entire loft and—from the look of the torrential downpour outside—the surrounding area as well. Her queen had not summoned her, and as advisor to the Summer Queen, she'd feel a call if Aislinn needed her.

The loft, though it was rebuilt for the current inhabitants, was not designed for holding this much water. There was a grate that opened, and once that was done, the flood that currently rose over Siobhan's ankles would sluice down into the open park that was the site of their revels.

Lightning flashed inside the aviary, and the birds all flew out into wherever they nested at such times. The blur of vibrant feathers looked like magic in the air, as if a riot of blossoms had been launched into the park.

She realized that she was laughing in glee as she sloshed toward the valve to open the grate. There was something invigorating about a sudden deluge, not quite a waterfall, but near enough that a part of her wanted to let the water build so they could swim.

The water was more than knee-deep as Siobhan finally reached the valve.

"Can you turn it?" Tavish was there, at her side, soaked and gorgeous. "Siobhan?"

Logic said not to let instinct rule.

Logic said she wasn't interested in rejection.

She said nothing as she gripped the old-fashioned valve and cranked. The water sluiced out, sucked past her legs and sending her toppling into Tavish's arms. She could've resisted, but why not enjoy it?

She smiled at him as his arms stayed wrapped around her. For all the faeries she'd met in the time she was a part of this world, and for all that she, too, was completely fey now, there was something about Tavish's inhuman beauty that left her breathless.

The silver strands of hair that were usually kept tethered in a braid had come loose, and the overall effect was a softening of an otherwise austere face.

"It is hard to trust you, Siobhan, when you look at me with cunning smiles," Tavish said finally, breaking into her reverie.

"Perhaps, Tavish, there are good reasons for those 'cunning smiles.'"

"Tell me."

"I haven't seen you look like this in years."

"Bedraggled?"

"Aroused," she countered. "My years as a Summer Girl might be coated in softer things, but my memory is not gone."

He said nothing.

"Tell me no," she whispered.

He leaned down and kissed her until she wasn't sure she'd still stand if not for the tightening of his arms around her. Her lips parted to invite him to deepen the kiss, and her hands reached up to tangle in the metallic silver that was so rarely free.

But he stopped.

"No," he said finally. "You are her advisor, Siobhan. To pursue this, one of us would have to abandon that duty."

Siobhan blinked to try to push her lust back enough to answer him. "Ash said that?"

"No." Tavish rested his forehead against hers. "I have served this court since the last king's father was ruler. How could I leave my responsibility? How could I abandon her for . . ."

"A meaningless fuck?" Siobhan finished, stinging with his rejection and lack of regard for her. "I suppose I could ask Irial if there are others in his court not so opposed to my affections."

"Then I suppose you should await the end of his meeting with Aislinn, to advise her and speak to him," Tavish said. "I would rather not speak to him at all."

Tavish stepped away, striding out of the room before she could reply.

And Siobhan was grateful that the rain was still dripping on her face. It helped hide her tears. No man had ever wanted her—not the Summer King who stole her humanity or the Dark Kings who saw her only as a friend and sometimes lover. Was it so impossible to find one who wanted her wholly?

Perhaps she was not suited for the Summer Court.

AISLINN STARED at the faery who watched her with such open and obvious affection. The room flooded, and if not for the bubble of sunlight she created around them, he'd have been drown. He'd not moved even as rain and thunder rolled through the loft.

"I can't do this," she repeated.

"Talk to me? We speak often, Aislinn." Irial stayed on the floor, but his voice had a comforting tone she'd rarely heard. Oddly or not, it upset her to have him worry over her feelings.

"We cannot be family. You are partner to the Dark King."

"And your partner is child to the High Queen." Irial lifted a shoulder in a half-shrug. "My other partner is friends with the Summer Queen, who is friendly with the Shadow Court, as well."

Aislinn sighed. "I assume Sorcha knows?"

"She cursed me." Irial shrugged again, but the look of pain in his expression was enough to make the coldest heart soften. "Your great-grandmother and I wanted to keep our daughter safe."

"Grams. You forgot about Thelma to protect Grams." Her grandmother, the sweetest and fiercest person Aislinn had ever known, was half-fey. She'd hidden it or . . .

"Does Grams—"

"Elena knows," Irial said. "We are to meet, and she has already told me that if I keep trying to send guards or buy her things, she will ask you to set 'my faery arse on fire.' I believe there was an explanation about a magnifying lens and sunlight. I seem to be an insect in this example."

The embodiment of Chaos, the former king of the worst of the faeries, looked positively charmed by Grams threatening his life. It was disconcerting.

"Aislinn?"

She met his gaze.

"Elena has a brother," Irial said softly. "He's not as human as she is. Some fey children are more human, and others are more fey."

"Like Ani and Tish." Aislinn felt a twinge for Tish, who had died in the months when Bananach was rampaging.

"They were like children to me," Irial mused. "I didn't remember then that I had children, but I wanted a daughter. I dreamed sometimes of—" He shook his head. "I would have given Elena the world if I could, but the only way to protect her and Thelma was to leave. If I stayed, Keenan would've discovered her. Or Beira would've. How could I let him touch my beloved? Or my daughter? Or . . ."

When Aislinn said nothing, Irial took her hand tentatively. She looked at him.

"Or you." Inky tears slid down his cheeks. "I missed a century of having my daughter. I'll never meet Moira . . . please, Aislinn, at least consider letting me into your life."

"We're almost friends, so . . ." she started awkwardly. "You're already here. And you're Chaos. Upheaval"—she stood and walked toward the door—"which you more than deliver. Surely, that's enough."

"Aislinn . . ." His voice broke.

She shook her head, back to him. "I had no father. No grandfather. I have no idea what one even does with a father, and it's not as if you seem much like a grandfather."

"Faeries are different," he began.

Aislinn looked at him. "I cannot offer anything easily. You must know that, Irial. I have duties. I am a queen to a court that was cursed. By you. I am a faery because of your curse."

"No," he said, walking to stand at her side. "You are a faery because I fell in love with your ancestor. I surrendered her and my children knowing then that I would meet you. I saw it, Aislinn. I saw the future; Sorcha allowed it. I looked into the now, and I saw you. You were the reason I was able to give up Thelma. I knew that you would exist, and that you would break the curse."

Aislinn stared at him. It was all she could do without letting the emotional storm inside escape.

"I knew you would be a magnificent queen, and that because of you I would again meet the daughter I once held in my arms." Irial's voice broke. "I remember it all now, the love I had for Thelma. The loss. I was ready to let the world die if it meant being with her and my children."

"Do I know my . . . grand-uncle?"

Irial shook his head. "Elena tells me he left home when he was young, and that she hasn't heard from him in almost forty years."

"So, there is a faery that knows who you are, who I am," Aislinn said, not sure what that could mean. "He's related to two faery courts by blood, and we have no idea what he's doing."

Irial nodded. "He will visit you or me now that we know."

"He's your *son*." Aislinn shivered. "I cannot fathom what he must be like."

At that, Irial grinned. "Elena is my daughter, and she's a magnificent, kind, gentle creature. A lady like her mother."

Aislinn laughed. "Can I be there when you tell her she's gentle? And ladylike?"

While Aislinn loved her grandmother wholly, she was well aware that Grams was as gentle as a lion. She could be sweet, but threats to her loved ones were not tolerated. In a flash of clarity, Aislinn realized then that she understood that impulse—and that she was looking at the faery from whom they had inherited their ferocity.

She turned to Irial and kissed his cheek quickly. "I need time. To consult with my advisors and . . . I cannot promise anything."

Irial looked like he had received a lifetime of gifts all at once. "Anything for you, granddaughter. Anything I can do or slaughter or bring."

She wasn't ready for his intensity. So, she nodded and repeated, "What I need is time. Please?"

"As you wish." The former Dark King, her great-grandfather, bowed deeply and strode toward the door, sloshing through water and floating flower buds.

And Aislinn had no idea what to do with this knowledge —other than begin to try to locate Grams' brother and figure out what this all meant for her grandmother, who was apparently over a century old and had been hiding that detail.

SIOBHAN WATCHED A MARKEDLY LESS cheerful Irial exit the queen's chambers. He seemed lost in thoughts—which undoubtedly did not bode well. She waited until he was at the door before stepping to his side.

Irial met her eyes.

"Does my queen have need of me?" Siobhan asked.

"You're her advisor these days." Irial studied her. "She'll tell you. She must. Before word and whisper circulate, she'll need to figure out what her thoughts are."

"On?"

"The news that my great-grandfather has been found," Aislinn said as she stepped into the room, not drenched as Siobhan was. The Summer Queen appeared as beautiful and radiant as always. Her once-black hair was sun-kissed, and her skin had the perpetual tan of days lounging at beaches.

"I was always here," he said, staring at her covetously. "I missed so much. I want to grant your request for time, but Elena . . . insists that I gain your consent before spending time with me, Aislinn. Her loyalty to you is a beautiful thing, but I want to know my daughter."

"Will Grams die?"

"We all die eventually," he hedged.

"Irial . . ."

He sighed. "I have no idea. The obstinate streak in her—" He pressed his lips together in a most un-Irial way. "She won't answer a thing until you consent. Visiting her would alarm people, as if I am a threat to my own daughter, so I am left hoping your request for time is not--"

"I need time," Aislinn said. "Grams is her own person; she does what she wants. And if the other courts are alarmed by your visit to her, I will manage it. I do not object to your visiting your daughter."

Irial bowed deeply, and when he stood, he was smiling as widely as Siobhan had ever seen him do. "You are a gift, my dear."

And then he was gone, presumably off to see the queen's grandmother.

His daughter.

Siobhan and Aislinn exchanged a look, and then her queen said, "You can tell Tavish." She sighed. "Be gentle with him. . . and let him know that if his feelings toward me change, I . . . I accept it. I cannot do more today. Tomorrow we will deal with whatever this means. Update Tavish. I will speak to you in the morning."

Aislinn turned and left Siobhan to break the news to her co-advisor.

SIOBHAN TAPPED at Tavish's door. "Tavish?"

"Enter."

She stepped into the room, struck by the sheer number of plants in his space. One wall held a number of faery-made weapons. Cutlasses, rapiers, and daggers, fashioned in fey-friendly metals hung in cabinets with glass doors. A sitting area, complete with comfortable seats and a wet bar, filled the left of the room. Off to the right, behind a thick wall of foliage, was Tavish's bed. Wooden, simple, and overflowing with luxurious linens.

"Things looks different," she said mildly.

"We are settled finally." Unmistakable pride thickened his voice. "Should I have no creature comforts?"

"Not a criticism." She met his gaze. "It's welcoming, the kind of space that says a lot about the owner."

He shrugged. "I do not have many guests."

"Ours is a court of pleasure." She stepped closer. "I remember you having regular guests."

Tavish stiffened.

"I remember being your guest." Carefully, she touched his chest, resting the flat of her hand over his heart. "Fondly, Tavish. I remember those nights and days with joy."

"Niall and I had a duty to the Summer Girls," Tavish said, voice low enough that she wanted to move closer still.

"Was that all?"

He swallowed audibly. "No."

"Then why do you reject me?"

Tavish sighed. "Siobhan . . ."

"I have appetites still," she said, no longer hesitant to admit things that she'd have denied as a mortal.

"No advisors to enjoy. No Dark King," Tavish said, nodding. "Are there no guards you could enjoy? Or perhaps one of the solitary fey?"

And Siobhan felt an unusual burst of guilt. She shouldn't, not in the Summer Court, but the fact of his seeing intercourse as a task made her feel rejected. Had he only lain with her out of duty? Had it been an onerous duty?

"I suppose I shall need to see if Seth or Irial have any willing victims," she said, heat shimmering in her voice.

"You could speak to Ash if you have immediate needs."

Siobhan stepped back from him. "Perhaps. Unlike Keenan and his advisors"—she held his gaze—"Ash doesn't send me to faeries' beds for information."

"Did you dislike going there?" Tavish sounded confused, as if being sent to spy was a joyous act.

"I enjoyed the act. Here. And in their court. I will not disparage the joy I took in the Dark Kings' beds—either of them." She shook her head. Over the decades, she'd been sent to the Dark King, and while she'd enjoyed the acts of intimacy at the time, the reality that she had been used was depressing. Because Irial had longed for Niall, the Summer King would send her first to Niall and then to Irial.

"But...?"

"Pleasure doesn't erase the lack of choice," Siobhan said. "I was Keenan's spy, his discarded lover, and . . ." She stopped herself and met Tavish's gaze once more. "Is it so wrong to have wanted one of them to love me? To know what foods I liked best or what flowers or what color even. As a Summer Girl, I was bound to the will of the Summer King because of the curse, but . . . to go from words of love to being asked to bed the friends of the man I thought I loved. . . to learn he was faery, that I was no longer human . . ."

"Were you forced?"

Siobhan sighed. "There is no true answer there. To love Keenan? No. To become a faery? Yes, but that was a curse."

"By the Dark King," Tavish frowned and rose from the floor.

"No. Niall was kind. He refused me often."

"The other one?"

Siobhan laughed. "Irial? Never. He always offered drink or meal or conversation instead of intimacy." She paused, weighing how much to admit, before adding, "I sought him out because he had the thing I wanted. Love. It wasn't love for me, but if I had been with Niall, if his touch and scent were recent on my flesh, Irial treated me as if I mattered."

If not for the faith her queen had in her, if not for the fact that Niall and Irial had reconciled, she would have left the sunlight for the shadows when she was freed. They had their charms, and she was a woman who'd appreciated those charms. Often. It had seemed like a fine plan at the time, but there was no place for her now.

Stiffly, Tavish said, "I have difficulty seeing any merit in Irial."

Siobhan sighed, stepped closer to Tavish, and prompted, "But do you understand what I sought?"

The look Tavish gave her was, perhaps, the most honest she'd seen him appear when dressed. "I spent nine centuries concentrating on my king's lovers. Bedding the ones who were not the queen, advising him on the next one, always the next one." He gave her a wry smile. "I've never been allowed the time to pursue a woman of my own interest, and my duty still prevents my desires. Unfortunately."

The guilt Siobhan felt over being a burden in her days as a Summer Girl twisted with heartbreak that he'd, apparently, found her so unappealing. Steeling herself so as not to reveal her crushed ego and wounded heart, she updated him on Irial's revelation.

"We shall speak with Ash tomorrow, then, about our court's plan."

"I'm worried," she admitted, voice barely a whisper. "The Winter Court will not respond well."

Tavish nodded. "Indeed." Then, he caught Siobhan's wrist. "Fresh berries with the dew still wet."

"What?"

"Your favorite food," he clarified. "You say it's fruit or berries, but the ones that make you happiest are those berries that are only just barely off the vine. And your color isn't one, but the way the skies look when the sun is about to rise. You said as much when we were in the southern continent."

Siobhan stared at him, mouth slightly agape.

"I've thought about what I wanted," Tavish said. "When you left to be in other beds, in other arms, when I was too old or too silent or too . . . me to have you. When I had to do my duties to my court and king." He cupped her face. "You were never a chore."

He brushed his lips over hers. Then, before she could react, he pulled back. "You were never truly mine, Siobhan, but that didn't change what I wanted. Duty merely prevents it."

Somehow, she found herself outside his room, alone and perplexed. She touched her lips. Tavish saw her. Not the girl she was when Keenan chose her. Not the woman who had been cursed. Not the advisor to the queen. Her.

And he was going to ignore his feelings—and hers—as if denial was romantic somehow.

Siobhan looked at the now-closed door. "You're a fool, Tavish."

BEFORE MEETING THE QUEEN, Siobhan had to see Tavish for a training session. This time, however, she was not opposed to being there in the makeshift gymnasium. She'd barely slept—

not only worrying over Tavish's revelation but also over the news that the Dark King delivered to their court.

Despite everything, though, Tavish acted as if there were no major events on the court's horizon. He treated her no differently, either. If she had any doubts about her own memories, she would be alarmed.

This was the faery who advised the emotionally excessive Summer King for nine centuries, who advised his father before him. He was not easily unsettled, and if he was, he certainly didn't reveal it.

Siobhan made it her personal mission to touch him as often and as inconspicuously as possible all morning.

By the end of the session, he was looking at her with flashes of either desire or fury in his eyes.

"Meeting," she reminded him with a casual stroke of his upper back.

"Siobhan." Tavish pinned her with his gaze.

She licked her lips. "Are you warm? I'm becoming desperate with this heat."

One of the Wild Hunt visitors said his name then, drawing him into a discussion about the efficacy of wooden weapons as an alternative to faery-made metals since the access to Faerie was now limited.

"Sorry to interrupt," she said cheerily. "Would you mind terribly if I borrowed your shower? We need to meet the queen soon, and I'm sweaty."

Siobhan ran her fingertips over her cleavage, drawing many gazes in the gesture. Admittedly, she didn't usually act that way now, but years of being a Summer Girl had a few advantages.

"Fine." Tavish stared at her. "I'll stay here until you're done."

She laughed. "Silly man. I don't mind being naked around you."

He gave her a look that seemed almost angry, but she knew how he felt now. If he hadn't wanted her to find a solution, he ought not have revealed his feelings.

Quickly, she stretched up and kissed just under his ear, on the side of his neck. "You're the best," she said lightly.

His jaw clenched tighter.

"Off to get naked," she murmured cheerily.

The Dark Court guest flashed her a wicked smile and walked away as Siobhan laughed. Sometimes she wondered if Tavish had hidden how ruthless he could be or if the war had changed him.

"Siobhan?" Tavish said, voice barely level.

She paused. "Mmmm?"

"Do warn me if you'll have a guest with you," he said.

"Not to worry, I can handle it myself," she teased. When he said nothing, she added, "Do you want to watch?"

He closed his eyes.

"Siobhan, are you coming?" Mae, one of the other former Summer Girls, said in tone that implied that the question was a repetition.

Tavish opened his eyes and stared at them both.

Siobhan blushed at the look he was giving her. Perhaps she'd pushed him too far. Forcing her gaze to Mae, Siobhan asked, "Coming where?"

"Shopping." Mae smiled with the sort of genuine happiness she'd only recently developed. The Summer Girls had been dependent on the Summer King for their entire lives. For all practical purposes, he had been the sun: they bloomed or wilted because of him. The end of the curse benefitted many faeries, not just the former king.

Mae all but bounced in place as she waited for Siobhan's reply. "Everyone is coming."

"Next time, ok?" Siobhan hugged her. "I need—"

"You really do. I saw that look." Mae grabbed Siobhan in a fierce hug and whispered, "Ask Tavish to train longer. A bit of grappling would be good for you both."

Siobhan looked back at her co-advisor. "Trust me. I know."

#

Aislinn wasn't surprised to see Siobhan walk into the study early. Of all of the faeries in the court, Siobhan was the one most likely to treat Aislinn with the comfort of a friend, rather than insist on distance. The others weren't unkind, but the ease with which Siobhan talked to her was rare. Whereas most of the Summer Girls, guards, and court members occasionally forgot the deference that said that she was their queen, Siobhan occasionally remembered it.

"I'm bored," Siobhan complained.

"I thought the girls were going shopping," Aislinn said. "Perhaps after the meeting . . ."

Siobhan gave her a level look. "If new frocks were exciting, why didn't you go?"

"I like shopping." Aislinn frowned as she said it, though. She hadn't used to like it, but there were times when being the embodiment of Summer had meant changing who she was. "Evolution" was what Tavish called it. She wasn't so sure she liked evolving, but she liked who she was and loved her court so she didn't ponder that detail overmuch.

Siobhan flopped onto one of the overstuffed chairs, and then almost immediately stood and paced, and then sat again. Her foot tapped on the floor, and her hands seemed to move constantly, sweeping her hair up into a twist, fidgeting with her necklace.

"What?"

"If I quit, would you hate me?" Siobhan blurted out.

Aislinn smiled. "Tavish?"

"He's a fool," Siobhan said. "I could totally advise you and do . . . be . . . well, whatever it is."

"Date him?" Aislinn supplied helpfully.

"That. I guess." She sighed loudly. "I could love him, I think, although"—she let out a muffled scream of sorts—"that's fucking terrifying. The last man I loved stole my humanity."

"I am aware," Aislinn said. "We'll figure it out."

She looked up and saw the door open as Tavish stepped into the room. He looked between them and his expression grew wary. "Has the meeting begun without me?" he asked lightly.

"No," Aislinn said in the same tone. "Siobhan was considering her resignation. She is having difficulty working with you, I think."

"Why?" He looked at them both, and then settled his gaze on Siobhan. "Did I offend you?"

"No." Siobhan glanced at her queen and muttered, "Thanks, Ash."

Aislinn burst into peels of laughter. "My pleasure. You've both brought this to my table, and I happen to think my choice of advisors is inspired, so we need a new plan."

"Aislinn?" Tavish prompted.

"Kiss her, Tavish. Woo her. Seduce her." The Summer Queen gestured between them. "It's the season for love. Why are you trying to argue with your queen?"

"Respectfully, your majesty, I am not sure that"—he lowered his voice—"intimacy between your advisors is a wise plan."

"Noted." She clapped her hands together. "This is the Summer Court, and if you don't want me to lose an advisor,

I suggest you stop being obstinate and romance one another."

Her advisors exchanged a look.

"Now," Aislinn continued, tone serious. "What shall we do about my dear old great-grandfather?"

SIOBHAN AND TAVISH EXCHANGED A LOOK, and for a moment, she wondered at his thoughts. Hidden behind dark eyes and stern looks, Tavish seemed like an odd fit for the summer, but she knew he was a writhing mass of passions, barely hidden some days. Talk of the Dark King rarely brought out his better side—and Aislinn knew that.

She was, however, young. She'd lived merely two decades, and of a handful of those years was as a faery. She was impulsivity embodied. In truth, knowing that the blood of the last Dark King flowed through her veins explained a few things. Aislinn had a courage that was more than human, more than fey. Add shadows to the Summer Court, and she was the result.

"I don't suppose we can murder him, and hide the evidence," Tavish said, voice light enough to make it sound like a joke.

"Bananach murdered him once already," Aislinn said cheerily. "Didn't take."

"Alas." Tavish downed a drink. "Perhaps we might speak to Niall first."

"And Donia," Siobhan added.

"I told Seth," the queen said. "Not who although I bet he already knows. He said he doesn't, but that's only true if it involves him." Aislinn scowled and muttered, "Future-seeing makes for confusing relationships."

Siobhan reached over and squeezed her hand, offering silent support. Then she asked, "How do you feel about it?"

Tavish had advised a cursed king and before him a frolicking king. Aislinn's age and gender were sometimes confusing to him, but Siobhan was relieved to see that the flinch gave way to kindness.

"He has redeeming traits," Tavish said, sitting taller in his seat. "He protects his court, Ash. Or did."

"I know." Aislinn scowled. "I just . . . I've never had a father or grandfather. I grew up with Grams. A house of women. Female friends—other than Seth but he was always more. What do you do with grandfathers or fathers?"

"He's probably not like others," Tavish offered.

A knock heralded a frowning guard. "Your Majesty?"

"There is a . . . cub. Well, two cubs," he said, as he stepped to the side. There, tumbling over themselves were a pair of small tigers. They were absolutely, without a doubt, the cutest, least appropriate thing Siobhan could imagine raising in the loft.

But the queen was already on the floor, snuggling a tiny predator.

"The note says—"

"We know who sent them," Tavish started.

Aislinn was giggling even as she said, "Utterly foolish man." Then she was growling at a baby tiger and asking it, "What in the world am I to do with you?"

"'Light and dark go well together. A little shadow doesn't undo the brightness,' it says." The guard looked at them, not sure what to do.

"Is it signed?" Siobhan asked.

"'Love from your . . . Pappy.'"

Aislinn scooped the tigers into her lap, and then set sun

spots across the floor so they could pounce on them. "I always wanted a kitten," she mused.

There was no work that would distract her then, so Siobhan and Tavish excused themselves.

Outside the door, Tavish looked at her, "We will need to speak to Niall about this."

Siobhan nodded. "At least they're cubs."

Tavish sighed. "Nature thrives around her, so it's not a crisis. What if it's the start of a habit? Where would we put a menagerie?"

At that, Siobhan was assailed by visions of nonstop gifts from a doting former Dark King who had always, apparently, wanted children. "Call Niall."

Tavish paused before turning away. "May I woo you?"

"Yes," Siobhan answered. "A million times yes."

He touched her cheek. "I want to take our time, do things right. I've watched both of my kings destroy women they loved. I've watched Irial destroy Niall. I don't ever want to hurt you."

Siobhan thought she might legitimately swoon. They'd been intimate many times, danced, spoken, fought, but this was different. New.

"I'd like that," she said, feeling oddly shy and young. "I want to take care of you, too." She leaned up and kissed him softly before pulling back just enough to speak. "And then, I want to have my way with you."

Tavish closed his eyes briefly.

"Over and over," she added, "until neither of us can walk."

He swallowed audibly and rasped, "That . . . would be good, too."

And before she could reply, he kissed her until she had to

lean on the wall for support. It would, in fact, be very, very good.

AISLINN KNEW who Urian was the moment he stepped into her court. Her great-grandfather's warning that he would come wasn't why. Urian looked like family.

Shadow-dark skin and what would've been a twin to her own dark hair before sunlight changed her. He stood with his father's arrogance, and something of a wicked glint in his eye. This was not a faery who had found his heart.

This was an angry faery.

"What shall I call you?" Urian didn't bow, didn't even lower his gaze. "Niece? Ash-Girl?"

Aislinn lifted a hand to stop the guards who started to move closer.

"Murderess?" he asked, voice lower.

Aislinn lifted her chin and stared back at him. "Queen."

He laughed. "Not *my* queen. I bow to no one."

Aislinn repressed a shiver of fear. She was strong enough to fight any faery in existence now—at least those in her world. That didn't mean she wanted to do so, and power didn't always overcome skill.

Urian looked around, smiled at Siobhan and winked at a guard. "I thought I should meet the woman who mattered so much that my niece died." He stared intently at Aislinn and said, "You are a strangely pretty little murderess."

"I didn't kill my mother," Aislinn started.

Urian brushed his hand to the side, shadows slid across the ground as if he was summoning them.

He shouldn't be able to manage that. The Dark belonged to Niall now, not this faery.

"No." It was one word, but it was enough. Her guards came in, a rush of vine and bark.

Urian smiled, cold and vicious. That was a look she remembered well from Bananach, madness tinged with fury.

"We are fine," she told her guard. She motioned for them to leave. Perhaps it was foolish, but she wanted to try talking to him. Tavish and Siobhan stayed, but no one else was near. Only them. If Tavish were anyone else in the court, Aislinn would feel unprotected. He was fierce—and Siobhan was brutal when provoked.

And Aislinn was the queen, a faery with the ferocity of summer inside her very skin. Her uncle was no threat to her.

"If you must, you may call me Aislinn."

"Aislinn," Urian echoed. "My sister's granddaughter. The last ashes of my family."

He might be family, but he wasn't the sort of person Grams was, not even the sort of person her mother had been— or that Irial was. At least not the Irial she'd met and known. Urian reminded her of the fey things that had been the stuff of nightmares for her growing up, vicious in ways she would never understand.

"Such an odd little mortal-turned-faery. You took my mother's crown, my niece's crown."

"Thelma didn't want it. She *ran* to avoid it," she reminded him. "My mother didn't either. She ran and died avoiding it."

"And you?"

"I fought to avoid it. This wasn't the life I wanted, but it's *mine* now. This court is *mine*."

"You like power, though. You've drawn the eye of the High Queen's son," Urian added. "

"I knew Seth before he was her son."

What makes you so interesting, Ashes?

"I don't know, Uncle. Why are *you* here?"

As Urian laughed, shadows skittered closer as if he was theirs somehow. It frightened her. A tiny part of her wanted to kick everyone here out and call the rest of her family, which was now both Grams and Irial as well as Seth, but Aislinn had doubts as to Urian's temper—and stability. He hadn't approached his father or his sister. He hadn't approached Seth, the faery who was de facto leader of the solitary.

"Seth," she said, latching on to that detail. "Is this about him? Some solitary fey thing?"

"Oh, it's about a lot of things, Ashes." Urian shook his head, as if he was sad, but it wasn't sorry glinting in his eyes. Rage and hunger simmered in him, so hot that she could have been looking into Bananach's eyes.

Without meaning to, a sword of sunlight formed in her grip, blinding bright and sizzling with heat.

Urian glanced at the sunlit blade. A smile that was identical to his father's curved his lips. "Do let them know I've come calling, Ashes."

Then he flung something glittering toward Siobhan.

"Siobhan!" Aislinn was halfway across the room before she finished the word, but Tavish was closer and almost as fast. He pushed Siobhan aside.

He was there, in front of his co-advisor. The blade that had been hurled at Siobhan stabbed Tavish's stomach. And then he was on the ground, blood pouring from his wound.

Her advisor. Her friend. Her brother-by-choice. Aislinn was livid. The sword that was in her hand a moment ago was there and raised. She met her uncle's eye and stalked toward him.

"Will you let him die, too?" Urian asked, taunting her with the sort of voice best suited for playground quarrels. "Or will you kill the son of the last Dark King? Whose life matters to you? What do you choose today? Death or life, Ashes?"

Her guards came in.

"No!" Aislinn called. "He is not yours to touch."

"Ash!" Siobhan called. "Tavish needs you."

"We aren't done," Aislinn said.

Urian merely grinned.

But when Aislinn turned toward her advisors, Urian walked to the door and left as quietly as he'd arrived.

"Sunlight?" Tavish asked.

Aislinn flinched slightly, not so much that it was obvious to anyone who didn't know her. She knelt at his side. "There are complications."

"I know," Tavish assured her, voice shaky from obvious pain. "The side effects . . . are acceptable. Appealing, even."

The Summer Queen said nothing.

"Siobhan?" he asked.

"I'm fine, you fool." She knelt on the floor opposite the queen. "You, however, have a scratch."

He laughed. "My queen? Sister?"

"You will escort Tavish to his room as soon as I fix this." Aislinn nodded at the oozing wound. The edges were blackening as if ink had poured there, and the skin started to writhe.

"Poisoned," Tavish whispered. "If you could heal me soon . . ."

The Summer Queen pressed her lips together tightly, and she lifted his torn clothing so that the bloodied skin was visible.

"Are you sure?" Aislinn asked. "We can call a healer and—"

He looked at Siobhan as he answered Aislinn. "Yes."

Siobhan wasn't quite sure what she was missing, but her queen looked her in the eye and said, "That yes was to you, Siobhan. Remember that."

Then, the Summer Queen began to glow. Sunlight seemed to radiate from her entire body, as if she had summoned the sun itself and somehow held it inside her small frame. The guards, the freed Summer Guards, assorted Summer Court faeries all started flowing into the room as if they were being called to their queen's side.

"Be well, brother, and be loved," Aislinn whispered, and then she brought her hands down on the wound, cupped them there at first, and then pressed down.

Tavish moaned, first in pain as she seared whatever poison had entered his body and then in a sort of agony as the skin sizzled and burnt. When the Summer Queen finally lifted her hand, a tattoo was there, a sun much like the blackened sun already on Tavish's throat.

"My queen," he whispered. Then he looked at Siobhan and murmured, "My beloved."

"Ash?"

"He's drunk on sunlight." Aislinn didn't sound much more sober. The room was erupting in flowers, and couples—or couples for the night—were kissing and caressing.

Tavish slid his hand over Siobhan's leg, at first caressing her calf but within moments his hand was above the knee and showing no sign of stopping.

Siobhan caught his hand in hers and asked, "What are you doing?"

"Seducing you . . . ?" Tavish smiled drunkenly.

Siobhan stifled her giggle. She hadn't ever seen him quite this drunk other than the week Aislinn became queen. That week, he'd kissed Siobhan until she thought her whole body might melt. The next day, he was as taciturn ever.

Siobhan vaguely heard Aislinn say, "Seth!"

And the queen's formerly-mortal lover stalked toward her. "Sorcha said you would need me, and I thought—"

"My uncle was here to murder someone," Aislinn said, sounding far too light-hearted. "But . . . can we . . ."

The queen and her lover were gone then, and Siobhan was left with her amorous, intoxicated co-advisor.

"What happens in the morning?" Siobhan prompted, catching and again holding tightly to Tavish's hand which had escaped her grasp.

"More sex!"

Siobhan started laughing. "That sounds wonderful, but I thought you wanted to think things through."

"Fuck it," he said cheerily. "Loved you for almost a damned decade. Had to watch others be where I wanted, but if you're mad enough to want me, I'm done arguing."

Siobhan helped him to his feet—and discovered that without restraint, his hands were everywhere.

"You have the perfect arse, Siobhan. Like a firm apple." Tavish had both hands on her bum, squeezing and caressing.

"I had no idea," she murmured, pushing him back slightly. Although she was sure he truly wanted her, feeling the obvious proof of his desire straining toward her, Siobhan also knew Tavish. Sober again, he'd be mortified that he was so amorous in public. He was a wonderful lover, but not as public about it as many in their court.

Siobhan started to steer him toward his room, trying to ignore the stares and even a smattering of applause and remarks of "it's about time" or "finally come to his senses, has he?"

"I shall compose a sonnet for each breast," Tavish declared, voice low enough that only she heard. "Two sonnets. One for the left, and one for the right. Perhaps a Rondeau on your apple cheeks, though."

"A what?"

"Lyric poem," he said, speaking in that exaggeratedly correct way of the truly drunken.

They'd made it to the edge of the room when Tavish looked at her and said, "Let me love you, Siobhan. Let me be impulsive and enjoy this sunlit madness."

"If you try to walk away in the morning, I'll stab you myself this time," she warned.

"As you should," Tavish said before kissing her thoroughly.

In a moment, she realized his hands were unfastening her buttons, so she half led, half dragged him to his room where they made love stumbling and drunken and desperately until he sobered—and then did so again and again with more care and soft words.

THE NEXT MORNING, Tavish and Siobhan met the Dark Court's guests. Aislinn had left Seth resting in her chambers, so it was only the regents and their advisors—and the two tiny tiger cubs. They rolled and romped as if they'd always been a part of the Summer Court.

The current and former Dark Kings had arrived; their semi-human consort, Leslie, was not there. And as Siobhan looked around the jungle-like room, she realized with a near human awkwardness that she was currently sitting in a room with her two past lovers, her future lover, and her best friend.

Tavish looked uncomfortable, so she leaned over and kissed him speechless. He was still sore from the injury Urian had inflicted, but he was upright and therefore determined to be at the meeting.

"Well done!" Irial said. "That's one way to keep the old boy in the Summer Court."

"Irial!" Niall and Aislinn said simultaneously. The tigers pounced into Aislinn's lap, and she gently put them on the floor.

Tavish shrugged slightly. "He's not wrong."

When no one spoke, he added, "I'd still rather we murder you than meet with you, but my queen, my friend"—he nodded toward Niall—"and my . . ."

"Lover," Siobhan filled in. "Beloved, I hope?"

He squeezed her hand and repeated, "and my beloved seem to think you have redeeming qualities."

"They are sometimes not evident, but they are present." Niall took a long drink of whatever libation he was consuming before adding, "The Dark Court appreciates your consideration and patience, Tavish."

Irial opened his mouth to reply, but a band of shadows covered it immediately. The former Dark King raised a brow and looked at Niall pointedly.

Tavish snorted as Niall ignored his own beloved.

"While Irial is not under the command of my court, I will give my word as Dark King that he has no ill will toward your court—or you." Niall looked briefly embarrassed. "And as both a man and king, I want you to know, Siobhan, that I had no idea at first of the way Keenan misused you."

Siobhan did not miss the key omission in that statement. Niall was, however, a creature who ruled the things of nightmares. He had become the Dark, and so he was—and previously had been—more shadowed than sunlit.

"You were good to me." Siobhan looked at Irial. "Both of

you." Then she shrugged and added, "If Ash didn't need me, I'd thought to defect to your court."

"I thought as much," Irial said quietly, as the shadow-wrought gag vanished. He looked immeasurably pleased with himself as he noted, "That's why I provoked him."

"What?" Tavish asked.

He tapped his own chest. "Chaos, my dears. Cha-os. My lovely granddaughter needs you, and love"-- Irial looked around at them—"love makes madness seem rational. If you love our girl Siobhan--"

"Woman," Siobhan interjected. "Not a girl."

"And not yours," Tavish added. "My woman."

Aislinn laughed. "Well played, grandfather."

And at that, Irial preened. "Love. For it, we would do the impossible."

"Yes, but could we address the topic at hand?" Niall's tone was stern, but no one there could miss the look in his eyes as he glanced at the embodiment of Chaos. The Dark King was in agreement—and in love.

"And perhaps after that, discuss the topic of what gifts one can send the Summer Queen?" Siobhan added.

"She likes them," Irial said, pointing at the sleeping tigers curled into the Summer Queen's lap. "It was an excellent gift."

Tavish lifted his glass to the Dark King and then to the Summer Queen. "I do not envy either you."

Irial frowned, but after a moment, he sighed loudly and said, "Now, let us address the matter at hand. My lost son . . ."

End

WINTER DREAMS: A WICKED LOVELY STORY

KEENAN

1990

he Summer King rarely missed his Mother's court. Keenan had been born as the child of Summer and Winter. He *chose* sunlight, that was the secret no one seemed to realize: He could have chosen ice.

Sometimes he thought he could have been happier in the Winter Court, but he had a duty to the leaderless Summer Court. Summer had needed him, and Keenan wanted to *matter*.

"Summer is dying," Tavish had whispered.

"You are so much like your father," Niall had said over and over.

"When you're of age, you'll save them," they both swore. "Better to rule a weakened court than be a servant to the Winter Queen."

But Keenan wasn't a mere child now, and his fantasy of rescuing *anyone* was barely a flicker of hope. He might not be a servant, but lately, he didn't feel like much of a king. The world was blanketed by snow more often than not. Crops died, and animals starved. His own faeries shivered under layers of furs and he was . . . useless.

And no one cared. No one noticed. No one seemed to realize he was on the verge of giving up. Somehow the Summer Court still believed in him, and his mother . . . the Winter Queen? She would gaze at him in fear, in hate, in shivering rage. They thought he was the kind of king he wasn't sure he could ever be.

Keenan doubted he'd ever be strong enough.

The curse meant that he was bound, unable to be at his true strength unless he found the one mortal in all the world who was carrying his sunlight. And he hunted for her, letting dreams guide him to this or that place. Somewhere out there a mortal was meant to be his, and the surety that every curse could be broken drove him when he wanted to surrender.

Today, he stood in a wooded area, and he clung to that truth. She was out there.

The trees, coniferous and towering, were dressed in ice and snow. The ground under his feet crunched as his boots came down on frozen grass and fallen needles. The air was chilled, reminding him that winter grew stronger and stronger. It was barely fall, and yet the earth looked like it was nearly Winter Solstice.

"I must find her," Keenan whispered.

The trouble was that finding his queen now carried a cost. He *had* found the one mortal in all the world, in all the centuries, who seemed perfectly suited to him. He loved her. Still.

Perhaps, he was doomed as his father once was—to love a woman who hated him. His own mother hated him enough to torment him because he reminded her of the man who betrayed her.

When Keenan was a child, he'd summon heat or spark life in plants buried under thick layers of snow. And every time he did so, Beira, the Winter Queen, would rage. The more she raged, the more Keenan realized that his mother was kindling her hatred of his father—and in that icy rage she felt for the man who wronged her, she hated all things Summer.

She hated her son.

He looked too much like the last Summer King, and so he dressed in clothes that were mortal-made, a gesture to remind the approaching Winter Queen that he was, in fact, not the king she still hated.

"Sweetling," the Winter Queen greeted as she arrived for the test to determine his latest choice's fitness for the role of queen.

"Mother." Keenan let sunlight fill him, pulled on the strength of his court so he could face his opposition. He glimmered, casting sunlight that danced over the plants that Winter had frozen in her wake.

"Shall we dispense with this one?" Beira asked. She'd arrived alone, save for one other faery. The Winter Queen still enjoyed some measure of pageantry, and she swept toward him as if they were in a palace. As she moved over the ground, the length of a thick, black fur cloak trailed behind her. He thought, briefly, that it might be a grizzly bear's pelt, but he chose not to ask.

Keenan gestured toward the clearing. "Let us commence."

He'd like to pretend there was a chance that Tracey, the mortal girl he'd chosen, was his missing queen, but faeries can't lie, and even the Summer King was not above that law.

Winter walked away, preparing for another trial. As no

one thought the outcome would be anything unexpected, Beira was almost pleasant.

The other faery, however, was not. Try as he might, Keenan could not stop the thrill that filled him as he looked at her. *Donia.* Although he smiled at her, the last woman who *had* loved him enough to risk the curse was now glaring at him.

"Another one who sees that you are not worth it," Donia said, voice no less musical than when she was a mortal. The ice that filled her only added richness to her words. "Tracey won't take the risk. She'll refuse."

"I know . . . and it's better that she doesn't." He paused, resisting the urge to touch her only because it would pain her if he did. His sunlight might be weak, but she was a creature of ice now.

"I still wish *you* were the one, Don," he whispered.

She looked away.

He still thought she was the most beautiful creature he'd ever seen. Her blond hair had faded to the white of a snow squall, and pallor made her lips seem blue, but she was still as beautiful as she had been before she'd taken over as the Winter Girl.

Together they walked over to the mortal he'd chosen, Tracey, for the ceremony that everyone knew wouldn't happen.

Tracey didn't love him, and he couldn't see her as the Summer Queen. He shouldn't have selected her. She was fragile in a way that he knew would make her an unlikely match, but she was lovely. He'd seen her dancing in patch of sunlight near him. He'd been *glamoured*, invisible to mortals. She was happy, dancing in the light, and he'd wanted her to live forever.

In that moment, that flicker of affection, he'd chosen her.

In truth, he hadn't truly encouraged her to risk the cold. He had, instead, spoken of a lifetime in the sunlight, knowing that she wasn't his destined queen and unable to bear the thought of her misery if she tried to accept the test. Lately, he wished none of the former mortals had to endure either of the curse's two options. If there was another way to break the curse without risking them, he'd do it.

"I wish you'd suffer the way I do," Donia whispered from his side.

"I do suffer, Don. I swear to you that I do." Keenan glanced at her, barely resisting the need to touch her. "You *know* I do."

"Tracey?" Donia said, louder now.

The latest in Keenan's long list of failed loves smiled at Donia and Keenan both. This part of the test was inevitable, the words unavoidable. Some traditions—and all curses--were as laws for faeries.

The Summer King knelt before Tracey. "Is this what you freely choose, to risk winter's chill?"

"Oh..." Tracey watched him—and he knew his skin glowed brighter as summer's flames flickered just under the surface. At such moments, he no longer looked anything like a mere mortal. For this moment, Keenan *was* Summer made flesh.

"Tracey?" he prompted, hoping she wasn't going to say 'yes.'

"It's not what I want," she said, sounding apologetic. "You're wonderful, Keenan, but . . . I don't want to be a queen. I'm not *her*. We both know that."

Curses were inflexible, though. Keenan had to say the words. Every single time, he said them. This was no different.

"If you agree to try and are not the one, you'll carry the Winter Queen's chill until the next mortal risks this." He paused, glancing at her, willing her to refuse. "Do you choose the test?"

Tracey shook her head. "I mean, I *understand*. . . and I'm sorry, but . . . I can't."

He whispered, "I know. . . ."

He beckoned to the Summer Court advisors, Niall and Tavish, who had arrived as soon as the test began. They gave Beira a wide berth, but both fey men watched her cautiously as they approached Keenan.

"Would you see Tracey home?" he asked.

Tracey hugged him. "You'll find her. I just know it."

Keenan wished silently that he still believed that.

Tracey giggled suddenly as the vines that wrapped every Summer Girl stretched and shivered over her skin. "They tickle."

"They *also* keep you alive and stronger," he told her.

"You saved me." Tracey smiled at him. "Someday, you'll find the person to save you."

Keenan nodded and looked at her, not sure what to say. She was a friend, but she was also his responsibility now. Every Summer Girl was. Like plants in need of sunlight, they stayed near him.

In a rare moment of kindness, Beira waited until Tracey left to behave in her usual way. "That was depressing," she said. "No one to *save* you . . ."

"Must we do this, Mother?" Keenan met the Winter Queen's gaze, seeking the remnants of the faery who had once loved him a little at least. Her love had always been capricious, but he remembered moments of it. Perhaps nothing of that maternal love was left under her bitterness and rage.

The Winter Queen's response was to exhale ice all around them, knowing the pain it caused him.

He stood in the sudden carpet of ice and snow, watching

Donia's eyes fill with ice and her lips tint blue.

"Well, isn't that the way of life?" the Winter Queen said. "You're pitiful and alone, again."

Keenan, however, wasn't sure if he was intentionally selecting those who wouldn't be his missing queen—or if such a person simply didn't exist.

What if she'd died? What if the curse was worded in such a way that the one girl he needed had died centuries ago? Or what if the Winter Queen had sent her minions to kill the girl when she was found? *Could* they locate her? Were they as unaware as he was?

Donia, the current Winter Girl, was the last one who'd attempted to be his queen and failed. That was almost half a century ago. Before her was Rika, who was currently living in the American desert, as far from the cold as she could be.

Keenan stared at Donia as he said, "My heart wasn't in it this time. It's already full."

Donia widened her eyes slightly. She stared at him, silent, but he knew she understood.

His mother, however, laughed in that horrible, chilling way of hers. "*Still?*" Beira asked. "After all these unfortunates, you're pining after *this* one?"

The Winter Queen stroked an icy hand over Donia's hair, leaving it glittering with snow crystals that, for a moment, seemed like diamonds. "Donia would've been a harsh queen once she realized how useless you are, Sweetling."

Keenan turned and walked away before Donia could answer. The truth was that he didn't deserve Donia. Fate had made that clear when she wasn't the keeper of the missing summerlight—but he loved her.

Still.

He feared that he always would, and the curse was so much more awful because of it.

When Keenan left, Donia felt the usual mix of longing and rage. As a mortal, her reaction to him had been far different. The mortals he romanced never knew *what* he was until they were near the point of changing. By then, it was too late. Their mortality was gone, and the only choices were risking the cold or being a part of his collection of vine-wrapped Summer Girls.

Donia wouldn't have turned back, even if she knew what he was. She wouldn't have surrendered the chance for eternity with him. That was the secret that she couldn't quite face. She couldn't entirely blame him—because she chose the risk. She chose love. She chose duty. And if she had to do it all again, Donia would still choose *him*.

Half a century ago, Donia had been young, poor, and dreaming of the sort of romance she read of in books. And there was Keenan, her own Prince Charming. He was everything. Handsome. Charismatic. And he listened to her, truly heard her ideas and thoughts. Of course, she thought he was *the one*.

He would arrive to see her, pulling up to her home driving

a beautiful green Jaguar convertible or a deep red Triumph Roadster. To own *one* car was unfathomable to her, but to own two? He dressed smartly, took her on wonderful dates where they'd dance and laugh, and she imagined a life of such joy. She thought they'd grow old, have a family, and dance forever. She'd felt so lucky.

Donia had loved him wholly and that love had not faltered when she discovered that he wasn't human. He was, quite simply, a faery *and* still her fairy tale prince. Keenan was perfection to her.

So, when she faced the choice Tracey just had, Donia had accepted the challenge—and she'd been living with the pain of her failure for half a century now. She'd lost everything for loving him, and he'd lost nothing.

"Pack your things," the Winter Queen ordered, forcing Donia's gaze away from the weakened Summer King.

"Already done." Donia knew the pattern.

"Good. He'll move us now," Beira said, and then she was gone, too.

Save for guards that Keenan tasked with her safety, Donia was left alone in a clearing. Tracey was escorted away, cared for by the Summer Court advisors. The Summer Girls always were. Beira went off to gloat. No one cared about Donia's aching heart—not when she lifted the staff and was filled with ice, and not now when she watched another mortal lose every-thing for Keenan.

The Winter Girl was always in the unique position of being hated by both Summer and Winter Courts. The Winter Queen never forgave those who loved her son enough to attempt to break the curse, and the Summer King was always at odds with her. Her very function in life—as a result of the curse—was to convince chosen girl after chosen girl that she should resist Keenan's affections.

Donia, like the others foolish enough to risk everything for Keenan, was cursed for loving him. Filled with ice as a reminder of her loss, each Winter Girl could only be freed if she *failed* and another foolish former mortal took the test.

"I don't need you," she muttered toward the Summer King's guards, who trailed behind her when she turned toward her current home. That home, too, was temporary. The Summer King never stayed long in the town where the last Summer Girl had been found. He'd follow some instinct or whim. Whatever the reason, he'd move his court, and Winter would follow.

For all that his power was bound, they were still beholden to his whims. The curse was placed about nine centuries ago, long before Donia was born, and the result was that the Summer King spent his life hampered, weakened by the binding of his power, ruling with half of his sunlight hidden away in a mortal. And he had to find *her*, one mortal in all the world.

Girl after girl had been romanced by the Summer King, given her heart to him and her mortality. He didn't *seduce* them physically. That was a particularly twisted bit. Those who truly loved him, who were willing to take the test to see if they held Summer, never knew him physically. Those who didn't love him, who refused the test, became Summer Girls. They knew him intimately—needed his touch to survive.

And Keenan knew they didn't love him.

In her calmer moments, Donia could admit that it was a cruel curse for everyone involved, but seeing the man she'd risked death for romancing other women year after year didn't leave her very calm. Feeling aches down to her very bones didn't make Donia feel forgiving.

Knowing Beira made Donia understand why the curse was so dark. The Winter Queen was a creature of rage and bitterness. Add that to all faeries' propensity for clever curses, and it was no wonder that the curse was awful.

Donia walked, invisible to mortal gazes, to her rented cabin. She'd liked living here, surrounded by trees. This, too, she couldn't keep.

Because of him.

Who knew where they'd end up?

They'd live in the new place for a few years until the Summer King found the next potential queen. It was a horrible way to spend an eternity: she had forever to watch him woo woman after woman, knowing that he was telling them the words he'd once said to her, whispering their names, listening to their dreams.

Donia was almost to the cabin when Sasha, the wolf who was her companion animal, loped toward her. Sasha, like most sentient creatures, tried to avoid the Winter Queen. No one with sense wanted to be in Beira's presence for long.

A twinge of empathy for Keenan filled Donia as she thought about growing up under Beira's loving care, but the Winter Girl had no time for sympathy, especially for him.

She walked in quiet peace, silent as the path grew thicker with snow and the areas where mortals lived were far from sight. This part, the peace of nature, was her one true solace in her life of late.

He'd steal that, too. He always did. And Donia, for all that she wished otherwise, still loved him. Love was her curse, her flaw, her downfall over and over.

THE WARMTH at her back let her know Keenan was there. He sought her out after every failed test, as if she were a consolation prize.

"You know, I still wish you were the one," he said.

"Can we not?" Donia continued walking, not looking back.

"Don . . ." He caught up with her, so they were walking side by side.

"Every time, Keenan, every single time this happens you come to me. What am I to do? Live an eternity with the scraps you have for me between your romances?" She glanced at him, hating the way her heart still reacted as he smiled. Fifty-some years had passed since she'd had the right to look at him with these feelings. Half a century of being the fallback prize stung.

"You know I—"

"No." Donia stopped and glared at him. "We talked about this. I will not hear those lies. Not again."

Keenan, as predictable as seasons once were, said, "We can't lie. You know that, Don."

Her breath was coming out in angry puffs that undoubtedly caused him pain, but instead of backing up, he reached out so his hand was near—but not touching—her cheek. "There is no one I *have* to romance today. So, why can't I be here with you?"

"Because there will be." Donia looked away from him, before she let herself give in. "I'm not her, Keenan. I will never, ever be the one you want."

"You will *always* be the one I want," he argued. "I want *you*, Donia. Now. Before. Later. That's not going to change."

"Fate disagrees," she pointed out.

"The curse not selecting you isn't about what I *want*." He moved so she was looking at him again. "I can't undo the curse, but if I find her, you and I will *both* be free. The Summer Girls will. The world will thrive again. I *have* to find my queen for all of us."

"When we met, you offered me everything, but look at my

life . . ." She shook her head. "I understand why you do it. I do. I just don't want to be the second-choice, too."

"You're not!"

She exhaled a plume of frigid air. "The curse says otherwise."

"The curse is about the girl who has my sunlight. She's a vessel." Keenan ran his hands through his hair in frustration. "That's not *fated love*."

"It is fated matrimony," Donia snapped. "And you *always* love them. How can you say you won't with the one who will be your queen? Arranged or not, once you find her, you are forbidden to me. I will not be someone's mistress!"

Keenan took a breath, visibly restraining his temper and sunlight. "Have I found her?"

"No."

"Then I am free to romance you, am I not?" The Summer King gave her a smile that made logic and restraint vanish, and she hated him a little bit for it.

At the end of this, whether the next mortal or several mortals from now, he was going to be belong to another woman. How was she to let her heart begin to heal if Keenan wouldn't let her go?

"Don, please?" Keenan knelt in the snow and stared up at her. "Let me have more time with you."

"Give me peace for now," she half-ordered, half-asked. "Speak to me again when we are moved."

He smiled, hearing her acquiescence. Over and over, he broke her heart, and Donia had no idea why she couldn't resist.

One day, she swore, *I will refuse for good.*

Irial couldn't explain why he felt so drawn to this town. He walked around Huntsdale, Pennsylvania as if there was something that would jump out and answer the anxiety plaguing him.

The main street of this little town was a mix of buildings that hadn't seen better days in longer than even he could fathom. Humans were so peculiar. Why did they stay here? Why did they let poverty and disease eat them alive instead of moving somewhere with work? The simple idea of permanence in misery confused the Dark King—and he and his kind fed on the ugliest of emotions. If he could feed on humanity's misery instead of only fey pain, he might set up a home here.

He couldn't, though, so why did he feel like he wanted to stay here?

Irial summoned the Wild Hunt, sending his summons out of the bond he had with the leader of their nightmarish crew. *"Come to me."*

As he walked, invisible to mortal eyes, Irial studied facades that were presumably once attractive, but now bore telltale signs of age and decay. Stubborn weeds sprouted from cracked sidewalks and half-abandoned lots. It was a mundane town, steel tracks and abandoned train cars. There was nothing magical here. Sure, there was a portal to Faerie, but he was the Dark King. He could always find entry there.

The Summer King and Winter Queen had both relocated there, and as much as he tended to try to stay clear of their drama, this was one of the times he couldn't.

He was standing under a building, staring up at it, when Gabriel drove the Hunt through the streets of the steel town.

The Dark King inhaled the roil of terror and panic that accompanied their arrival before he turned to watch them. Cars, motorcycles, and beasts surged through the city. In Faerie, forever ago now, these steeds could wear whatever form they wanted all of the time. When invisible, they sometimes still did, but as centuries slipped away they became increasingly likely to take forms of machine over creature. A few skeletal horse-like steeds exhaled noxious clouds as they panted from whatever speed they'd used to reach him quickly.

Near the front of the mass of writhing, straining creatures and machines, stood the faery who was as close to a brother as Irial had in either world. Once he would've used that word for the long-dead Summer King, Miach, but he was centuries dead now. And while the Dark King wouldn't admit to Gabriel that he was always relieved to see the Hound uninjured, Irial still allowed himself a moment of thanks that his oldest living friend was here.

"Getting slower with age," Irial said in greeting.

The massive Hound snorted and swung a meaty fist toward Irial. The laughter it elicited in all of them eased the worst of Irial's anxiety. They were neither slow nor easily countered.

"Why am I called to you?" Gabriel grumbled.

Irial studied him. "Busy?"

"Later," Gabriel muttered, glancing back at his mate.

As Irial looked over the assembled group, he noticed the increased presence of piercings. The toxic metal caused them pain, as it did all things fey other than royal or unusual exceptions. The Dark Court fey had developed a recent predilection for piercings that were popular among mortals, as if creating their own pain was pleasure. Admittedly, they tended toward silver, but Irial saw a few scattered Hounds with a steel ring or stud in his or her skin. They'd switch out, but Irial couldn't help but appreciate the pain-pleasure he drew from them.

"I will expect answers," Irial said.

"See Rabbit," Gabriel muttered in a low enough voice that Irial had to wonder what crisis that would lead to, but today was reserved for the uncomfortable need Irial had felt to find and guard the missing mortal girl.

He walked over to stare up at the unsightly iron-coated building, closer than most fey could go. From above him, he saw the curtain slide to the side and a woman stare down at him. She looked familiar, although he couldn't imagine why. As he stared at her yet again, his memory tickled. Could she be the child of a faery he wasn't recalling? There were reasons this mortal called out to him, eliciting protective instincts.

"Why do I care about *this* one?" Irial asked as Gabriel approached, a roll of fear accompanying his steps as if it was a tangible cloud.

"This one?" the Hound echoed.

"*She's* here," Irial said quietly. He didn't need to specify that he meant the one human in all the world who could change the shift of power between the faery courts. The girl the Summer King sought was here. As creator of the curse, Irial knew. He'd always known.

"Here?" Gabriel motioned out toward the dying city.

Irial caught his eye and then looked up at a window of the building. The curtain dropped closed, so it was simply a covered window, but she was in there. "No. *Here*."

A look of worry came over the muscular Hound. "And what do you ask of the Hunt?"

"I want her protected, from all of them, from us," Irial scowled. "The mortal and her mother."

Gabriel scowled. "Protect . . . *mortals?*"

And despite not understanding why, Irial felt a tightening around his chest that made no sense whatsoever. It felt like a *geas*. What vow had he made, though? When he tried to understand, he felt an absence, a missing space in his mind that was only possible if the High Queen had been sinking her magic into his skin or if he had been cursed.

"Iri?"

The Dark King shook his head. "Keep them safe. I need to run an errand."

"Chela could do this," Gabriel offered. "I'll be at your side on the errand. If the other courts are here, you'll need to pay your respects to Beira."

Irial clasped his friend's arm. "I need to go to Faerie first."

At that, Gabriel stepped back. He wasn't eager to step foot back in the place where they'd been first formed. It might be the original home of the fey, and the Wild Hunt might be allowed free roam there, but the wild energy that the High Queen wielded was disquieting to the steeds that made up the Hunt. They preferred this side of the veil—and so the Hunt trusted that instinct.

"We shall guard them," Gabriel vowed. Ogham marks spiraled over his skin, confirming the Dark King's orders, and with that, Irial turned away from the window that had drawn his attention so strongly.

For reasons he couldn't explain, he paused and looked

back. "She has the Sight. Moira Foy. She's Sighted, and she has . . . she has fey blood, Gabriel. Dark Court blood. I feel her, not just because of the curse on the Summer King. Her mother, too."

The entire Hunt had heard.

Irial met the gazes of the steeds and Hounds alike. "She might be *their* missing mortal, but she is of *our* court, somehow, too. Someone I know is parent to these mortals. No High Court fey may know of their heritage."

He thought of the fate of the Sighted. Eyes gouged out. Lives cut short. The fey were notoriously private, not liking their affairs to be the business of mortals. Those who saw them knew not to speak to them, not to spend time with them, not to be near to them at all if possible.

And as much as he needed answers from the High Queen, he decided not to share this detail. She collected the Sighted, but these mortals had Dark Court blood.

"Protect them," Irial stressed, sending the message out over the lines of connection he had with the entire Dark Court. "No Summer or Winter may harm them. Your lives for their safety if we must."

No one questioned his orders. They wouldn't when he was willing to unleash the Hunt to protect them, but he questioned it.

Why do these mortals matter?

When they arrived at the dingy town of Huntsdale a few weeks later, Donia thought she might have to seek out the Summer King and question his sanity. She had decided she wasn't agreeing to his request to court her, although she would have to see him soon to share that decision. Her heart missed Keenan, but her head wasn't seeing the point when the courting could lead to nothing.

Her heart objected.

And so she'd avoided any contact with him. Now, however, they settled in this new town, undoubtedly to find the next mortal girl.

The town was not thriving. She remembered the poverty she'd known and seen in her mortal years, but this wasn't much better. The town had a lot of alcoholism, despair, and a desperation to "get out." She'd seen that over the years, sometimes in the girls Keenan chose. She wouldn't admit it, but sometimes she thought he knew this or that girl wasn't the one he needed, but he still wanted to save them. In a few cases, Donia had wondered if the curse of eternity with the Summer Court was anything other than a *gift*.

Trust him to find ways to use a curse to help people.

Donia smiled to herself. He really did have a good heart and a drive to rescue those in need—which was why she was questioning why he'd brought them here to a city of steel and sorrow. Huntsdale was thick with steel-laden train yards and steel buildings, brick structures decorated in wrought-iron balconies.

The ground outside the city even had an unusual stink of iron in the soil itself. The majority of the fey who were seeking shelter here would find the town deadly. Donia was no exception.

"What are we doing here?" she whispered. Only the guards might hear, but the worst that could come of her question was a conversation after a guard reported her words to the Winter Queen or the Summer King.

"It's covered in steel," Donia continued.

Sasha, her wolf companion, joined her as Donia found them a cottage outside the iron-laden city. Her temporary home was in one of the few wooded areas in reach of Huntsdale. It was small and isolated, and she knew that both the Winter Queen and the Summer King would hate it. Beira was fond of old elegant homes and servants. Keenan had never moved beyond the need to live with a crowd.

Donia couldn't blame him entirely. The Summer Girls depended on him the way plants relied on the sun and soil. Having his advisors there was another matter altogether. For centuries, they'd shared homes, and to be truthful, she found it peculiar. Keenan argued that families lived together, but it wasn't the same. Sasha was all the company Donia needed— and Sasha was out roaming as often as possible.

The way Keenan filled whatever home he had with caged wildlife was another confusion point for her. Birds weren't meant to be indoors; she was certain of it. Admittedly, however, the reptiles Keenan collected likely benefitted from the Summer King's presence. Many living creatures did. He was the sun, warm and nourishing. He evoked joy and passion. His temper might be fierce and destructive, but rage was rare. Mostly, the Summer King was a pleasure to be near.

I would benefit in his presence, she thought. The Winter Girl reminded herself of that often. Keenan had chosen her, and now she was in daily pain. His love was bad for her.

Even though it felt so natural and right.

Feelings weren't always enough. Relationships—especially with a king—were not easy. Keenan was a cursed faery king,

He's not mine.

Donia felt a bit like an old woman sometimes, and lately, she'd realize that she'd been in this world as long as many a grandmother. And she'd been alone for most of it. No child. No spouse. She'd spent years as if in stasis. Her body, however, was not changed from when she'd been a girl. Loving Keenan had led to immortality, and as time passed, she started to think that eternity, at least, might have been a gift.

She was as strong as when she was mortal. Her health was unchanged—aside from the weakened state that iron caused and the constant chill of winter inside her body. Unless she was murdered, Donia had eternity in front of her. Sometimes she thought about the future, but in her imagination Keenan was still there. What foolishness it had been to fall in love with a faery!

I can resist him.

She thought about Rika, who had no love left for Keenan but whose heart was as surely walled up as if it had been made stone. Suffering under a curse did terrible things to a woman's ability to trust—and worse still, the only ones she could love were faeries. Mortals aged and died. So, Donia was caught in an in-between, nurturing her mistrust for faeries because of the curse, yet somehow still loving Keenan.

In truth, she was lonely.

She always thought—*hoped*—that eventually the fey could have their revelries among the trees near where she would make her home. In every city, she thought of it, hoped for it, but they never did. They wouldn't. No one got too close to her, as if Keenan still had a claim—or maybe they were simply afraid to draw the attention of the Winter Queen.

Beira was the worst of winter. She seemed to have forgotten the beauty of the first snow after a hot summer, or the gentle breeze that swirled snow into ephemeral images. Beira had become rage, blizzards, and pain. And many faeries were terrified of her.

Sometimes Donia was, too.

The rush of warm air outside the door heralded his appearance. There was no way to avoid the Summer King.

Before he could knock, Donia opened her door and stepped back. "Come in."

He smiled, beautiful and tempting, wicked and lovely, and her heart broke a little more. "You said when we arrived at the next place."

"It usually takes longer," she pointed out, stalling on telling him that she couldn't let him court her.

He shrugged. "I wanted to see you."

"But *here?*" Donia motioned outside. "This city is not . . . normal for you. There's so much steel. A thriving railroad, and--"

"It's where a faery queen would hide," Keenan explained. "The steel would protect her. I'd felt summoned here before, but I'd resisted, thinking I was wrong. Now, I feel it again. We've never looked in such places, thinking she couldn't bear the stench of iron either. If she carries the sunlight, surely, she'll be like us in some ways . . . but what if that was wrong? I thought this was what we missed, and when I felt called."

"You felt called here, then?" Donia pressed. She wasn't entirely sure how it worked. Why this girl but not that one? How did he know? Or was it completely random?

"She's mortal, Keenan. She doesn't know she should hide." Donia shook her head.

He shrugged. "Maybe I'm wrong, but if I am, you and I shall simply date longer while I wait to find the right possible mortal."

A small sliver of her heart thrummed at the realization that he'd rushed everything, endangered all of them, so he could romance her. Fey and mortals alike needed him to succeed—not avoid his quest.

Keenan loved her in his way, and as much as she hated the reality of what that meant, she still gloried that her feelings were returned.

"But do you really think she's *here*?"

He paused, guilt clouding his face, and then he said, "I can feel her here, Don. It's different this time."

Donia sighed. "You always think that. She's never where you look."

"I know."

Suddenly, Keenan looked so despondent that despite everything, she felt a rush of guilt this time. She hated the well of compassion that bubbled up inside her, and from the way he smiled at her then, he knew what she was feeling. He *always* knew. It wasn't magic, or faery gifts or something. It was simply him. No one had ever understood her as he did.

"I want to be with you," Keenan whispered. "Sometimes I'm afraid I'm not looking enough because I spend my time dreaming of you. I picture you as my bride. Consort. . . lover."

Although she was nowhere near a girl in years lived, Donia still blushed like one as he looked at her.

"I think of you like that," Keenan continued.

Donia shuddered, but forced a laugh. "We'd destroy everything. Ice and heat, Keenan. It hurts just to touch you."

"Is it worth it, though?" Keenan stepped so close that Donia's clothing felt like it would burn her.

She let out a small sigh, a soft cloud of icy air. Her decision burned up in the heat from his nearness, and without a word spoken between them, Keenan knew.

He saw the opening, her weakness, and asked, "Come out with me tonight? No one needs to know."

"Fine." Donia shrugged, as if it meant little. She stared at him and insisted, "It's not a date, Keenan. It's two friends who—"

"We're friends?" He sounded far too excited by that, as if it was a gift, an unexpected one at that.

"We aren't enemies," she allowed. There wasn't a word for what they were. They weren't simply acquaintances. "Lovers" was wrong, but so was "enemies." He looked so hopeful, as if her admission changed something. It didn't, but she still understood that hope. The Summer King was wrought of hope and joy. Believing impossibilities came naturally to him, despite everything.

Donia held his gaze. "We might as well be friends."

"I'm glad." He took her hands, squeezing them carefully.

And Donia tried to keep the ice inside her body controlled, much as he obviously was keeping the sunlight under control. His touch hurt, but it was worth the pain.

"I miss you when we are at odds, Don," he whispered. "I hate the way you dwell on my weaknesses, and I know you *must* because of the curse, but . . . I hate it. I hate you, of all people, thinking about all of my flaws month after year after decade."

"I am as bound by the curse as you are." Donia resisted, tugging away as he pulled her closer. They'd done this too many times, this apart-and-together dance. She wasn't his mistress, but sometimes *that* was the closest example she had to what they could be—and it wasn't enough.

"What would happen if I kissed you?" he asked.

"Don't." Donia pulled her hands away. "You break my heart over and over, Keenan. What would *you* do if I found a lover? What if I fell in love?"

Sunlight sparked in his skin, like a firestorm caught inside his body. His already glimmering hair looked like copper-strand left under a midday sun. Donia winced at the pain, the glare of it.

"You wouldn't," Keenan half-asked, half-ordered.

She gave him a sad smile. "The way you feel right now is the way I feel every single time you leave me. You'll make me believe in us again, and then you'll leave me. I can't do this. Every time it breaks my heart just a little more."

His sunlight blinked out. "Don . . . the curse . . ."

"It's not the ice, Keenan. It's *you*. You destroy me," she said, trying to impress the truth upon him. Glimmer of sunlight slid over him, making the frost falling around her glow and melt in tiny puffs of steam.

He kneeled before her as he had the day she accepted the test to be the Summer Queen. "Once more, please? Let me have one more chance to court you."

"*Why?*" She crossed her arms and stared at him. "You need a queen. I'm not her. I'll never be the Summer Queen, Keenan. You know it. I know it. Your advisors. Beira. Why can't you let me go?"

"Because I lo—"

"No." Icy tears clung to her eyelashes. "What would make you let go?"

"Give me the holidays?" Keenan took her hand. "Can we have that dream we once shared?" He paused and offered, "If you give me this, I'll stop pursuing you and focus on finding my queen."

*W*hen Donia dipped her head, giving the slightest of nods in agreement, Keenan let out a *whoop* of joy.

Summer was meant to be happy, to revel in the things that were a part of the season—merriment and dance, languid kisses and long nights. Keenan was never sure if it was the curse or his parentage that made him fall into fits of depression. Did it matter why though? It was who he was, and he had no idea how to undo it. All he could say for certain was that Donia was the cure to his worst moods. In her, he found solace and joy.

"You make me happy," he told her. It was the simplest, truest thing he could say. Loving her was hard, and he was well aware that they had no chance at eternity. Today, though, he could love her—and the Summer Court was very much about finding joy in the moment.

He wanted every moment, as if he'd starve without them.

Daring her temper, he leaned in and brushed a kiss over her lips, knowing that it would sting. The brief taste of her lips was better than magic. He felt like he could spark volcanos or scorch deserts. Donia, even now, made him feel invincible. *Love* made him feel that way, as if his every weakness was gone.

She pulled back, but he wrapped his arms around her and rested his face against her icy hair.

"It should have been you," he whispered against her ear. Then he stepped away. Too much touching was dangerous, and not just to his heart. She was ice, and he was sun. There was no way to touch safely, not as often and truly as he wanted.

Someday, when the curse ends, I will make love to her.

That dream was almost as much a drive as freeing his court from the pain they suffered because he was a bound king. In that sliver between freeing his court and reigning with his destined Summer Queen, he would steal a few moments with the one woman he'd truly loved. He would know that joy before he fulfilled his duties. It wasn't enough, but he would have it.

"You're absurd," Donia said, stepping away and giving him a look that he knew well.

He wondered what she'd say if she knew his thoughts. He grinned. "So, we can date until the next one is—"

"Fine." She turned and walked into her cottage. Her voice drifted back. "I expect true romance. Impress me."

She sounded like she was laughing, and he felt lighter at the sound.

"Tonight, then, when the sunlight is calmer," he called back.

Her hand waved behind her, a shower of ice and snow swirled in the air, and then she was inside—and he had a date to plan.

$\mathcal{I}$rial reached out to touch the fabric that divided the two worlds, the veil that now separated the world of mortals for the home of his kind.

He pushed his fingers through the fabric and parted it. The material twisted around his hands, holding him captive for a moment. It had always done so, recognizing him as its own, as if it would pull him back to Faerie. In theory it wasn't sentient, but one of Irial's theories was that it was an extension of the High Queen's will.

Irial parted the veil and let himself fall into the world he was technically to co-rule. Balance was the proper system for all of the fey. Each court had a balance—Dark existed to balance the logic and order of the High Court, and Summer existed to keep the ice and cold rage of Winter in check. There were those outside the courts, solitary fey, and there were those that defied classification. The embodiment of War, Bananach, lingered in the Dark Court, but she wasn't truly *his*. Devlin, brother to the High Queen and War, stood at the High Queen's most trusted. And Niall . . . the faery who now stood as advisor to the Summer King had once been Irial's beloved, his intended heir, and in his sorrow, Niall had sought haven here in the arms of the High Queen. He was solitary before all of it.

"You dream of your love," Sorcha said, lowering herself from a swing that seemed tethered to the sky, which for reasons Irial didn't ask, was currently nearly purple with thick clouds.

The weather here was often expression Sorcha's moods, so Irial was cautious, as he took another step closer.

"Push me," she ordered.

There were moments when Irial missed Faerie. This was one of them. He'd missed being around a faery queen who was capricious and lovely and not trying to skewer him with ice-wrought knives. The Summer King had no love or even tolerance for the Dark, and the Winter Queen seemed angry at all times. The High Queen, however, was the sort of mad that Irial enjoyed. Sorcha was both clever and intriguing. He'd spent enough hours and days with her to know that avoiding boredom mattered more than power.

No fey other than Lady War or Death could have more power than Sorcha. What the High Queen sought in their negotiations was something else entirely. She wanted joy and unpredictability. Irial made it a hobby to offer her exactly that.

"Do you have a secret to share with me, Sorch?" he invited, lowering his voice as he teased.

Sorcha cringed at his bastardization of her name, as she always did, even though Irial felt her spike of pleasure at the act. He tasted her emotion, all fey emotions, and it was the weapon he used to know best how to manipulate other regents. The beauty of dealing with the High Queen was that the tightly controlled emotions of the High Court slipped just a touch in his presence. It was, he thought, why she tolerated his visits.

Once he acquiesced to her demand and gave her swing a push—which obviously she could have achieved on her own—he asked, "What shall I convince you to tell me?"

Sorcha smiled. "I have nothing save for secrets. Which one shall I refuse to tell you?"

"Does it have to do with Niall?" Irial stopped the swing and stepped in front of her. He looked into her eyes. Theirs was an odd honesty, a bond they'd shared over centuries. And the Dark King was well aware that she wasn't this open with most faeries.

"Ask me no questions, Irial, about the things you have forgotten." Sorcha reached out and cupped his face in her hand. "There was a time you asked me to take this knowledge from you. I will not give it back."

"I *asked* to forget?"

Sorcha gave him a small smile. "Yes. You asked. It was your idea, your request to me."

"When?"

Sorcha stared at him, as if she had no idea how to answer that, and Irial was reminded that time was complicated for the High Queen. She saw the threads of the past, the now, and many varieties of the future.

So he tried another question, "Would the future be better or worse if I knew?"

"Worse."

Irial was stunned that she answered so quickly. It was typically a hard question, one that took weighing many lives and many potentials. Carefully, he tried, "Will my lack of knowledge create balance?"

"In some time," the High Queen said.

The Dark King had spent other days, sometimes many in a row, trying to glean truth from Sorcha. "Will she—"

"I cannot answer questions about these halflings," Sorcha said.

He startled. The High Queen rarely allowed such half-fey beings to live in the mortal world. Cautiously, he said, "The curse was that a mortal girl had the sunlight."

The High Queen stared at him and in a droll tone pronounced, "Someone chose to bed one of the mortals who would be Summer Queen."

"Who would dare?" Irial thought about it, the arrogance it must take to risk eternal winter for ruining the terms of the curse. No wonder he had chosen to forget. His rage at such a person must have been intense. He thought about the fey he knew within his own court who might be so bold. *Niall? Gabriel?* Niall claimed not to be Dark Court, but truth will out in time.

"I recognize the feel of Dark Court." He watched Sorcha, seeking verification.

She smiled, knowing full well what he was doing, and he felt the laughter she didn't let slip. After a moment, she confirmed, "No one but the Dark King will notice her ancestry."

The swing backed away from him, pulling the High Queen backward into the air by way of a pair of long tree branches that had grabbed the sides of the swing.

"Even I cannot lie directly, " she said. "I will speak plainly: you, Irial, asked me to take this knowledge from you. It was a curse, devised by you, and I placed it on you. You will forget *again* after this one either is chosen or is not. Your court will forget. The Hunt will forget."

Such a curse was extreme. What had prompted it? Why had someone been so foolish as to bed the mortal meant to be the Summer Queen?

"Did he love her?"

"Thelma?" Sorcha asked. "Yes, he loved her enough to remake the world. And I . . . cared for him enough to make it so."

It *had* to be Niall. Sorcha had always been fond of Irial's beloved *gancanagh*. Irial stared at the High Queen, thinking about the questions he could ask. As she hurtled back toward him, Irial let the shadows that were extensions of his court loose. They caught her and slowed her, so that she was perfectly still in front of him.

His shadows held her aloft there and he asked the only thing he could, "Why?"

The High Queen leaned in and covered his mouth with hers, stealing his question and offering a distraction.

The swing vanished, and Irial felt a willow tree behind the High Queen. The branches of the willow draped around them, creating a curtain of greenery that granted them privacy.

When he paused in their kisses, Sorcha was crying. "One day you will have your answers. Between the young king's choice of her and the future, you will forget again. You *must*. Do not ask me more, Irial. Do not try to find these answers. Death will come if you do."

And that was all she would say.

Back at the house he was renting, the Summer King was greeted by the scowling expressions of his advisors. Tavish and Niall had been at Keenan's side his whole life. They'd advised his father—and when Keenan was a child, they were his only guests from the Summer Court.

They were his family, and like any family they had secrets and discord.

If not for the intercession of the eldest faeries, those who lived in Faerie, he'd have only known Winter until he reached his eighteenth year. Tavish and Niall had been the ones who started to counter the stories his mother told him. In time, they'd become treasured friends as well as advisors. After nine centuries, they knew him better than he knew himself.

Today, however, Keenan was not as grateful for their insights. He didn't miss the assessing looks they gave him.

"My king," Tavish started.

Keenan shook his head. "No."

"I understand that you have feelings for the Winter Girl." Tavish shoved the long silver plait over his shoulder in a tell-tale sign that he was agitated. He was very loyal to the court, and his tolerance of the Winter Court or Dark Court was minimal at best.

"Stop." Keenan had listened to more than enough lectures on duty. He knew his duty, and he'd see it through in time. When he'd told Donia he thought the girl was here, Keenan had been serious. He was drawn here, to her, and oddly, he'd been drawn to this area before. He met Tavish's patient gaze and said, "I will take my joy where I ch—"

"Take it with the Summer Girls," Tavish interrupted. "They require your time. *She* does not."

Nearby, Niall sighed and rubbed his head. The second Summer Court advisor was the more emotional of the two faeries—on every topic save duty. There, Niall was quiet where Tavish had been willing to take risks that Keenan wasn't sure he could accept.

Niall was not at ease with conflict. Still. He'd fight, and he'd sometimes allow himself pleasures that were beyond the typical court debauchery. He disliked quarrels, though.

"Are you sure you need this?" Niall asked, drawing their gazes. He rubbed his hair with both hands anxiously. His shorn wood-brown hair stood out at odd angles, and for a moment, Keenan had a thought that he might let it grow finally. It wasn't mere vanity to hope that for him, but a wish that his advisor might finally heal. His close-cropped hair was kept that way to make certain no one missed the long scar that ran from his temple to the corner of his mouth.

"Tavish," Keenan rebuked, glancing back at Niall.

"Joy matters," Niall said with a shrug. "You know that, Tavish." Then to Keenan, he added, "You should see her—unless it will make you hate yourself later."

Those were words Keenan had said more than once to Niall, referring to the Dark King, though. His advisor, for all that he was loyal to Summer, had been a creature of the Dark

Court before Keenan's birth. And it took no genius to see that a part of the *gancanagh* still missed the other court. That was one of the many things Summer did not discuss.

The Summer Court was a place of frolic, of leisurely naps in the sun, and naked dancing in the rain. They were not so serious, and they had little time for regrets. In that they were more akin to the Dark than to the Winter Court or High Court.

At that thought, Keenan grinned. "Summer does as it wants, and I want Donia."

Niall laughed at Keenan's boisterous proclamation. He understood impulsivity better than most any fey thing. He'd gone from Solitary to Dark Court to Summer Court. In every iteration, Niall was driven by emotions and *need*. He'd joined the Dark for either love or lust, and he'd left out of rage and betrayal. He stayed with Summer out of some mix of those passions.

"Wanting Winter resulted in your father's death," Tavish said. "The curse we bear now—and for all of these centuries— is Winter's doing."

"And Irial's," Niall muttered.

Keenan couldn't argue, but there were perks to being king. Not as many as he'd like, what with being cursed his entire life, but one undeniable fact was that the king answered to no higher laws. He shrugged. "I do my duties, Tavish. I shall continue to do so. Sometimes, to enable me to do so, I need to remind myself why."

"For a mortal who is *not* your queen?"

"No," Keenan corrected. "She's a woman—a *faery* woman thanks to the curse—and one I love. Breaking the curse will free her and all of them"—he gestured into the house where Summer Girls were giggling and running—"and the world. Forgive me if I need a reminder of why I don't give up."

Tavish sighed and walked away, leaving Niall and Keenan in the room alone.

After several moments, Niall spoke, "I understand."

Keenan waited, knowing his friend well enough to know there was more to say. Finally, Niall met his gaze and added, "The past is the past, though. You can't live in memories."

"The past is why I am cursed and you are my advisor," Keenan said. "My father's past. *Your* past."

Niall said nothing for several moments. He was never at ease discussing his time with the Dark Court, as if ignoring it would erase it. Keenan didn't have that luxury. If he didn't break the curse—and stop Beira's ever-growing power—his court and then the mortals that populated the world would perish.

Logic and hope both said he would find the missing Summer Queen, curses were meant to be broken. The Winter Queen might think she was invincible, but Keenan had faith. Somewhere in the world was a mortal who would save them. He simply had to find her.

Tonight, though, he was going to absolve himself of kingly responsibilities and simply pretend he was a faery who had the joy of romancing the love of his life. He knew that he would lose her when he found his queen, but regrets were the stuff of other courts. He might be a bound king, but he was still the Summer King.

He would figure out how to romance Donia, and he would *also* meet his obligations. Keenan paused as he headed toward his room, snagging a few Summer Girls who spun by him.

"Niall?" Keenan waited until his advisor met his gaze. "Please inform the Dark King that we are here. I saw the Hunt, and I know they are near."

And Keenan pretended not to see the flash of shadows in

Niall's eyes. He wasn't sure if his friend knew they were there, but Keenan saw it. The raw truth was that Niall would always have divided loyalties, one even he denied. Eventually, he would need to face whatever he felt for the Dark King. If not, Keenan would be forced to admit to Niall that the element that healed him was not, had *never* been, sunlight.

IRIAL

When Irial left Faerie, he was no more informed than when he arrived. He had once known these mortals—or at least known of them. Tonight, he stood staring up at their building. He was unsurprised when he felt the approach of the one being he'd ever loved. Was the mortal one he'd rescued from the *gancanagh?* Had he hidden them because the eldest one was addicted to his beloved Niall? Or was she the child of his beloved? Why had he asked Sorcha to curse him?

Did Niall know he'd had a child?

Gabriel was the only other faery Irial could imagine protecting, and the Hound had a child already. A half-ling son, and if Irial's suspicions were right, he had at least one more child who was half-mortal.

Niall's daughter.

Irial strolled away from the building until he found a park. Once he was situated, he sent messages over his connections to his fey. *"Bring me my gancanagh. Gently. Trick and whisper."*

The minutes ticked by as Irial found himself at a table

at the edge of the park. He sat inside, alone, at a wooden table in a small bar. The building was stone and wood, brick and mortar. Niall could sit here with him in relative comfort.

"Dark King." Niall's voice came from behind him.

Irial felt his abyss guardians, shadows that were both part of him and somehow sentient, surge toward him. He felt the twist of guilt, longing, and lust that Niall quickly crushed. And under it all, Irial tasted love. It was buried, but it was still there. With that, Irial's tension lowered just enough to hide his own feelings.

"Did you miss me, love?" Irial said as he glanced back at Niall.

Although it didn't show on Niall's face, Irial could taste it. *Like honied fire.* Niall had always been such fun.

"No guards," Niall asked. His concern had an edge of genuine curiosity now. "I know you summoned me when you heard I was seeking a formal audience."

Irial pushed out a chair. "Sit."

"Not your lackey."

"Please, Niall?"

Whatever he heard in Irial's voice was enough for his curiosity to flare even brighter. He took the chair, although he pulled it back as if Irial couldn't resist touching him.

Irial smiled to himself. Someday, he'd wear down Niall's fears. He no longer looked at the Dark King with only hate in his eyes. The love—and the lust—were always obvious again.

"Do you ever think about the days where no bed was forbidden?" Irial asked. "Where a woman would slide from my arms to yours? Where—"

"Not if I can help it." Niall's expression tightened.

The wave of lust from Niall that washed over Irial was enough to make the Dark King pause. He shook out a cigarette, tapped it on the table. "Do you ever think of children?"

Niall stilled, and for a flicker of a moment, Irial watched him. He wasn't sure if he could force the question. Did Niall know?

"Have you any?" Irial asked.

Niall took Irial's unlit cigarette and sniffed it. Carefully, he held to his lips and looked at Irial.

Stunned, Irial lit his cigarette. He didn't let himself think of other times when Niall had allowed him other intimacy that ended with cigarettes and silences. "Feeling bold?"

Niall took a long drag and exhaled. "Earlier, my king mentioned that although he does what's needed to fulfill his duties, sometimes, to enable that, he needed to remind himself why."

Irial watched him curiously.

"I am here to tell you that we are in this town, that my king will commence seeking his queen here." Niall smoked and stared at him for several moments. "I am reminded that I risked death to leave you."

"Do you think I wouldn't risk death to tempt you back?" Irial took Niall's cigarette and lit his own with it. After a long moment, Irial asked, "Are you trying to see if I'll seduce you tonight?"

"I'd refuse."

Irial smiled. "Tonight? Probably. You're not meant for the sunlight, though, Niall. We all know that."

"I have no patience with Winter." Niall still held his gaze, as if whatever urge was riding his nerves tonight was going to tempt him toward actions they'd both regret.

"I wouldn't tell you no," Irial whispered. "But the things you're thinking are no good for either of us."

Shame surged in Niall, and Irial drank it down. Such guilt

and shame and lust and anger made time with Niall intoxicating.

Despite that, Irial confessed, "I would never refuse the things I see in your expression tonight, *gancanagh*. I miss that." He clasped his hands together to resist taking Niall's hand or starting a fight that would lead to a way to excuse what Niall was craving. "But what I still want is something else."

Niall scoffed. "I don't recall propositioning you for *anything*."

"Answer me this: do you have children in this world?" Irial asked, again tasting the feelings that told the truth in a way no words could: Niall was confused. That meant that if those were his relations, Niall knew nothing of them.

Had we both forgotten? Was it Niall's secret and that's why Irial had asked to forget? There was no one else Irial truly loved.

"What game are you playing?" Niall asked, his voice dropping lower in suspicion.

Irial stood, unable to answer and unwilling to lie.

Then Niall grabbed his arm—and Irial let their connection gape open. He shoved his own lust, need, fear, and possessiveness toward Niall. He stood watching Niall shudder as if he was swallowing rich wine.

Niall pulled his hand away.

"Don't grab me unless you want to hold on," Irial whispered. He hated that the only times Niall touched him for centuries were when he was injured and didn't remember their kisses, nights when Keenan summoned him to press shadows into the injured body of the faery he wished he could drag home tonight.

Or anger.

Irial enjoyed both, but neither was enough.

"I will do what I can to protect what you have made, *gancanagh*." Irial offered his vow, even though Niall wouldn't understand. The vow was binding nonetheless.

Then he slipped into the night, because protecting Niall's child was more important than giving in to the terrible longing in Niall's eyes. Giving in, despite the pleasure it would bring, would make Niall hate him later.

So Irial made his way out of the bar, and as he walked he sent the lust that was boiling over slide along the tendrils of connection with the court. He knew Niall well enough to know he'd return to wherever the Summer Court was staying and find his pleasure with Summer Girls.

"*I am in need of satisfaction.*" Irial sent the invitation to his court. He'd think of his *gancanagh* doing the same elsewhere in this horrible city, and then soon, he'd approach the halflings that his beloved had surely fathered and find a way to protect them from the Summer King.

There was no way that Niall's granddaughter was the mortal who would be Summer Queen. Irial would help her flee Huntsdale, and then in a few years perhaps he could come to terms with the idea that the missing Summer Queen could be a young woman several generations removed from his beloved.

I may have to ask Sorcha to re-curse me.

*P*laying mortal used to be easier, but knowing this was Niall's family made his plans fall apart. The girl, Moira, was the granddaughter of a *gancanagh,* of his *gancanagh,* and that made everything seem wrong.

She wasn't mortal.

She wasn't a stranger.

Irial knew better than to speak to the girl's mother. That one, Elena, looked at the fey with the clarity of one with the Sight and anger to go with it. She shimmered in that way that the Sighted always did for him, as if they weren't wholly present. A part of him wondered if the Sighted had fey ancestry—but he noticed these two because of the curse or because they were of his court in some way.

"You're staring," she said, pulling Irial's mind to the moment. The girl was braced against a wrought iron fence, and if he had been most faeries, it would intimidate him. The Dark King was immune to the pain of iron.

"You know what I am," Irial said, not even trying to play at being mortal.

"Maybe." Moira tilted her chin defiantly.

"Good." Irial leaned against the iron fence and shook out a cigarette. "Smoke?"

She hesitated, but it didn't last. The girl had Dark Court blood, Niall's blood, *gancanagh* blood. She leaned toward the forbidden. And with a smirk that made him try to remember another face, Moira said, "Light?"

Irial flinched a little and handed her a lighter. She sounded like she was flirting, and Irial . . . couldn't. Although the Dark King was supposed to embrace taboos, the mere thought of debauching this girl appalled him. Moira was likely Niall's grandchild. That was the only explanation he had that would explain his reactions, and it made Irial slide to the side, putting more distance between them.

"Are you why they all watch me?" she asked after lighting her cigarette and pocketing his lighter.

"Any in particular?"

"Icy ones," she whispered. "And the one who glows brighter. Like you but"—she shrugged—"warm?"

Irial nodded. "There was a curse once, a foolish man cursed a girl, and her daughters and her daughters' daughters."

Moira waited. She shrugged again, paused to fling her thick dark hair over her shoulder, and said, "So?"

"So I want to protect you. I need to keep you safe," Irial said, wondering why the need to do so was so urgent. "They must not see you. One, in particular . . ."

"Him."

The Dark King nodded. "When you're ready, I'll help you run."

"I can't leave my mother." Moira folded her arms over her chest. "You don't under—"

"I'll protect her. My court," he swore. "No one will hurt your mother."

Moira Foy stared at him, as if trying to figure something out. "Do you know why? Why the Dark Court—"

"You know who I am." Irial smiled at the girl. By all rights he ought to react much differently to a mortal Seeing and learning of the fey, but she wasn't just a mortal, was she? Moira Foy and her mother Elena had Dark Court fey blood along with mortal blood. Elena, the girl's mother, felt older than she looked. Irial was certain that one was more fey than mortal. He wasn't sure about the girl beside him. If Keenan saw her, she'd become fey as part of the curse.

"She can't know," Moira whispered. "That you're watching her."

Irial nodded. This one was clever for her age. *Niall's blood.* He pushed off the fence. He wasn't about to linger and draw eyes to her too soon.

"Once he sees you it's too late," Irial warned.

Moira said nothing as she turned and walked away. She certainly had the spirit to lead the Summer Court. Irial tried to see a trace of Niall in her walk or her hair or something. He couldn't find it, but with everything he'd learned from Sorcha and his only reactions, the girl had to be Dark Court. These were the descendants of someone he valued enough to seek a curse.

That detail concerned him. The only love he actually felt was romantic love for Niall and brotherly love for Gabriel. And Gabriel's children were not secret to him. That left Niall, but Irial saw none of his traits in the girl.

Watch these two for ever after, Irial thought-ordered his court. *They are of ours.* He let them see Moira and her arrogance despite fear and he let them see of his memory of her mother, Elena, staring at him not in fear but that same arrogance he saw in many of his court. She was a force.

Irial was still watching the street near Moira's house when

Beira approached him. She stared at him in a way that reminded him of long-gone days where they were friends of sorts. When she was in love with Summer, when the three regents flitted from court with comfort. Friends. In maudlin moments, he missed *that* version of the Winter Queen as much as he missed the late Summer King.

"There was a time we all laughed," he said to her. "Do you ever laugh that way?"

"I was weak." Beira shrugged it off. "And I suffer still for it."

Irial kept silent. He despised her statements that were openings to either argue or lie. Irial couldn't *say* that Beira's suffering was a choice, and he couldn't *lie* to say she was right. Trust Her Icy Temper to have found a way to make the *geas* on honesty a way to torture him.

"Do you recognize her?" Beira asked, and Irial didn't need the Dark Court ability to taste emotion. Her curiosity was writ large in her voice and posture.

"Some mortal that wanted a cigarette," he said, not technically lying.

"That's all?" Beira prompted. "Any urge to *seduce* the girl?"

He shivered involuntarily.

The Winter Queen leaned close and whispered, "Or *protect* her?"

"From *what*?" Irial scoffed.

Laughter shouldn't ever make him shudder like hers did. Her sharp-edged laugh thing filled him with horror. *Did she somehow know that Moira was the missing mortal? Had she always known?*

Beira pressed her red-painted lips against his cheek, leaving her make-up kiss over a frost-burned mark. Painting her blue lips didn't change how dangerously cold she was. "That child is a halfling, Irial. We both know it."

Irial stared at her. Whatever he'd forgotten, she knew in part.

"Perhaps. Those are Sorcha's interest not mine." The Dark King could misdirect well, but he saw no need to try to do so when the truth was undeniable. "Talking to a halfling is not the same as *protecting* them."

"Despite her parentage?" Beira asked, somehow sounding both disbelieving and amused simultaneously. "Isn't that why you watch her? Knowing about the *father*?"

"I owe you a gift, Winter Queen, if you do not harass these halflings." Irial met and held her gaze. "My word that the debt I owe is equal to the worth of these halflings."

The weight of his vow was violent. The *value* of these halflings was immense, even if Irial didn't have logical reason to think so. The Dark King's shadows, the abyss guardian, slithered all over him as if they recalled. He wanted to know the thing he'd forgotten, but Sorcha's words that death would come with his knowledge held him back.

"Vow accepted," Beira murmured. "My court will not tell the High Queen about these halflings. Nor will we take their eyes."

"Or tell the Summer King?" he prompted.

"I thought I already killed him," Beira said cheerily. When he stared at her, Beira added, "Fine. I won't tell my child either."

"You underestimate the kingling," Irial warned her. All curses end, and if there was any chance of peace between them, Beira needed to start treating Keenan as an adult.

Beira scoffed. The Winter Queen didn't take any critical word lightly. She also apparently didn't know Moira and Elena's greatest secret, but he still needed assurances that

Beira wouldn't draw his gaze their way. Keenan had already been drawn to the city where his intended queen lived.

The curse is weakening.

If Moira stayed, the curse would be broken. Irial knew it, and as much as he was ready for balance, that wasn't best for the Dark Court. They fed on the darker emotions of the fey, and as such they were almost as powerful as Winter currently.

And it'd not be best for the girl.

Irial walked back to the girl's house, waiting for her to gaze down at him. When she did, he tapped his wrist and whispered, "Time to go."

EPILOGUE

"Her name is Moira Foy," he announced, sounding more certain than he ever had before when they'd done this. "It's *her*, Don. I know it."

"Keenan," Donia snapped, a cloud of frigid air slipping out with her voice. "She doesn't like you."

"She will." Then he said the words that'd sealed so many mortal girls' fates. "I've dreamed about her. She's the one."

Keenan glowed more than she'd seen in fifty years. There was a spark in his eyes, a flicker of fire she hadn't seen when he's looked at the other girls. He grabbed her hands regardless of the pain it caused in her skin and her heart. "Things are going to get better."

"Congratulations . . ."

"She was leaving town, but I asked. She'll be back in a few days." Keenan glimmered with the sunsparks. "I've found her, Don. I'm sure this time."

And Donia was equally sure. This felt different, but she said nothing.

"Once she says 'yes,' we'll both be free. You won't hurt, and I'll be at my full strength." Keenan brushed his lips over hers. "I feel it. This is the start of the end of the curse. We can still--"

"I still have to convince her not to love you," Donia pointed out. "I'm as bound as you are."

He nodded but he didn't believe her, not truly. She could see it in his eyes, and as she looked at the way he was smiling, Donia had no doubt she could convince Moira Foy to reject him.

Keenan was half-in-love with Moira already.

It was the nature of the curse, even though he was Donia's beloved, he wasn't hers to keep. She could admit to herself that he was and would always be her "one," her fairy tale prince, even though he wasn't destined to be hers.

What we just had was nothing more than a winter dream. And as the Summer King stared at the building, that dream evaporated. A mortal girl was slowly becoming fey, and soon she'd either reject him or take the test.

Either way, Keenan was no longer looking at Donia. The curse made this sudden love he felt for mortal after mortal inevitable, but that didn't mean it didn't hurt.

"You'll see," Keenan swore. "She's the one, Don. Everything will change now!"

And Donia blinked away her tears before leaning in and kissing his cheek. "I believe in you, Keenan."

She did, and even though she would try to convince Moira to refuse Keenan, Donia now also wanted him to succeed. They all needed Winter to stop growing in power, and Donia needed to be free of him before the love in her heart turned to hate.

The End

AUTHOR'S NOTE:

THIS STORY of Ash Foy's mother—as addressed in my first novel, *Wicked Lovely*—is the story of a young woman who ran away from the metaphorical "demons" pursuing her. In Moira's story, those are faeries. In the real world, there are other demons many of us have wanted to run away from, or spite, or defeat. Ash's mom in the story chose death over the Summer Court. I want to remind you though, that this was a fictional world. Out here in the real world, we keep fighting to overcome. We ask for help. We find a resource. I've watched loved ones struggle with depression and with crises. I've lost friends to suicide, to addiction, and to deaths hastened by other kinds of deadly choices. I have considered suicide, but after some rough patches I decided to seek help. Look to your local resources, trusted friend or family, or suicideprevention-lifeline.org.

A**vailable now:** *Cold Iron Heart*

How far would you go to escape fate?

In this prequel to the international bestselling WICKED LOVELY series, the Faery Courts collide a century before the mortals in *Wicked Lovely* are born.

Thelma Foy, a jeweler with the Second Sight in iron-bedecked 1890s New Orleans, wasn't expecting to be caught in a faery conflict. Tam can see through the glamours faeries wear to hide themselves from mortals, but if her secret were revealed, the fey would steal her eyes, her life, or her freedom. So, Tam doesn't respond when they trail thorn-crusted fingertips through her hair at the French Market or when the Dark King sings along with her in the bayou.

But when the Dark King, Irial, rescues her, Tam must confront everything she thought she knew about faeries, men, and love.

Too soon, New Orleans is filling with faeries who are looking for her, and Irial is the only one who can keep her safe.

Unbeknownst to Tam, she is the prize in a centuries-old fight between Summer Court and Winter Court. To protect her, Irial must risk a war he can't win--or surrender the first mortal woman he's loved.

REVIEWS:

"Set against the lush backdrop of 1890s New Orleans, Marr's spellbinding prequel to the Wicked Lovely urban fantasy series invites readers back into the world of the fae. . . . The resulting conflict delivers all the magic, intrigue, and romance that Marr's fans expect. Readers will be pleased." -- Publisher's Weekly

"WHAT A DELIGHT TO discover how much I loved being back in the Wicked Lovely world, discovering details about beloved characters that made me want to race back for a series reread. This is Irial's story set in 1890s New Orleans, brimming with faerie court drama and steamy romance. Can we. and should we, outrun fate? And if so, are we prepared for the consequences? I could not put it down." --Angela Mann, Kepler's Books, Menlo Park CA

"SET 100 years before the events in Wicked Lovely, Cold Iron Heart finds Irial, the king of the Dark Court, in New Orleans and entranced by a mortal. Is his interest in Thelma Foy just a passing fascination, or could it change the course of her life and the world forever? Melissa Marr masterfully rises to challenge of writing a prequel by both expanding on the mythology of the original series while telling a story that exists wholly on its own. Fans of the series will inhale this delicious glimpse into Irial's past."-- John McDougall, Murder by the Book, Houston, TX.

. . .

ON THE AUDIO EDITION:

"In this prequel to the Wicked Lovely Novel series, narrators Kristin James and Tim Paige--both gifted with rich, easily distinguishable voices--immerse the listener in the elegant, fascinating, deadly, and intriguing world of the Summer and Winter Faery Courts. Lovely jeweler Thelma Foy, who has the second sight and can see faeries, catches the eye of the Dark King himself. Unbeknownst to Thelma, she is the key to ending the battle between the two courts. James has a lilting, lush, and whispery voice that perfectly captures Thelma. Paige has an affected mien that is equally perfect for the gorgeous and hedonistic king. This listen is wicked--wickedly enjoyable." --A.C.P. © AudioFile 2020

"I loved *The Wicked and The Dead*! A sassy, ass-kicking heroine, a deliciously mysterious fae hero, and a wonderful mix of action and romance. Add that to Melissa's usual great world-building, and I'm already looking forward to book 2!"
— Jeaniene Frost, *NYT* Bestselling Author

The Wicked & The Dead is AVAILABLE NOW!

In near-future New Orleans, *draugar*, again-walkers, are faster and stronger than most humans, but not venomous until they are a century old. Until then, they shamble and bite. Since not everyone wants to see their relatives end up that way, Geneviève Crowe makes her living beheading the dead.

But now, her magic has gone sideways, and the only person strong enough to help her is the one man who could tempt her to think about picket fences: Eli Stonecroft, a faery who chose to be a bar-owner in New Orleans rather than live in *Elphame*.

When human businessmen start turning up as *draugar*, the queen of the again-walkers and the wealthy son of one of the victims, both hire Geneviève to figure it out. She works to keep her magic in check, the dead from crawling out of their graves, and enough money for a future that might be a lot longer than she'd like. Neither her heart nor her life are safe now that she's juggling a faery, murder, and magic.

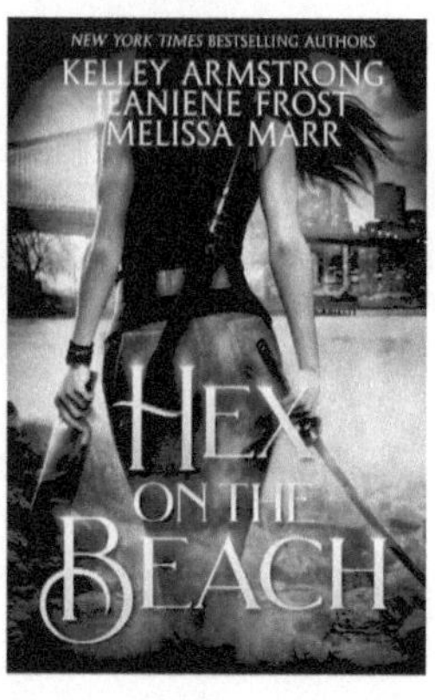

HEX ON THE BEACH is COMING IN JULY!

Girls Night Out has never been so much fun--but what are they going to do with all these bodies?

NEW YORK TIMES and USA Today Bestselling Authors Kelley Armstrong, Jeaniene Frost, and Melissa Marr deliver a sexy summer read with this novel-length anthology containing three all-new stories from their Cursed Luck, Night Huntress, and Faery Bargains worlds. Kennedy, Cat, and Gen are just trying to enjoy their respective getaways, but when immortals, vampires, and witches come out to play, things are bound to go awry. Let the supernatural hijinks begin!

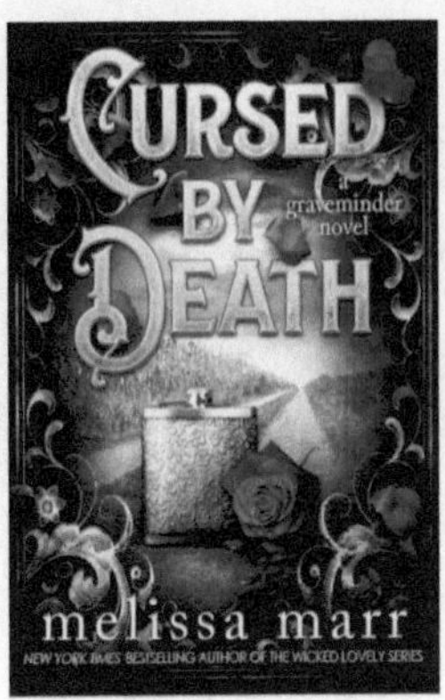

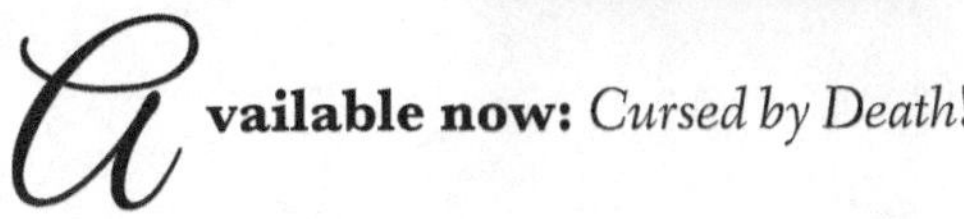

$\mathcal{A}$vailable now: *Cursed by Death*!

THE DEAD DON'T ALWAYS STAY dead in Claysville . . . and in the afterlife, Death himself can't be trusted.

AMITY BLUE HAS BEGUN to remember strange impossible events, her ex trying to bite her and people vanishing like mist. Everyone in town swears a mountain lion is responsible for the recent deaths, but Amity is sure that there's more to the story.

After a stalker—a dead stalker—appears at the bar where she works, Amity discovers that the dead don't always stay dead in Claysville. Along with the current Graveminder, Rebekkah Barrow, Amity seeks out the enigmatic Mr D, who seems to be Death himself, only to discover that the centuries-old contract to protect Claysville has been broken.

Caught between life in a cursed town and Death himself, Amity and Rebekkah must find a way to put the dead where they belong—because if the Hungry Dead keep rising, everyone in town will be lost.

Return to the world of Graveminder, Goodreads Choice Winner for Best Horror Novel in this stand-alone Graveminder novel (also includes two Graveminder short stories.).

and what happens to us when we refuse them—matter to us as much as the multiple cases of heebie-jeebies she doles out..." —NPR.org

"Spooky enough to please but not too disturbing to read in bed."—*Washington Post*

"Dark and dreamy. . . . Rod Serling would have loved *Graveminder*. . . . Marr is not tapping into the latest horde of zombie novels, she's created a new kind of undead creature. . . . A creatively creepy gothic tale for grown-ups."—*USA Today*

"Plan ahead to read this one, because you won't be able to put it down! Haunting, captivating, brilliant!" —*Library Journal* (starred review)

"Marr serves up a quirky dark fantasy fashioned around themes of fate, free will—and zombies. . . . Well-drawn characters and their dramatic interactions keep the tale loose and lively." —*Publishers Weekly*

"The emotional dance between Rebekkah and Byron will captivate female readers. . . . Fantasy-horror fans will demand more." —*Kirkus Reviews*

"No one builds worlds like Melissa Marr." —Charlaine Harris, *New York Times* bestselling author of the Sookie Stackhouse series

"Welcome to the return of the great American gothic." —Del Howison, Bram Stoker Award-winning editor of *Dark Delicacies*

ABOUT THE AUTHOR

Melissa Marr is a former university literature instructor who writes fiction for adults, teens, and children. Her books have been translated into twenty-eight languages and have been bestsellers internationally (Germany, France, Sweden, Australia, et. al.) as well as domestically. She is best known for the Wicked Lovely series for teens, *Graveminder* for adults, and *Bunny Roo, I Love You*. In her free time, she practices medieval swordfighting, kayaks, hikes, and raises kids and chickens in the Arizona desert.

Visit her online:
http://www.melissamarrbooks.com

facebook.com/MelissaMarrBooks

twitter.com/melissa_marr

goodreads.com/melissa_marr